BLEAK NOVEMBER

Rohan O'Grady was the pseudonym of June Skinner. She was born in Vancouver, British Columbia in 1922, the daughter of an Irish-American forester and an Irish-Canadian mother. She graduated from Lord Byng Secondary School in 1940 and during World War II worked as resident assistant manager of the Capilano Golf and Country Club. After the war she worked in the library of the *Vancouver Sun*, where she met and married newspaperman Frederick Snowden Skinner, with whom she would raise three children. She published four novels under the O'Grady pseudonym: *O'Houlihan's Jest* (1961), set in 18th-century Ireland and an ode to her own Irish heritage; *Pippin's Journal* (1962), also published as *The Curse of the Montrolfes* and *The Master of Montrolfe Hall*, a historical Gothic novel; *Let's Kill Uncle* (1963), her most famous book, a darkly humorous tale of two children who conspire to murder their wicked uncle that was filmed in 1966 by William Castle; and *Bleak November* (1970), a creepy Gothic novel. She also published *The May Spoon*, a young adult novel, in 1981 under the pseudonym A. Carleon. She died in 2014.

I0636656

Bleak November

Rohan O'Grady

Valancourt Books ★ Richmond, Virginia 2025

Dedication: To A. L. Hart, Jr.

Bleak November by Rohan O'Grady
Originally published by The Dial Press in 1970
First Valancourt Books edition 2025

Copyright © 1970 by June Skinner

Published by Valancourt Books, Richmond, Virginia
http://www.valancourtbooks.com

ISBN 978-1-960241-38-2 (paperback)
Also available as an electronic book.

Cover by Roderick Brydon
Set in Dante MT

Tragic Aftermath of Bank Hold-Up

See also pictures on page five and stories on pages two and three

CHAPTER ONE. How does one start a chronicle of horror? It was in the bleak November ...? But it wasn't. It was in spring, after what had seemed like an abysmally long winter, and I noticed, on my way home from work, the first fronds of daffodils pushing their way up boldly through the sour earth of the West End gardens.

This didn't start out as a diary and it isn't one. Whatever I have begotten—and I'm hard put to pin a label on it—its birth was due to the fact that as a legal stenographer, I am almost incapable of not taking notes.

I had kept notes for years (nothing of importance of course; I'm a rather dull person) so it wasn't until we bought the house that I became caught up with enthusiasm. It was then my notes began showing copious details. I started out with what I thought were useful records of household accounts and duties.

Though I intended to write merely a compendium of prices, objects purchased, grocery lists and future tasks to be faced, there also emerged shapes, sometimes grey, sometimes etched too precisely for comfort, of feelings, disappointments, hopes, conversations, and fears. In the course of transcribing them I have attempted, most of the time, to put them in chronological order.

Although years of training enable me to dash my thoughts down at a hundred and seventy-five words a minute, I haven't the makings of a diarist. Diarists, despite what they may say to the contrary, strike me as usually having a pretty sharp eye on posterity, and it takes a great deal more self-confidence and extroversion than I have to assume that my every thought, burp, twinge, and prickle of fate is of interest to the rest of humanity.

Imagine my surprise then, when I reread this motley assortment (kept at the office in a black looseleaf binder) and found I had a record that would have done credit to Mr. Pepys for trivialities.

Even more surprising though, was that the thing, like the genie escaping from the bottle, had a certain form, that behind the tedious commonplaces were sinister turns of events and patterns that emerged, until the genie stood full-fleshed before me.

More to clarify the mounting confusion of the atmosphere of this house than actually to record or tell a story, I began to type my notes up during slack periods at the office, leaving out many superfluous details. Finally I took the binder home with me and kept adding to it faithfully. Its form and tenses are erratic, dictated either by my fears at the time of actually writing the notes, or my mood while transcribing.

I have gone over my notes, trying to be systematic; and as usual, there's only one place to start. At the beginning.

Spring, and the flowers of the gardens gave me the same sense of joy that the Icelandic settlers must have felt when they brought their emaciated cattle from the dim, evil-smelling byres to the spring pasture grounds. Spring. A time for life and rejoicing, a time for beginning things—and we were. We were beginning a new life in what was for us a new home.

That spring night we moved into the house. We were all there: I, my husband Eric, his mother Laura, and Bernard Kielty, the real-estate man who had sold us the house. Igor wasn't there because at that time we didn't know him too well.

The combined furniture from our little apartment and Laura's looked lost in that vast, lovely old home; but despite the bareness, the atmosphere was one of festivity, and we certainly had no fear.

Then.

I had not told Eric, but a month previously I had handed in my notice to the law firm I worked for and I was due to leave the day after our move. Oh, what a relief it was to think that never again would I type one of those endless documents with their "signed, sealed and delivered in the presence of" rigamarole.

It was a big, impersonal company; my work was dull and exacting and I felt no pangs of nostalgia on leaving it. I had been there for four years; much to my surprise, the sixteen other stenographers had banded together and bought me a lovely little antique table with an inlaid top.

I had contributed to many a going-away present, but I'm not much of a mixer and had never become close to anyone in the office, so it hadn't occurred to me that I myself would be the recipient of a gift, particularly such a tasteful and expensive one. If I was touched by this gift, I was dumbfounded when Mr. A. P. Turner, one of the senior lawyers, called me to his office and handed me a check for a hundred dollars. I hadn't realized he knew I worked there.

"We are sorry you will be leaving, Mrs. Burton. It's difficult to get women as conscientious as you. If you ever decide to come back, even on a part-time basis, we'll always be glad to discuss it with you."

I thanked him, fervently hoping that day would never dawn.

Well, finally, it was moving day and a huge van picked up Laura's things and then ours. Like the grasshoppers in the fairy tale, we—feckless, landless lot that we had been until now—managed everything with our usual improvidence. Fortunately Bernard, who by this time was more a friend than just another real-estate salesman, took a proprietary interest in us. It was he who remembered to get the phone installed and the water turned on, to put in light bulbs, and to order enough groceries for breakfast. He even remembered toilet paper. Then, beaming like a large, sheepish schoolboy, he presented Laura with an antique blue and white Wedgwood bowl.

"A small housewarming gift." It was typical of his thoughtfulness, and Laura was delighted as she placed it on our white marble mantelpiece.

We had forgotten to make plans for dinner, of course. Bernard phoned out and got enough Chinese food for a banquet, which we held in the kitchen, as the empty dining-room looked like an unoccupied railway station.

Laura had splurged on a bottle of wine, though, so we toasted each other and our new house. Bernard was anxious to try out the chimney in the living room and we collected scraps of lumber and lit it. It drew beautifully, despite the fact that the whole house had been moved. Laura's divan and our old chesterfield looked lonely in that vast room, but we all sat around watching the firelight dance cosily on the paneled walls.

After the wine was gone, the party began to wear thin, and Eric yawned ominously. But Laura and I were so keyed up by moving that we knew we wouldn't sleep, and when Bernard suggested that he fetch a bottle of Irish whiskey from his car so we could all have Irish coffee, we responded with enthusiasm.

When he returned waving the bottle over his head and shouting, "Up the Jamesons," Eric looked uncomfortable and mumbled something about Amy having to go to work pretty early. Little did he know, and Amy said she'd love some Irish coffee. Eric gave me a dirty look.

Perhaps I should explain. Eric is a writer, a former newspaperman, who has now taken two years off to write the great book of the century. I am the breadwinner until such time as we reap the bounteous fields of his genius. At least, I was the breadwinner until I quit because Laura inherited a legacy from Eric's long-lost father and bought this house. Eric saw nothing untoward in living off the avails of his wife, but he drew the line at what he referred to as "sponging off Mother." Fortunately for me, Laura did not share his lofty ideals.

Bernard, like a big pink elf, switched on Laura's radio, and sweeping her up in his arms he waltzed about the huge, empty living room. I liked Bernard.

I went to the kitchen and put on the coffee, and I was feeling good myself, since *I* knew I wasn't going to work in the morning. I tuned in the little transistor radio on the kitchen windowsill to the same station as the one in the living room and did a merry jig as I set out the cups and saucers.

When I went back to the living room to wait for the coffee to perk, a surprise awaited me. Laura's radio was turned off and only the thin sound of the little transistor radio on the kitchen windowsill could be heard. Laura and Bernard were no longer dancing but stood in the middle of the room with their arms still about each other and a strained expression of listening on their faces.

"What is it?" I asked.

Their eyes turned to Eric, who was standing in the front hall, by the door.

"Didn't you hear it?" asked Laura.

"Hear what?"

Eric left his post at the door. "A dog. It was howling."

The three of them exchanged glances.

"It scratched on the front door," said Bernard. "When Eric opened it, he thought he saw a big black dog."

"I didn't think I saw it. I did see it. It was the size of a Shetland pony and it ran away when it saw me."

Bernard, subdued, served the Irish coffee, which he made much too strong. It wasn't laced with whiskey, it was bound hand and foot.

"This is delicious!" Laura knocked back two without turning a hair, as did Bernard; but Eric barely touched his, and twice he went to the front door, opened it, and gazed out.

"Maybe somebody abandoned it." He looked glum.

Laura and Bernard were dancing again, and Bernard, having cut out the unnecessary frills of coffee, was drinking straight whiskey.

Eric's mother, bless her, suddenly vowed she was drunk, which she was, and she fell giggling onto the chesterfield. We've never been able to afford liquor very often, and this, our first night in our own home, did call for a celebration, but Eric looked tired and irritable.

"I think you've had enough to drink, Mother."

"Nonsense," she said. Around her neck she always wears a long necklace of amber beads, which she now proceeded to swing as though it were a bola. "Bernard, dance with Amy. I'm done in."

Like so many heavy men, Bernard was remarkably light on his feet and twirled me around as if I were a cardboard mannequin.

Then Eric switched off the radio again.

"Listen!" he commanded.

There was complete silence. Again he went to the door and opened it. Only the night.

Still swinging her amber necklace, Laura began to hum.

"Turn on the radio again, Bernard. Oh, sit down, Eric! You make me nervous prowling around and poking your head out the door every two minutes."

"But I heard it again," said Eric. "I don't understand."

"Maybe it was Black Sutch." Laura's red wig was slightly askew, she was still giggling, and she winked broadly at Bernard.

"Who?" asked Bernard.

"Black Sutch. A big ghost dog who haunts the lanes of the north of England. My nurse used to threaten that he'd get me if I were naughty when I was little. Been around for centuries."

"Come on, Eric, have another drink." Bernard poured whiskey into Eric's coffee cup and Eric made a face as he drank it.

"Party pooper," said Eric's mother. I couldn't help but laugh. I had never seen Laura have more than a glass of wine before. She's a good old scout and I wished Eric wouldn't play the straitlaced son on our first night in the new house.

The bottle was now empty and Bernard rose to leave us. Despite the fact that he had been drinking before he arrived and had had a fair amount here, he was as steady as a rock as he bade us good night.

"He'll look like W. C. Fields in another ten years," mumbled Eric, as he went around locking doors and checking windows.

We actually had a home of our own and a roof over our heads that wasn't rented! Eric took his duties as master of the family seriously.

"Oh, Eric!" Laura winked at me this time. "What if Bernard does drink a bit too much at times? He's always pleasant. As a matter of fact, I think he's delightful. Don't you, Amy?"

Amy was thinking that she felt just a wee bit guilty about a certain piece of news she would soon impart to her husband.

"Amy, hadn't you better hit the hay?" asked Eric. "It's been a long day and you're going to be awfully tired for work tomorrow if you don't get some sleep."

"Not yet." My apprehension increased. I stretched out in

front of the fire. "What a luxury. We ought to have a fire-screen, though. The sparks are liable to land on the carpet. And we should have apples or chestnuts or marshmallows to roast. Or mulled cider. That's what they drink in England, isn't it, Laura?"

Laura deliberated before answering. "Well, perhaps the farmers," she finally conceded. "Father always drank port."

"Amy," said Eric, "It's nearly twelve."

"I know," I said, taking a deep breath. "I quit."

"Quit what?"

"Work."

His mouth dropped open. "You didn't."

"I did."

Laura glanced anxiously from Eric to me.

He was furious. I knew, of course, that he would be.

"Well, that's just dandy, isn't it! A fine housewarming for me. I suppose I can bloody well chuck my book and go back to the newspaper. Is that it?"

"No," I said. "You can do what you like. I'm taking in boarders."

When we, or rather when Laura, bought the huge house, Eric suggested facetiously that if our financial situation ever became dire, I could take in boarders. Little did he know on what fertile soil that remark fell.

I kissed Laura's cheek.

"It was *his* idea."

Boarders. Yes, it did sound terrible, put in words, but it was practical; and though Eric, exercising the prerogative of the artist, is not practical, I am.

I was in bed in the master bedroom when there was a knock on the door. Laura entered, and there being no other place to sit, she perched on the edge of the bed. She looked old and unhappy and I felt like a brute for spoiling her evening. It didn't sound like such a good idea now and I supposed I would have to scrap it.

I had had other bright ideas for a cottage industry that would allow me to quit that deadly legal stenographer's job. Before we moved, when we were still in our cramped little apartment, I used to lie awake and wonder how I could make enough money to support us and yet be a housewife and a mother. A future mother, that is.

Those ads. You've seen them. "Earn six hundred dollars a month in your own home. Write away for our salesman's kit. Enclose $15.00." Cosmetics? Magazines? Mrs. Amy Burton's Pound Cake, Made on the Premises from an Old Family Receipt? No. Boarders were not as bad nor as ridiculous as they might sound. However, if both Eric and his mother found the idea *that* repulsive, I would either have to come up with something else, or go back to work.

"All right," I said meekly to Laura, "I give in."

"No, you won't." She shook her head. "My mother would have been shocked, but I'm too old and I've worked too long to have much false pride left. And I know you don't want to be entirely dependent on me. I'm upset only because of this friction between you and Eric. He's a lot like his father in some ways, Amy, and he'll have to start adjusting to the rest of the world. We've made a lot of concessions to him, you and I, trying to make up for something else, I suppose. Well, I think boarders are a splendid idea, if you can manage, and if you prefer that to working in an office, it's your business. I won't interfere. I promise you."

I sat up.

"Laura, you're the limit," I said. "Where did Eric ever get a mother like you?"

She was standing in the doorway. "He'll sulk for a day or so, then he'll come round. I know him. He can't stay angry. Oh, before I forget, here. It's for furnishings. Whatever you want."

She tossed me a check. It was for three thousand dollars. Then she said, "I wonder just what that dog was? Eric may be a writer, but he's not that imaginative. There must have been *something* there."

I was too excited about the check to think much about the dog. "How can I ever thank you?"

She smiled. "Don't. The greatest pleasure for me in finally having money is to be able to give you and Eric what you need." She paused, staring out the bedroom window. "Perhaps it was lost, poor thing. Do you think that perhaps it was lost, Amy?"

I gave the check a big kiss. "I don't know. I only hope it isn't a bad omen on our first night in the new house." I was so happy about the check that I was laughing.

Laura waved good night to me and closed the door softly. Overhead a jet screamed for a split second, leaving that strange vacuum, as if all the other sounds in the heavens had disintegrated, and I pulled the covers up closer.

It was well after midnight when Eric came to bed, and he must have been unusually angry because he was unusually silent. The old adage of not letting the sun set on one's anger seemed particularly fitting on this first night in our new home.

"Good night, Eric."

"Good night." He turned his back to me, but five minutes later he sat up and lit a cigarette. "I wonder why it came here? I know I didn't imagine it. It sounded like a soul in anguish."

Then he remembered he was mad at me, stubbed out his cigarette, and plunked himself back on the pillow.

"Black Sutch," he mumbled, just before he started snoring. "What a hell of a name."

I was too excited to sleep. Our own home. Finally! Now I could be like other women and forget the past and that accident. Housework, gardening, cooking! And children.

CHAPTER TWO. Transcribing these notes with some degree of order is like playing snakes and ladders. You're at the top and making headway, then, zoom, you have to go back.

Back I slide, back to the square of Laura's birthday, before we moved and when we were still in our little apartment. I remember it so well, with the usual useless hindsight, that I hardly need my notes. It is clear to me now that despite her apparent artlessness, Laura was already deeply involved in the affair of the house.

It was about five o'clock, Eric was seated at the card table in the living room, his head bent over Roget's Thesaurus, and his Savonarola nose almost touching the pages.

"What I want," he said, "is a word to express nostalgia for a place, but on the lines of 'weltschmerz.'"

I shrugged and went back to the kitchenette, where the angel food birthday cake was ready and iced. It was her sixtieth birthday.

The drop-leaf table was set up in the dining end of the living room and I thought for possibly the millionth time how much I hated this open-plan style of apartment, all scientifically designed. Scientifically designed to the last miserly inch to give you claustrophobia and whatever they call it when you hate your fellow man due to too close physical association. There is a name for it. I read an article on it and even rats become so neurotic they can't be bothered getting up in the morning or raising their off-

14

spring. They just sit on their crowded little perches until they fall off in a coma of stupefied rage and indifference.

"God, English is a clumsy language."

He was standing behind me, that is to say, one foot in that glorified cupboard, the kitchenette, and the other in the dining area.

"Try homesickness," I said.

He gave me the glance he reserves for me when I am more than usually trying, or, as he puts it, obtuse, but I noticed he sauntered back to the card table in the bedroom and jotted something down on the yellow pad he uses for notes.

I had bought a few flowers for a centerpiece. They cost the earth and looked tatty, but they were better than nothing, even if they were in a pressed-glass salad dressing bottle from which I had removed the label.

"What's the celebration?" He was back again, eyeing the cake.

"Your mother's birthday. She's coming for dinner."

"Her birthday? That's in March."

"This is March."

"Oh, hell." He sighed and reached around me to open the fridge door. I obligingly flattened myself up against the stove. Actually, I had no choice.

"Isn't there any beer? Damn. I was going to really work tonight. Things are going smoothly for the first time in days. It's as if I were plugged in to some idea machine and the thoughts just pour out. I suppose she'll stay all evening."

He lifted a fork from the table.

"This is sterling!"

"I know," I said. "I bought a place setting for myself on my last birthday."

He has gypsy eyes, black, hard and bright. Now they were cold.

"You what?"

"Look, everybody has to have a few nice things. We can add just one spoon or fork or knife a year, and before you know it we'll have enough to set an attractive table."

He was going to start, I knew it. The lecture on Economy. The Russians have their five-year plans, while ours is on a two-year basis; and like them, I had a feeling it would be a fifty-year plan if I didn't put down roots. The Book, which was to shape future generations of literature, must come first; all frills must be sacrificed on that hallowed altar.

On he went. I knew what I was getting into when I married him. I had made a bargain. Gone into it with my eyes open. We would both work. I at my job as legal stenographer. He at The Book. After two years he'd either be with his shield or on it. He'd been honest with me. And if I bloody well didn't like it, why did I marry him?

Why, indeed. Well, I won't go into that now, but after eleven months of this confinement, voluntary as it was, we had already worn down our incisors on the bars of our communal cage and were now prepared, blunt as they were, to use them on each other.

Thank heavens his inspirations could only be composed in longhand—otherwise I would have been pressed into service after office hours, a sort of Canadian Mrs. Tolstoi, recording the precious words in shorthand. All I knew about the book was that it was fiction, and that's all I wanted to know about it.

I heard Laura's silver bracelets and bell earrings tinkling along the corridor outside our supposedly soundproof pen.

"There she is. For heaven's sake don't spoil her birthday."

He is genuinely fond of his mother. For that matter he is genuinely fond of me, although a casual observer would be hard put to prove it most of the time. I haven't any creative ability at all, and the single-mindedness, the absolute—well, selfishness, to be quite honest, of an original mind has to be seen to be believed.

"Amy!" His mother jingled into the room, kissed me, then Eric, and flung her hands up to straighten her wig. She has four. If Eric were reading this he would say, "Four what? Hands?"

"Happy birthday," I said.

"Happy birthday," said Eric.

She saw the cake, the flowers, and the silver, and tears came to her eyes.

"Amy, thank you!" She turned to her son and smiled. "I know you well enough to see it was Amy, not you. He can't even remember his own birthday, let alone mine."

She paused, picked up a knife. "Why, Amy! It's sterling! Louis

XIV, isn't it? I wish you could have seen mother's table when she was entertaining. I don't care what anybody says, it does make food taste better. Oh, Eric! Take that look off your face. I told you when you married Amy that man does not live by bread alone."

It is proverbs, or, as Eric calls them, aphorisms like this that make him say that Nero wasn't quite the villainous offspring history has made him out to be.

"How is the book coming, dear?"

One never asks a writer that. He tells her so every time she asks, but she always asks anyway.

"There isn't any beer," he said.

I got a bottle of wine out of the top of the fridge where I had put it to chill and I opened it myself because the last time we had wine he managed to break the cork and shove it into the bottle and I had to pick it out with tweezers.

It was a successful little party. I like cooking and fortunately Eric and Laura will eat almost anything. We toasted her health in plastic juice glasses and when she wished and blew out the candles she no longer looked so tired.

Where she got a son like Eric is beyond me. They don't look alike, think alike or act alike. He has her long, slender hands, but on a man they simply manage to appear inadequate and out of place.

Eric lit a cigarette and leaned back.

"How are things at the tearoom? Put Conrad Hilton out of business yet?"

Laura toyed with her plastic glass as if it were Waterford crystal.

"We served seventy-four sandwich specials today. Mrs. Mac's teacup reading is really paying off. If only I had had her years ago. Women come in and then tell their friends and before you know it the word has spread around. If this keeps up we'll make a decent profit. That is, if they don't raise the rent when the lease is up. But you can't tell with those Chinese. They'll do anything to get an extra penny out of you. I wouldn't mind if they would keep up the repairs, but no—just because they live like coolies themselves, they expect us to."

Eric mumbled something about the white man's burden and poured himself a glass of wine.

Laura was on her third tearoom. The first was owned by a Greek, and she hated all Greeks. The second shop was leased from Jews, and though decency forbade her from being openly anti-Semitic, she did say that while most of them are just like you or me, trust her to get one of *those*.

She doesn't mean anything by it. She's been a non-fit grass widow competing in a business world for far too long and it's comforting for her to have someone to blame.

"Father traveled extensively in the Orient, so I know what I'm talking about. You have to bribe them for every little thing. Constantly. They just don't understand the British code. Oh, he'll raise the rent, all right, I know that. I suppose I'll just have to develop some Asiatic traits and resign myself to it as the will of Buddha or whoever it was."

"This is excellent wine, nice body," said Eric, pouring himself another glass.

Actually it wasn't excellent. Not the cheapest, of course, but it certainly didn't taste as if it came from any old ducal cellar.

Laura turned the bottle around to read the label.

"South Africa."

Eric's face got that look.

"Amy! There's domestic wine, there's Australian wine, there's California wine, there's European wine, and there's Israeli wine, to name a few! Why the hell did you have to buy South African wine?"

"What's the matter with South Africa?" asked Laura.

"It's a fascist state, that's what's the matter with it!" shouted her son.

Nevertheless he had two more glasses.

Laura insisted on helping me with the dishes, although I didn't want her to. She'd been on her feet and working hard all day, and it was her birthday.

When Eric went back to the bedroom to write, closing the door, she and I began to chat, and it wasn't until she was leaving that I remembered we hadn't given her her present.

It was only a little silver charm for her bracelet but it might have been the Hope diamond, from her reaction. Dear old Laura.

As she kissed me good night she nodded her head toward the bedroom door and whispered.

"I know he's difficult to live with, but I can't tell you how happy I am to have you for a daughter-in-law. You've done so much for him. He couldn't have stood it much longer reporting and trying to write at the same time. I haven't been able to give him what he needed or deserved in the past and now he has the most precious gift in the world. A chance to prove himself."

There are day people and there are night people. If Eric lived in Tokyo and I lived in New York, everything would be dandy; but I do try to be diplomatic where his writing is concerned, so after the teeth and cream routine, I crept into bed and pulled the covers up to my ears.

The typewriter was going like a machine gun and his monk's head had not moved when I entered.

Two minutes later he stopped typing abruptly and glared at me.

"Must you?" he said.

"Must I what?"

"Breathe in that stertorous, hideous manner."

I was going to make the obvious rejoinder of pardon me for breathing but thought better of it, turned my back to him, and pulled the covers up higher.

I heard him groan and light a cigarette.

I sat up. "Now what's the matter?"

"Will you please stop interfering with my thoughts?"

"Will I stop what? Good grief, all I'm trying to do is to go to sleep."

"You're *thinking*!" he said.

There was an angry clatter as he prepared to move into the living room.

The amount of paraphernalia necessary to woo the muse staggers me. First there was a pile of yellow pages of penciled notes, then the handwritten preliminary drafts, also on yellow paper. A third pile was of semicompleted and corrected pages, and finally a fourth of corrected pages on white bond. All these were in separate typewriter-paper boxes with extra paper for each box. There were also pens, pencils, erasers, cigarettes, ashtray, the typewriter and the card table, and a folder of newspaper clippings.

I looked through the folder once and it contained such disparate items as the mating of a captive panda bear called An-An, an earthquake in Turkey, an article for flooding the Mojave desert, Atlantis rediscovered, a genealogy on hemophilia in the royal houses of Europe, the yearly score of the Toronto Maple Leafs and a recipe for candying rose petals. He had forbidden me, on pain of instant abandonment, to read any drafts of his Book. As a matter of fact, I don't want to. It's his baby and I know him too well not to realize who would end up dandling it.

And there were the books. He is always surrounded by one pile that are apart from his reference books. Apparently they keep him company and he seems to take a swig out of one or another, the way a sly drinker sneaks to the kitchen during a dry party. Then there were the indispensables: the Oxford dictionary, Bartlett's Quotations, the atlas, Roget's, Cruden's Concordance and the Bible.

It was now eleven o'clock and it took him another ten minutes to transfer everything to its usual pristine disorder. From the living room drifted anguished sighs, nose-blowings, pencil-sharpenings and scuffing noises; then at last the typewriter began to stutter.

An hour later when I woke up and went to the bathroom, I passed unnoticed. He was writing in longhand again, and a cigarette with a two-inch ash smoldered in the ashtray as, interspersed with the odd congratulatory chuckle, he alternately grimaced, smiled, admonished, muttered, and growled to himself.

Veteran Policemen Sickened During Investigation

Most Appalling Crime in City's History, Says Chief

CHAPTER THREE. (Saturday) Met Laura and Mrs. Mac for shopping. It would have been a busman's holiday for them to go out to tea, so after looking in the stores, we went to the King George Hotel for lunch.

"Eric needn't know," said Laura.

Mrs. MacLean, who has only been out from Scotland five years, shook her silvery head. "It is rather expensive."

"It's my treat," said Laura. "It does one good to splurge occasionally."

She was wearing her red wig and a sort of poncho cape in Donegal tweed. With her heavy Mexican silver jewelry she looked like a refined, elderly hippie.

"My word, when I remember the meals we used to have when we weekended at Portchester it makes my mouth water. Of course, there were scads of servants in those days and we took it for granted."

She smiled as she put a cigarette in the long holder she used and turned to Mrs. Mac.

"Things are certainly different these days, aren't they, Jessie? Of course, we belonged only to the cadet branch of the Pontifax family and meals at the Vicarage weren't on a par with the Castle, but I still remember breakfasts at home. The maids in their stiff white caps and aprons, the sideboard and the silver and the lovely smell of grilled sausages and liver and bacon and kippers. It's like another life, rather than another era. Eric never saw any of it. He belongs to this generation completely, while I'm afraid I'm not really in either."

"Eric was only two when he left England, wasn't he?" I asked.

Laura nodded. "Yes. Well, I made my bed and I've had to lie on it. If only I'd listened to Father. But then, I suppose young people never do."

"Eric never speaks of his father," I said.

"He really doesn't know a great deal about him," said Laura. "He hasn't shown much interest and I thought it best to let sleeping dogs lie. Father warned me. Said I'd be cut off without a penny and they'd never see me again if I married Agar and that's just what happened."

A combo band started in the corner of the dining room and I leaned over to hear Laura better, but she had sunk back in her chair and was studying the ornate molding on the ceiling.

"I suppose Eric doesn't remember him at all," I persisted. Since the mysterious Mr. Burton was to be the grandfather of my future children I felt my curiosity was not entirely rude and misplaced.

"No," said Laura.

"What was he like?" I asked.

Laura suddenly snapped to life and sat up.

"Agar Burton? He was a blackguard. An out-and-out scoundrel. He deserted me, left me without a penny when Eric was twenty-two months old. I've never seen him since, I am happy to say, nor do I wish to."

A thousand questions popped to the surface of my mind. Did Agar Burton drink? Or was he a gambler? Did he beat her, or had he perhaps been a philanderer? Had he money? Was he a gentleman? Somehow I couldn't see Laura marrying him if he weren't.

"I suppose social codes were much stricter then," I ventured. Laura did not rise to the bait.

"It seems rather harsh," I continued, "for your parents never to have contacted you again. Surely they must have been concerned about Eric's future?"

Mrs. Mac, who had been sitting like a nice, comfortable old granny, spoke up.

"I think the salmon steak sounds very nice."

Laura stubbed her cigarette, finished her sherry and studied the menu.

"I'll have the Crab Louis, with consommé first. I've put on five pounds in the last six months. No, Amy, my dear," she continued in the same breath, "I had my pride too. I don't know whether they realized Eric even existed. I certainly didn't tell them. He was born in the charity ward at Guy's Hospital in London, you know. Agar had, by that time, run through the small inheritance I had received from a trust fund at the time of our marriage. We muddled through, laden with debts for nearly two more years, and then one day, he just walked out. I sold my jewelry, packed, and came to Canada; and that, my dear, is the end of my rather drab little saga."

It wasn't, of course. Eric had let enough remarks pass so that I could fill in the picture, and it was not a very colorful one. Just wearing, commonplace poverty, with never enough of anything. Laura had worked as a chambermaid, a waitress, and a housekeeper; and once she had saved up enough to open a small dress shop. With her lack of business acumen she had gone broke in a year.

But no matter how reduced the circumstances were, she had never boarded Eric out or put him in a foster home. She had never abandoned him. When he was fifteen, she had had pleurisy and for three months they had been on welfare until he got a job as a copyboy on a newspaper.

It was his lack of formal education for which Laura could not forgive herself. He was the only male in her family in eight generations who had not been a Cambridge man.

Eric, with his usual unpredictability, apparently didn't give a damn one way or the other. By a similar token, her sacrifices and my supporting him were viewed with the same lofty eye.

But anyway, despite psychologists' theories to the contrary, I don't think his unorthodox upbringing made much difference to a man as fundamentally unconventional as Eric. He would be the first to agree that fitting in with anybody's well-laid plans, buckling down to an academic schedule, or growing up a little gentleman among her formal and formidable family was just not his cup of tea.

He saw nothing unusual about himself. On the contrary, to him it was Laura who didn't conform. As he had told me just before I met her for the first time, "You'll like my mother. She's a bit of a nut."

"I hope," said Laura, removing the parsley and sliced green pepper from the top of her salad, "that you'll be firm with him about this two-year plan and not let him talk you into extending it. I'd like to have a few grandchildren before I'm too old to enjoy them. Whichever way I look at it, I did miss a lot of his childhood, having to work."

It was a delicate subject for me.

"Let's hope the book is a success," I said. "Tell me, Mrs. Mac, do you really feel psychic inspiration when you read teacups, or is it just a game of make-believe to keep us superstitious females happy?"

Mrs. Mac wears spectacles as thick as plate glass and, trite as it sounds, she does look owlish.

"My family have had second sight for generations," she said. "Unfortunately you can't turn it off and on like a light switch, and a good deal of the time I just spout off the top of my head. At other times it surprises and even frightens me. For instance, about two months ago I dreamed my sister in Edinburgh was writing me a letter about her house. Half way through the letter she tossed it in the fire and I saw it burn and float up the chimney. Ten days later I got an airmail letter saying her house had caught fire, the very night of my dream. Fortunately the fire department was able to control it. I really don't think it is coincidence. It happens too frequently."

"Do a reading for Amy," said Laura. "You've never done her, have you?"

"Oh, no," I said. "This is supposed to be Mrs. Mac's day off."

"Oh, I don't mind." Mrs. Mac's a sweet old soul. "Give me your hand, dear."

Somehow I didn't like the idea, but Laura insisted.

Mrs. Mac gave me the usual trip-over-water, letter, good-news, small-amount-of-money routine, and then her magnified eyes seemed to stop looking, rather like a person caught in a candid camera shot. "I see children. Many children. Six—seven—maybe eight."

Her eyes clouded up and she folded my hand shut. "That's all, dear."

"That's enough!" Laura was chuckling. "Poor Amy! I once asked mother if my birth had been a difficult one and she said, 'Well, I don't know how it was for *you*!'"

She and Mrs. Mac laughed, but I didn't.

When I got home Eric was sitting at the dinette table reading the newspaper.

"I got you some new undershorts and socks," I said.

"Why?"

"Because I was ashamed to take your others to the laundromat any more, that's why. I also bought myself a shift dress for summer. Do you like it?"

I held it up. He nodded and went back to the newspaper.

"Lord, I'm tired," I said.

He stood up and put his hand on my shoulder. "I'll make you a nice hot cup of tea. Okay?"

He brought my slippers and put them on for me.

"I put the roast and potatoes in at three. Was that right? Here. Read the other half of the paper. Tea will be ready in a jiffy. Do you want a sandwich or anything before dinner?"

I shook my head. Just when I am ready to kick him into the middle of next week he always does something genuinely and unexpectedly kind.

I sat sipping my tea and reading. It was Saturday afternoon and I didn't have to go back to work until Monday. It was a lovely feeling.

"I see they're subdividing up the old Danby estate," I said.

"Let me see it. I did a story on that place years ago."

I gave him the paper. He read it through without comment and handed it back.

"I wonder why they're turning the house into an officers' club?"

"Taxes are too high for the heirs, I guess."

"'The rest of the estate, fully landscaped,'" I read, "'will be converted into acre and half-acre lots.' I suppose they will sell for a fortune in that neighborhood."

"Not necessarily. They're too close to the new airstrip. With the sonic boom it would be like living through the blitz."

"Let's drive out tomorrow," I said.

"Why?"

"Why not, for crying out loud! It won't *cost* anything. We could take your mother. It would be a nice outing for her."

He didn't answer.

"Well?"

"Well what?"

"Oh! You infuriate me!" I threw the newspaper at him, then stalked to the bedroom. It was knee-deep in books and papers, the bed was unmade, an overturned ashtray was spilled on the floor and I slid, believe it or not, on a banana peel.

"Couldn't you even make the bed!" I shrieked. "I'm sick and tired of this place looking like a pigsty!"

He stood in the living room with a pained expression on his face. "Ever since you walked in that door"—here a fine thespian flourish—"you have been looking for a fight. I have done everything humanly possible to placate you. You are behaving like a spoiled child, Amy, and I do not intend to stand for any more. When you come to your senses and are reasonable, I will treat you as one adult treats another."

After delivering this homily he calmly put on his jacket and left the apartment. I sat on the edge of the bed, fuming, biting my knuckles and wondering if it were worth crying about. Finally I decided it wasn't, so I made the bed, cleaned up the room, had a shower, got into my housecoat and baked a lazy-daisy cake for dessert. It wasn't until I put it under the broiler to melt the brown sugar topping that I remembered it was his favorite. It says a great deal for my character that I did not throw it out.

Fortunately I am no more capable of sustained anger than he is.

He strolled in just before dinner and we both acted as if nothing had happened. When he saw the cake, he smiled. "That's the girl. I knew you'd see reason." He magnanimously patted my behind as he walked past.

We did not start on Sunday because the car would not start on Sunday.

"What's the matter with it?"

"How the hell would I know? Do I have to be a mechanic too?"

"Too what?"

It turned out to be the ignition and we didn't get it fixed until Wednesday because payday wasn't until Wednesday.

We went the next Sunday. It was a glorious day and when we reached the Danby place we found we were not the only ones to take advantage of the weather. Dozens of cars were parked around the estate and people milled about as if the grounds were a public pleasure garden. Eric wanted to go back but Laura and I wouldn't hear of it.

"But it's illegal," he said. "It's trespassing. I thought we were just going to drive around it."

"Nonsense," said Laura. "It can't be illegal. Everybody is doing it."

"And they can't arrest all of us," I chimed in.

Eric is the most scrupulously honest person I have ever met. For instance, he won't even let me keep my foot on a public weighing machine till he steps on so we can both get weighed for a penny. Now he tagged along behind Laura and me with the self-conscious air of a man committing a public felony.

The mansion stood lonely and empty, surrounded by huge poplars. We strolled through the estate, which must have consisted of twenty or thirty acres. There was a formal Italian garden in front of the house and tennis courts behind it. To the left of the courts was a beautiful sunken Japanese garden with stone lanterns and bridges and pools in which carp swam between gum wrappers and empty cigarette packages thoughtfully provided by the public.

There were greenhouses and several acres of lawn and a kitchen garden, but what caught my eye was a small walled orchard about an acre in area.

The old red brick wall was ten feet high and Laura and I immediately tried to figure out a way to climb it, but Eric, who had gone ahead, called to us.

The front of the wall, facing onto a quiet street, had been torn down to allow passage for a huge, flat deck truck on which was perched precariously—or so I thought—on great square timbers, a house.

Laura squeezed my arm as we clambered over a heap of bricks.

"It's just like *The Secret Garden*," she whispered. "Do you remember?"

I did indeed. I remembered our attic on a dark prairie afternoon with the rain drumming on the roof and flashes of lightning snapping across the sky as I sat eating apples, Northern Spy apples, and reading that magic tale.

At the back of this orchard was a wonderful old cherry tree in bud, and espaliered against the warm, worn bricks were apple, peach, almond, plum and pear trees.

"They've been let go badly to seed, if that's the word," said Laura, caressing the lichened, scabby bark of an apple tree. "I wonder if they'll ever come back."

Neither of us paid too much attention to the house—then. . . . We were too enchanted with the garden.

Eric was talking to a powerfully built young man in white overalls who was standing on a plank leading up to the house.

We joined them.

"Oh," Eric said, "this is Igor. This is my mother and my wife, Miss Pontifax and Mrs. Burton."

Laura will persist in using her maiden name, which causes a certain amount of confusion during introductions.

Igor apparently saw nothing untoward.

"Hi," he said.

"And you mean there's no damage done to the house, picking it up by the ears, so to speak, and leaving its roots?"

"Naw," said Igor, patting the siding of the house. "The feet of the chimneys had to come out and strengthening scaffolding put in, but this old place is really solidly built, not like these shacks in developments now. They'll have to put in a new basement and foundation, of course, but if I had the money, I'd buy this place in a minute, rather than a new one."

It was two and a half stories high and far from small. How they ever moved it was beyond me.

It came from the city, said the young man, where it had been marked for demolition to make way for a new high-rise. It had been moved, truck and all, across the bay by barge in the middle of the night so it would not interfere with traffic.

"It's too bad," said Igor, accepting a cigarette which Eric offered him. "The previous owners had started to remodel it, done a good job of what they done, too, before they decided to sell it."

"I wish we could see through it," sighed Laura. "It looks perfectly lovely." She turned to me. "The Vicarage was half-timbered like this, and with leaded windows just like those, too."

"Sorry, I can't let you through, lady, I just work for the house-moving company," said Igor. "The real-estate agent is a fellow called Kielty. Stick around. He'll probably show up soon."

What was the use? The three of us couldn't have raised a thousand dollars between us.

"Oh, let's wait," said Laura, looking from Eric to me.

Much to my surprise he merely shrugged and said it couldn't do any harm.

He and Igor walked around the truck as Igor explained how one went about the task of moving a house.

Laura spread her Donegal opera cape or poncho or whatever it was on the long grass, and we sat leaning our backs against the rose-colored wall.

"It surprises me, Eric being so interested," I said.

She smiled.

"It's the garden. I used to read a lot to him when he was little and *The Secret Garden* was always his favorite. He used to say, 'Oh, Mummy, someday we'll find a rusty key and we'll open an old door into a secret garden, and we'll walk in and we'll build a little house for ourselves and we'll never live in flats or other people's houses again.' "

Good old Eric. I didn't know he had it in him. I could never imagine him as a child, although I suppose there is no reason why there shouldn't be sardonic, misanthropic little boys.

There was no sign of Mr. Kielty so finally Laura and I approached Eric and his new friend.

They were in the midst of a spirited discussion.

"But there's a dichotomy"—here Igor see-sawed his hands —"between capitalism and labor. You take a guy like me. What chance have I got of running for Parliament to change the system, like? I gotta do it through organization of my peer group."

"Yes, I see what you mean, but the more unions raise wages, the higher costs are. Somebody has to pay. And you know who does?" Here Eric tapped Igor's broad chest. "You."

"Yeah, but if the state controlled labor, like, then terms could be dictated so that——"

Eric cut him short. "Then you'd have dictatorship."

"Jeez, what's the matter with that? Why should those bigwigs in Ottawa be pulling down thirty thousand a year for standing, yes, standing, like, on our necks?"

Eric noticed us and, slapping Igor on the back, said, "Igor and I are having an interesting talk about dialectical materialism."

Igor ignored us.

"A writer like you, an intellectual, ought to think this thing through. Hell, I'm not a commie. I don't want any politburo telling me what to do, but the present government is really hung up on this. Too conservative to ameliorate management to the population. You ask me, I bet they're afraid to give the little people a chance."

What in heaven's name was he talking about?

"What little people?" said Laura. After sitting in that enchanted garden I think she was bewitched with visions of elves with green pointed shoes and crocks of gold.

"Igor's writing a book too," said Eric, and his eyes were snapping with mischief. You never know what he'll come out with, and Igor was built like a Cossack, broad, thick-necked and even slightly bowlegged. I hoped Eric would keep his big mouth shut.

I needn't have worried.

"It's been a pleasure talking to someone of your intellectual status, Mr. Burton."

Speaking of dichotomy, Igor seemed to teeter between an adolescent and an aged professor of economics. He began to quote something he had obviously memorized. I forget the content; all I can remember is his delivery, and at the conclusion I felt I should cheer and shout that we had nothing to lose but our chains.

"In a progressive society a man of your culture should be supported by the state," continued Igor.

Eric demurred with becoming modesty. If he was putting on our friend Igor, he was doing a good job.

"We really should be going," said Laura. "I left the Sunday joint in the oven." We were to dine with her in her tiny apartment that night.

Women obviously had no place in Igor's brave new world. He disregarded both of us.

"You ask any ordinary guy, Mr. Burton———"

Another crowd of sightseers pushed into the orchard and Laura saved the day.

"It's been charming meeting you, Mr.—uh—ah— . I do hope we'll see you again. Come along, Eric."

She took his arm and led him toward the street, with me following.

"Hey! Just a minute!" Igor caught up with us. "Here's one of Kielty's cards if you want to get in touch with him. You see, there's another example. He sells a house like this and clears maybe three thousand in an afternoon and he's never done a hard day's work in his life. Hey, wait! I'll put my number down too. I sure would appreciate talking to you again, Mr. Burton. Maybe we could help each other with each other's books."

Eric pocketed the card and saluted Igor, who began walking slowly to the back of the garden.

I know that in women's magazines the hero always stalks or glides or strides—in short he does just about everything but walk—but this fellow, with his powerful neck, mighty shoulders, and trim behind *did* pad along with the ease of a big cat. Eric looked willowy and uncoordinated by comparison. Igor had gone about twenty feet when he suddenly stopped full in his tracks, and slowly turning his head, looked directly into my eyes.

It was at that moment that I got the strange feeling he could read minds. At least, that he could read mine. His eyes were tilted and so dark that the pupils were indistinguishable from the irises, but it wouldn't have surprised me if those irises had been vertical. For a second that seemed like eternity our gazes locked, then he blinked lazily, the way a cat does, turned and sauntered on. It left me with a déjà vu sensation, as if we had spent eons together in the past and that I knew him and he knew me.

Tigers. Indifferent, cruel, and beautiful. Jim Corbett, the tiger hunter, wrote that he was convinced predatory animals were psychic, that they had to be in order to anticipate the flight of their victims. After looking into Igor's eyes, I was inclined to agree with Mr. Corbett. He was, I'd be willing to bet, cruel, and he was beautiful, strange as that word may sound in describing a man.

It was one of those odd moments that change the course of your life, but neither Eric nor Laura seemed to notice anything unusual.

Eric and I hurried to catch up with Laura, who was walking ahead of us now.

"Well," I said, "what's he going to call his book? *Mein Kampf* or *Das Kapital*? Whichever one, it would improve his if he learned to speak the Queen's English correctly— like."

Petty of me, perhaps, but that man's eyes had disturbed me and brought back memories I preferred to forget. I unsnagged my nylon from a bramble.

Eric looked amused. "Alas, Amy, we are not all privileged to graduate from that ancient and ivy-hallowed pile, the University of Saskatchewan."

"It was the University of Manitoba, as you well know, and I did not graduate, as you also well know."

He turned suddenly, his eyes dark and gentle.

"Sorry, love."

As I have said, when you least expect it, Eric is always kind.

"What an extraordinary young man," said Laura as we got in the car. "Actually it's been an extraordinary afternoon. You know, I was going to ask you to drive me out here to see that lot when you suggested it."

"Well, it doesn't cost anything to dream. Like." said Eric, crashing the gears as usual.

**Constable Graham
Under Surveillance
By Police Department
For Two Months
Prior To Murders**

CHAPTER FOUR. (March 4th) What a gorgeous day! After work I took a bus to the park and walked through it to get a breath of air that hadn't been exhausted by several hundred thousand other lungs. The whole downtown and most of the West End seems choked with high-rise apartments, office buildings, and humanity; what a blessing the city fathers had the foresight to leave miles of sweet-smelling nature alone. Seeing life unfold according to the design of the season rather than man was an escape to another planet, although it did make the return to the flat even more depressing.

We hadn't seen Laura since going to the Danby estate, but that night while Eric was watching TV and I was washing my hair, there was a knock on the apartment door.

Eric answered it, and wrapping a towel turban-fashion about my head, I joined them in the living room.

"Hello, Laur—" Her manner made me stop. She looked like a sleepwalker.

"Sit down," said Eric. "What's the matter?"

She sat looking up at us for a full minute, then her eye was caught by a bunch of mending on the arm of the chesterfield. I had been turning the collars of Eric's shirts.

She rose, picked them up, walked to the kitchenette and dropped them into the garbage container.

We watched her as if she had lost her senses.

"You won't be needing those any more. You can get new ones. Sit down, both of you."

We did.

"Would you like a cup of tea?" I asked, half rising. The air was charged and Laura always said there was nothing like a cup of tea during moments of stress. She motioned me to sit.

"Eric," she said finally, "I don't know quite how to tell you this, but there's no use me being hypocritical and pretending sorrow, so I may as well out with it."

She looked at me and then back at him.

"Your father is dead. He died suddenly in England several months ago. The solicitors had trouble tracing me and I just learned today."

"Oh," said Eric.

"I don't suppose it comes as any emotional shock to you. At least, I don't see how it possibly could. You were less than two years old the last time you saw him and he couldn't have cared about us or he wouldn't have behaved as he did."

Eric shook his head slowly. "I suppose you're right." Then he shook his head again. "Still, death is death, and he was my father."

"A fine father he was! Do you know the sort of life you could have lived if it hadn't been for him? The things you could have had? The person you'd be? Do you know all the things, the things that rightfully should have been yours, that he cheated you out of?"

"Shhhh, mother." Eric kept shaking his head.

"Well, he's dead now. And I'm not sorry. But that isn't what I came here to tell you. If that were all I probably wouldn't have mentioned it. What would be the use after all these years? When I think of the shabbiness of our lives, of you going out to work, still a child—oh, I'm not blaming just him. I cheated you too, by marrying him. Apart from my father, you would have been my uncle's heir. Half a million pounds sterling, prewar value, Eric, a town house, an estate, stables, furniture, silver, paintings. Oh, between him and me, we did a terrible thing to you!"

Eric rose, sat beside his mother and put his arms around her. "Mother, it doesn't matter. It's all in the past now. It never did matter to me."

She gave a short laugh, but I could see she was on the verge of tears.

"My poor boy. You are selfish, Eric. Maybe you don't care, but look at Amy. Do you think it hasn't nearly broken my heart seeing her working so hard for you? And me not able to do anything? Oh, I know she doesn't begrudge it to you, but it hasn't been fair to her either."

"I don't mind, Laura," I said. "I knew what I was getting into."

Laura smiled for the first time.

"My children. My dear children. Well, I have some good news for you. You won't have to scrimp in this beastly little flat any more. Things are going to be different from now on."

She turned to me.

"I think I'm ready for that cup of tea now, dear."

She followed me to the kitchenette, talking over her shoulder to Eric.

"It's the only decent thing I have ever known your father to do."

I switched on the element, filled the kettle and turned to Eric. His eyes met mine and he shrugged and lifted the palms of his hands.

"Laura, what are you saying?"

She suddenly gave a little sort of goat leap in the air and clapped her hands.

"We're not poor! Not millionaires by a long chalk, but Agar left me a considerable sum!"

We were too flabbergasted to speak, so we both just stood there and Laura made the tea.

"It's the first decent thing he ever did in his life," she repeated, opening the fridge door. "Where's the milk, Amy?"

Poor guileless Laura. Doomed to preordained failure in all her pathetic little business ventures, year after year. And now this! It was like a fairy story.

A lump rose to my throat and Eric still looked stunned, but not for long. A minute later he was the same old Eric and his black eyebrows drew together like a Grand Inquisitor's.

"Mother, you know I have always been against inherited wealth. It's yours. Amy and I will get along."

I was holding the tea pot and I could have clapped him over the head with it. Oh sure! I felt like screaming, the perfect utopian gentleman, to the very last. To the very last gasp of breath I have in my body and the years go by without children until perhaps it's too late.

"Nonsense, Eric," said Laura. "There's enough to go round. What good is it to me if I can't help you and Amy? And the first thing we're going to do is get you out of this wretched little hole and into a decent home where you'll have privacy to write, and Amy can live as a real wife."

Bless her! I had never spoken to her of Eric's views about parenthood, and knowing him I was positive he hadn't.

The years, the years! How long could I keep up the pretense? Eric may be so self-absorbed he doesn't notice but someday somebody would. And it might be too late.

"Just over two weeks ago I received a letter from a firm of solicitors in London asking for proof of my identity in regard to a legacy. Naturally I thought someone in my family had relented or their consciences were bothering them. It never occurred to me it might be *him*. Remember I said I wanted to go and see that lot on the Danby place? It was just a hunch, or really a daydream on my part, but it's going to come true, children, it's going to come true!"

"The Danby place? My God, that would cost a fortune!"

"Nonsense," said Laura. "Have you still got that card the young man gave you?"

I had thrown it out. I recalled doing it as I was sorting laundry and thinking it was like keeping an old Irish Sweepstakes ticket long after the race had been announced and won by somebody else. Besides, it had his name on it, and I didn't want to think about him.

"I threw it out," I said.

"Oh, well, never mind. There are other houses."

Eric is the one with the elephant memory. He may not be able to tell you what day it is or what he had for lunch, but he can recite the repeal of the corn laws verbatim, or recount a 1926 debate from Hansard on freight rates.

"What was that man's name?" Laura asked.

"Igor."

"Not him, you ninny. The other one. The real-estate man."

"Kielty," he said, and he spelled it out.

"We can trace him through the real-estate board," said Laura. "I doubt if there'd be two with an unusual name like that. I've dealt with them before with leases and things and they're always very helpful."

It would be a fine fancy to say that after Laura left we went happily to bed rejoicing in our newfound fortune.

I was far too excited. Eric sat in front of the TV with the picture flashing but the sound turned off.

I whirled around the room.

"Isn't it wonderful, wonderful, wonderful!"

He didn't answer.

"What are you thinking about?"

The dark eyes met mine. "My father."

I stopped dancing and stared at him. Like Laura, I am practical.

"It's a little late, isn't it? I mean, I hardly recall you even mentioning him. Did you ever really think about him before?"

"A few times. I suppose he never thought much about me either. We must have been a lot alike."

March 8th. Had only four days passed since I walked through the park brooding because I wasn't getting my due share of oxygen?

That walled orchard outside the heart of the city was another new planet. The three of us got out of the car and stood involuntarily taking deep breaths. Even Eric, who is no fresh-air fiend, was sniffing like a beagle.

"The country!" gasped Laura.

It wasn't, of course, but it was close enough for us.

It was our first meeting with Bernard Kielty, who was standing in front of the house. He was a fat, jovial man of about forty with a pink and white complexion that would have done credit to a baby.

Don't ask me how, but the house had been moved from the truck and stood on the huge, piled-up timbers. A plank was laid from the ground to the front door.

"We haven't put in any foundation yet. We thought it best to wait until the house and lot were sold so that the new owners could decide what they wanted in the way of construction. Now, are you ladies nervous about heights? Do you think you can manage this plank so we can have a look through the house?"

I for one was very nervous, but Laura bounded up like a chamois. Eric followed her more slowly and stopped in the middle, waiting for me.

"Come on," he said, holding out his hand.

Mr. Kielty gallantly took my arm and led me up to Eric and I finally got to the door, which was open.

Comrade Igor, looking as though he had misplaced his steed and knout, was standing in the hall, and his face broke into a grin when he saw Eric. Me, he ignored. And I didn't know whether I was sad or glad.

"Hi! Going to buy this place after all, Mr. Burton?"

Eric nodded to Laura.

"She'll decide. I'm just along for the ride."

"Now this," said Mr. Kielty, as though fearing we might confuse it with the kitchen or bathroom, "is the front hall. I think I told you that the previous owners had partially renovated the house. This tiling is genuine terrazzo. Never requires waxing—a damp mop will keep it gleaming. And here, to our left, is the living room, or—," with a coy glance at Laura, "I suppose you'd call it the drawing room. The old floors were in pretty bad shape and have had plywood laid over them as a base for wall-to-wall."

It was a lovely large room, running the full length of the house, with bay windows and window seats at both ends. The mantle of the fireplace was white marble and very elegant.

"Now across here is the kitchen, which has been fully renovated, as you can see. Walnut cabinets, dining area, heavy wiring, and behind is a nice old-fashioned pantry with bins for flour and sugar and bread. And through here is the dining room. All the light fixtures have been removed but a very lovely cut-glass chandelier hangs right there. Well, here we are back in the front hall."

A curved, open staircase led to the upper story where there were six, yes, six, bedrooms and three bathrooms—two, as Mr. Kielty informed us, 'en suite.'

"Up here," said Mr. Kielty, with a flourish of his plump hand, "is an attic with enough head room so that it could be finished if additional living space were needed. It can be reached by stairs behind that door next to the linen closet."

An attic! It might not sound like the height of luxury to most people, but after that apartment it was like the dome of St. Peter's to me.

Mr. Kielty opened the door of the main bathroom and hastily closed it after we had had a glimpse.

"The other bathrooms are completely modernized. As you can see, this is still in the transitional stage."

The walls had been ripped out and were roughly covered with plywood. There were no fixtures.

Mr. Kielty led us downstairs again.

"I can't," he said, "take you to the cellar because at present there isn't one."

He laughed heartily at his own little joke and out of politeness Laura and I joined him. Eric looked glum.

"Well, Miss Pontifax, how do you like it?"

Laura sighed.

"It's beautiful."

"And you, Mrs Burton?" He winked at Eric. "We have to please the ladies, eh?"

"Perfect," I said, and I meant it.

"Now, Mr. Burton, it's time for your opinion."

"Where'll I write?"

"One of the bedrooms could be used as a study," said Laura.

"Yes, indeed, or, Mr. Burton, when the basement is built you could have a complete lower floor, with study, bar, bath, recreation room, fruit storage room, trunk room, laundry. There is no end to the possibilities."

Eric brightened.

"It could be soundproofed," he said.

"It could indeed," said Mr. Kielty.

"I could have shelves built for my books, and a table as big as a pool table, so I could lay out all my stuff."

"Yes!" Laura's eyes were shining. "And a fireplace, I do think every room should have a fireplace. At home that's the way it was. Of course, bedroom fires were only lit when one was ill. But a fireplace gives a room a focal point, don't you agree, Mr. Kielty?"

I'm sure that no matter what Laura said fireplaces gave a room, Mr. Bernard Kielty would have agreed.

We left Mr. Kielty and went back to our apartment to talk it over. It was just a formality. We were already sold on the house.

"What's the price?" I asked. Strangely enough, that had not occurred to me until now.

"Well, I'd get a special price if I paid cash, Mr. Kielty says. Mr. Kielty says the house is owned by a trust company and they are anxious to dispose of it. Mr. Kielty would handle all the details for me. Of course, the furnace and the foundations and the fireplaces and all that would increase the cost. Mr. Kielty reckons about twelve thousand dollars extra."

Eric whistled.

"I could manage and still have enough left over for an annuity when I quit working."

It hadn't occurred to either Eric or me that she would continue at the tearoom.

"Working?" said Eric.

"Certainly. I don't propose to stop now just when we're making a decent profit. Besides, I've worked for so long I wouldn't know what to do with myself if I didn't. Amy, I thought I'd have the bedroom next to the linen closet, if you and Eric hadn't set your mind on it. I expect you'd rather have the master one, though."

I don't know why we were surprised. After all, why should she go on living in her little apartment while just the two of us rattled about in that big house? Nevertheless, neither of us had thought about Laura living with us. I certainly didn't object. It was her money, and for that matter, her house.

"Mr. Kielty says we can be in in six weeks. Some of the interior work may not be completed, but that won't matter too much. It's not as if it were winter, or anything."

Laura left, saying she would see Mr. Kielty in the morning to start negotiations for the purchase and that Mr. Kielty would look after all the details.

It still didn't seem possible. A house. A home. Of our own. Well, practically our own.

March 11. The next three days passed in a flurry of excitement.

Of course, it had completely slipped our minds that we didn't have enough furniture to furnish one room properly. Laura said not to worry, she would pay for the essentials and we could collect other items gradually after we had moved in.

With what, she didn't say.

When I started to write a list of the essentials, I was appalled. A fridge, a stove, a washer and dryer came to an astronomical amount by my frugal standards, and these were only the beginning. There were lamps, tables, chairs, curtains, carpeting, to mention only a few. Luxuries such as dishwashers, freezers, electric mixers, polishers and lawn mowers were not even mentioned.

"Good grief," I exclaimed, "we don't even own a garden hose."

"Garden furniture!" cried Laura. "We must have garden furniture. What's the use of that lovely garden if we don't use it? Put down a hose, Amy, and garden furniture."

Until now I had assumed I would give up my job when we moved, but it began to look as if I would have to go on working. Well, at least I would be working for something tangible.

But how could I work and look after a house that size as well?

"Oh," I said to Eric after Laura had gone, "there are always strings attached to things. We simply can't ask Laura for anything else and we need so much. Hell's bells, I'll be working until I'm a hundred."

Eric raised his head from his book.

"You could always take in boarders. God knows there are enough bedrooms."

He was joking, of course.

But I thought it was a splendid suggestion.

Later that night when I was in bed and Eric was getting undressed, we started the old fight.

"I should have known!" Eric threw a shoe savagely into the clothes closet. "I should have known no woman would keep a bargain! Damn it all, what do you want? You're getting a house free. Isn't that enough? Why do you have to bring that up again?"

"But two years is such a long time! We could manage somehow, even if we had to take out a mortgage!"

"Good God, woman! The house isn't even bought yet, and furthermore, as far as I know it isn't even in our name and I'm damned if I'll ask her to turn it over to us."

I could manage. I knew it. I had the vision of my boarders before me. If the downstairs were finished with an extra bedroom, we could accommodate four—maybe six, if we had couples sharing a room. I didn't mind the work and there wouldn't be rent to pay anymore.

"You made a bargain, and by God, it so happens that this is one I can make you stick to. As long as I'm taking the precautions there won't be any children. Get that straight and through your head now!"

I began to cry.

"Now stop it, Amy. Stop it!" He sat on the edge of the bed. "Listen, there's more to my attitude than you are willing to realize. Face it, Amy, with this family background we wouldn't be doing a child any favor bringing it into the world."

I sat up and slapped him across the face as hard as I could.

"I should have known you'd bring that up!" I screamed.

"Shh—keep your voice down. Do you want everybody in the building to hear you?"

"I don't care! I don't care! I should never have told you!"

There was a look of horror on his face and he took me by the shoulders and shook me till my teeth rattled.

"I didn't mean you! What sort of a monster do you think I am? Do you really think I'm cruel enough to throw that up to you? I'm selfish and I'm inconsiderate and I'm sorry, Amy, but I'm not that sort of a bastard!"

I had stopped crying. I felt terribly, terribly tired.

"Then what do you mean?"

"Honey," he stroked my hair back from my face, "I mean my family."

When I lay back he leaned over me and put his arms about me.

"It just won't wash, Amy."

"It's another excuse, that's all. Hundreds, thousands of men abandon their families. It doesn't mean any hereditary instability. You're looking for a way to have your cake and eat it too, as usual."

He stood up, pulled the comforter from the bed, and went to the living room to spend the night on the chesterfield.

I had come this far. I couldn't give up.

It was all a dream. A nightmare.

"I'm ashamed to hold my head up in this town. Even an animal has more decency than that!"

"It isn't as if we were just anybody here! People look to us to set an example!"

"Amy! Amy! How could you do this to me? Your own mother! Surely you could have told me, trusted me? Thank heavens Grandmother is dead. Three generations we've lived here and there's never been a breath of scandal."

"Well there certainly is now, thanks to her. The best thing she can do is clear out of here. Dad, don't you agree?"

"It will ruin business. People don't forget things like this overnight. Not in a town this size! I wish you had never been born!"

"We'll say she's gone to Europe, Dad. I've got my future ahead of me and there's no reason I should be stigmatized because of her! We'll just say she's gone to Europe. Indefinitely."

Gone to Europe. Gone to Europe. Gone to Europe. Gone crazy. Gone crazy.

The walls are beginning to slither and drip. They don't put people like me in places like this. This is for crazy people. I'm not crazy! Statistics prove one out of three persons requires psychiatric care at some period of life. I'm not crazy! You don't understand! I didn't want you to find out, Mama. That's why I didn't tell you. It was all so terrible. But I didn't mean to! I don't know what happened but even the doctors said it was an accident, you know that! At first the police questioned and questioned me, as if I did it deliberately, but that isn't true! Even they admitted I didn't! You do believe me, don't you, Mama? Father?

Now Amy, take your medicine like a good girl. You want to get better, don't you? Of course you do. We'll take our two little pills and soon we'll be asleep . . . asleep . . . asleep. Of course it's not a prison, dear. It has bars on the windows because it's a hospital for people who are sick as you are sick.

Now Amy, swallow your pills or we'll have to ask doctor to give you a needle and you know you don't like needles. That's the girl, dear.

Eric shook me awake.

"It's all right," he whispered. "You were having that old nightmare. Everything's OK now."

He lay beside me, and with his arms around me finally I slept again.

Who Wore Red Wig?

Police are still searching for either a middle-aged man disguised as a woman, or a woman of about sixty, wearing a red wig. He or she is believed by police to be an accomplice of Constable Graham in the robbery of the Canadian Investors Bank. Witnesses' descriptions vary, but all agree the accomplice was about five feet seven, thin, not young, and wearing what was obviously a wig.

CHAPTER FIVE. On March 15th at Laura's request, Mr. Kielty visited the apartment with several sets of plans for the lower floor and foundation. Laura had hoped to retain him in an advisory capacity for business dealings in completing the house, and we were fortunate he agreed to accept. I took the precaution of checking his standing with the real-estate board. It was excellent.

Laura's choice was wise, for Bernard Kielty had a remarkable grasp of architecture, building, renovation and contracting. Beneath that plump, old-maidish façade were discriminating taste and a large amount of plain horse sense, of which the rest of us realized we could have done with an extra portion.

I don't know what Laura paid him, but I do know he earned it on the plans of the lower floor alone. Laura insisted on Eric and me having a share in the planning, and between us we managed to change our minds half a dozen times. Bernard Kielty was a patient and good listener, but when one of us proposed a plan that was patently ridiculous, he didn't hesitate to say so, as he did in the case of Laura's billiard room.

It would take up one-third of the total lower floor area and since none of us could play billiards we saw the sense of his objections, although Laura did say a little wistfully that it sounded so nice to have a billiard room.

"Try to think of it as a pool hall," said Mr. Kielty.

There were the usual hitches but by April 25th construction had gone ahead to the stage where the house was habitable. I hate to think of the results or the time element if we had been left on our own. Material had to be first-class and the workmanship first-rate or Bernard, as we now called him, held back payments until the jobs suited his standards; and his accounting and rendering of bills to us was exemplary.

As the house was being made permanent, it became more and more attractive and seemed to grow into its setting as if it were meant to be there from the beginning.

Although bulldozers snarled and roared on all sides of us, we felt secure and more than a mite smug behind our sturdy brick walls. We used to drive out nearly every soft, spring evening, and with the bees buzzing chummily in the blossoming fruit trees, we strolled about and inspected the day's progress.

While I sat under the cherry tree jotting notes or just plain lazing, Laura bought some gardening tools and started a flower and vegetable plot at the rear. Eric, ashamed, I suppose, to see his elderly mother using a pick-ax to break up the sods, had actually dug the beds for her. Although I had never known him to be ill, his sedentary indoor life had given him a stooped, scholarly appearance, but after a few days of working in the sun his usually sallow complexion was a rich dark color and he could have passed for one of the Italian masons working in the neighborhood.

May 1st . . . Three days before the great move. I went to the house to supervise the installation of the broadloom on the main floor. The carpeting was a pale gray nylon, guaranteed for fifteen years average usage. My supervisory capacity seemed to be limited to getting in the way of the men from the rug company, but they were a good-natured trio, who, if anything, seemed to enjoy extra company.

I had brought along a thermos of coffee and sandwiches and we had an impromptu picnic in the kitchen when they were through.

"What happened to the last carpeting that was down here?" asked their foreman.

"There wasn't any," I said. "The old flooring was in such bad shape they just covered it up with plywood before moving the house."

He looked puzzled, then he shrugged. "They had something on the plywood. The tack marks are still there."

"Maybe it was old plywood they laid down," said his assistant.

"Maybe," said the foreman. "Well, good luck to you in your new house, Mrs. Burton."

"My old-new house," I replied. "They were in the midst of remodeling it. Thank you all."

The foreman gave me a curious look.

"Old?" he said, then he shrugged again and raised his coffee mug to me. "Well, good luck anyway, Mrs. Burton."

Continued from Page 1

and his family had lived in the $85,000 traditional Tudor-style home for six months. It was purchased by Constable Graham three years ago, when it was completed by the Gravesend Realty Company Suburban Development.

CHAPTER SIX. Yes, we finally made it. On May 3rd we moved in, lock, stock, and barrel, and apart from that puzzling affair of the dog the night of our move, everything went smoothly. Even my quitting work was accepted by Eric, as his mother had said it would be. He sulked for just one day, then it became too much of an effort, and with the exception of his writing, anything that is too much of an effort for Eric goes by the boards. The day following his sulk he was in his soundproofed study by eight-thirty. I took down a tray at noon and when he answered his door, his blank expression of total concentration was one I knew well.

"Why hello," he said, as if we'd bumped into each other in the park. I followed him in and put the tray on a corner of his table, which was already crowded.

He sat down and resumed his typing.

"Don't forget your lunch."

He looked up, smiled, leaned over, grabbed his dessert—a piece of pie—and ate it with his eyes still on the longhand script he was transcribing.

"You're supposed to eat the sandwich first."

He didn't answer, but a minute later, without raising his eyes, he fumbled around and found half a sandwich. I left him eating and making penciled corrections on the manuscript.

That evening, we had our first visitor. Laura brought Mrs. Mac home for dinner.

We went through the "And this is the pantry" routine, and I smiled as I remembered Bernard shepherding us around that first afternoon. We were as bad as he was. When we went to show her the upstairs, she stopped at the foot of the staircase.

"What's the matter, Mrs. Mac?" Eric had linked his arm through hers as we toured the downstairs and main floor, and now he stood, one foot on the first stair, looking down at her.

She shook her head slightly, the way you do to wake yourself from a doze.

"Jessie, are you all right?" asked Laura.

Mrs. Mac straightened her back and began walking up the stairs with Eric. Halfway up she stopped and looked back to Laura and me and the magnified eyes behind the thick lenses had a baffled expression.

"This house has a strange aura. A very strange aura. I noticed it as soon as I walked in the door."

Eric, who regarded lady teacup readers as combinations of con men and pixies, smiled.

"I thought people, not objects, had auras."

Mrs. Mac takes her profession seriously and her glance was reproving as she continued up. But she walked more and more slowly. She said nothing as we showed her the bedrooms but when we came to the main bathroom, which was still unfinished, she came to a sudden stop.

"Don't open that door!"

Eric, Laura, and I exchanged glances, and I felt my spine tingle.

"Whatever's the matter, Jessie?"

She didn't answer. She marched resolutely downstairs, put on her gloves and adjusted her hat on her silvery head.

"You're not going?" I said. "But Mrs. Mac, dinner is——"

"No," she said. "Certain places disturb me. This is one of them. I wouldn't spend a night in this house for a million pounds."

We thought it was quite nice.

"What's the matter with it?" asked Eric.

"Jessie, do you feel all right?"

"Has something happened to upset you, Mrs. Mac?"

"Vibrations," she mumbled. "Destructive! Impossible! I don't know how you can bear it."

She was off without a good-bye, not at all like our old Mrs. Mac, leaving the three of us standing looking at each other.

"Well, I never!" said Laura.

"She must be ill," I said. "I've never seen her like that before."

"Come on, let's eat," said Eric. "The poor old thing has been reading too many teacups. She's dotty."

"Jessie is no such thing," said Laura as we went into the kitchen for dinner. "I can't understand it. Something must have upset her before she got here."

We had a let-down feeling. We had been looking forward to showing off our new home.

"She must have been overtired. More salad, Laura?"

"Thank you. Yes, I suppose so. But I can't get over it. It was rude, and Jessie is never rude."

"Pass the vegetables," said Eric. "She wasn't being rude. Be sensible and face facts. Nobody would take up that line of work unless they had a screw loose to begin with."

Laura put down her fork.

"Jessie is a sensitive. Ordinary people like you or me can't appreciate her feelings because we haven't her gifts."

Eric smiled as he helped himself to the vegetables.

"I don't know about you, old girl, but I am not ordinary. Nor am I insensitive. I have all the feelings I can handle, thank you, mum. Seriously, though, people who fool around with the occult have a tendency to go off the deep end. Fortunately most of them are women so you hardly notice the difference."

Mrs. Mac never entered the house again, although as a house-warming gift she sent over a lovely little watercolor of the Isle of Skye which she had brought from Scotland

May 10th and for the following week, realizing it was necessary to have furniture before boarders, I went on an orgy of buying, going to auctions and secondhand dealers and answering ads in the paper.

I got an old, beat-up mastodon of a dining room suite including buffet and china cabinet for two hundred dollars. It was scarred and spavined, but at least one layer of it was walnut. We put it in the downstairs storage room, and the three of us worked for four evenings, stripping, sanding, and revarnishing it. Eric peeled off the old, rotting, leather seat covers and Laura and I redid them in black and white striped linen. After it had been rescrewed, reglued and refinished, I was amazed. It looked rather like an antique.

I splurged and bought a handsome Madame Récamier type of sofa for the living room. It was secondhand, but we sent it out to be professionally upholstered and French polished. At an auction I also bought two red velvet wing chairs, a set of brass andirons and two pictures with heavy gilt frames. The pictures themselves were pretty awful, one of a pair of cows in a meadow looking as if they had been stunned by lightning and the other of a black-smith shoeing what Eric referred to as a fat-assed horse's ass of a horse. He said he could not live with them. Laura thought they were beautiful. I liked the frames.

We furnished the two extra upstairs bedrooms, one with a bird's-eye maple suite which could have come straight from the set of "Sunset Boulevard"; but we did buy a new mattress for it. I sanded off about twenty cigarette burns and water marks from the dresser and sprayed on a plastic coat. When Bernard saw it he clapped a dimpled hand to his forehead and offered me a thousand dollars for it on the spot. I presumed he was joking. I was becoming fonder of Bernard every time I saw him.

Eric's study cost little to furnish. One of the carpenters built a large, plain table and installed plank bookcases. These and a straight-backed chair were all Eric wanted.

Our old dinette suite was in the kitchen and I was all set for business. There were a good many other things we still needed, but I wanted time to think over my choices and I hoped to pick up some really good pieces in the future.

I was now faced with another problem. I hadn't the vaguest idea how to go about getting boarders. Obviously one couldn't buttonhole them on the street.

I called Bernard and he suggested an ad in the paper, with his business telephone listed. Since he had some insurance forms for Laura to fill out, he dropped in.

"But why your number?"

"Zoning regulations."

"Zoning regulations?" Laura and I cried in concert.

He explained that boarding houses were not permitted in our area.

"This is a fine time to find out." Eric, of course.

"It's all right, it's all right," soothed Bernard. "These things can be got around with a bit of finesse."

Eric began arguing that it was dishonest and that he would have no part in it.

"Oh, do be quiet," said Laura. "This is a family dwelling, and they'll just be part of the family, so to speak."

Always overawed by authorities, I was worried; but Bernard said the bylaw was not strictly enforced as long as people did not abuse it flagrantly.

"Just don't get any flagrant boarders," Eric muttered, and added by way of comfort that if anything did go wrong he had never seen me before.

I don't remember exactly when it happened, but I think it was the night after this that both Eric and I were awakened by a dog howling.

"There it is again," I whispered. "That dog you heard the night we moved in."

Eric rose and went downstairs. When he returned he merely shrugged. "Black Sutch strikes again. Well, whatever it is, it's gone now. Sleep tight."

And writers are supposed to be hypersensitive.

"I can't sleep," I said. I felt jumpy. "Do you mind if I read in bed for a while?"

He was almost asleep again and gave a grunt of what I took to be consent, so I went down to his study to get one of his library books.

I chose the dullest-looking one, as luck would have it a scholarly treatise by an eminent anthropologist titled "The Myth of the Wendigo among the Northern Plains Indians."

Well, it might have looked dull from the outside, but after the first six pages my hair stood on end and I closed it with a snap and crept close to Eric's back.

The Wendigo! My God! Compared to that fearsome spirit

Count Dracula seemed as innocuous and wholesome as Mickey Mouse. Trust me. I left the light on.

A couple of days later Comrade Igor turned up. He had quit his job with the house-moving company and gone to see if Bernard knew of any work for him. Bernard suggested we might have some odd jobs, and so we had our first family retainer.

I felt hesitant about having him around. To tell the truth I didn't know whether it was him or myself I didn't trust. I needn't have worried. He sat opposite Eric at the kitchen table, gazing at him as if Eric were his guru. Me he ignored.

He informed Eric he was only engaged in this menial occupation to tide him over to a fall semester in political science and modern poetry at the new university.

"I don't know just how much needs to be done, or what we can pay you," said Eric.

Not to worry. His father owned a grain store in Regina and was staking him. All he needed was pocket money and some intellectual stimulation to see him through the summer. His father wanted him to join him in the grain store, but with a lassitude that would have done credit to a Romanoff, Igor said that that, of course, was out of the question. He was dedicated to the arts and his book.

"I think Amy wants the upstairs bathroom finished first," said Eric, for once being practical. "She tells me she's going into the boarding-house business. Come on up and have a look at it."

I half expected Igor to be offended by such a prosaic request, certainly an abrupt change from the finer things of life; but on the contrary, he seemed pleased that Eric needed him.

He was not a sensitive.

His eyes, with their slight Tartar tilt, roamed over the plywood walls and floor of the bathroom.

"Feel any vibrations?" asked Eric.

"Whaddaya mean?"

Eric winked at Laura. "Mother's friend thinks this place is haunted."

"That's a lot of horse—," Igor paused, then in deference to Laura, said, "that's a lot of nonsense. Say, how old did you say this place was?" He rapped his foot on the plywood floor.

"I don't know. Do you, Amy?"

I shook my head. As a matter of curiosity, I had intended to inquire, but with one thing and another, I hadn't got round to it.

"What do you want to pay me good money to do this for? There's nothing to laying tile. You could do it in an afternoon."

I was about to say, "Are you kidding?" but Eric beat me to it.

"Look, Igor, let's just say I'm not handy."

Igor scratched his broad chest and asked for a pen and paper.

"What color tiles you want?"

Eric shrugged and Laura said whatever I decided. I didn't know.

"The walls. You want plaster? I'm not so hot on that. Or maybe those sheets of little waterproof tiles? Or arborite? They use a lot of that now."

We didn't know, of course.

"Well, I'll get some samples and you can choose. I think you'd better get a real plasterer in. If you're going to spend five, six hundred dollars for fixtures, you don't want an amateur job, like. Got a tape measure?"

Laura fetched one from her sewing basket and we watched Igor measuring and figuring.

"You know if your plumbing and wiring are up to specification?"

"Hell, you moved the house," said Eric. "Don't you know?"

Igor scratched his chest again. "Seems to me this was already ripped out then."

"Bernard says the previous owners had everything approved and ready for installation. It's just the walls and floors and fixtures," I said.

"Well, there isn't much else in a bathroom, is there?" said Eric, glancing up at the plastered ceiling.

Igor looked up too. "That's the original ceiling. What's that hole up there?"

"The light fixture?" Eric suggested.

"No. That's in the centre. I mean that hole about the size of your fist in the corner. Well, we can get it patched when the walls are done."

Igor wrote down some more figures and turned to Eric.

"I tell you what. I got a friend who's in the wholesale business. She," and here he indicated me with a jerk of his thumb, "can meet me in town, say tomorrow, and choose what she wants and I can have it delivered in a day or so and get busy here. Save you thirty percent."

Laura decided to go to bed, but Eric, Igor, and I trooped down to the kitchen for coffee.

"How's your book coming?" asked Eric.

Igor fumbled through his pockets.

"Got a cigarette?"

Eric supplied him with one and lit it.

"Well, I'll tell you," said Igor, exhaling deeply and tapping his temple. "I got all the ideas here. What I'm looking for is somebody to collaborate with me and put them down. I'll do the thinking and they can do like the pedestrian work. You know, the typing and spelling and writing and that sort of stuff."

A wicked little smile curled the corner of Eric's mouth.

"You've got the right system, Igor. Now, why didn't I think of that? Well, it's too late now, I suppose."

"What I mean is, Eric, say, you don't mind if I call you Eric, do you? Good. What I mean is, Eric, I don't want to waste my creative energy. The concept of capability ought to be synchronized."

Eric nodded wisely. "How about rustling up a couple of sandwiches, Amy?"

"There isn't any bread. There's nearly a full cake here, though."

Eric cut huge pieces for himself and Igor, and I poured coffee.

I had the temerity to speak. "What's your book about?"

He had not, as yet, spoken directly to either Laura or me. Whether he considered us undeserving of his lordly attention or he was just plain boorish, I wasn't sure.

"Well, it's like this," he said to Eric. "I feel a functional society ought to be a projection of interplanning from the organization level."

"Maybe you've got something there." Eric cut two more huge slabs of cake. "Don't you agree, Amy?"

"Oh, absolutely," I said. Half of the cake was gone.

"You read Nietzsche?" Igor asked suddenly.

Eric nodded.

"What do you make of him?"

Eric pondered. "Well," he said finally, "I feel his total logistical contingency is predeterminedly abstruse."

Igor digested this for several minutes, munching on my cake with a formidable frown.

"You may be right. Say, you wouldn't like to go in on this book of mine with me, would you?"

Eric shook his head. "Sorry, but I'm sort of hung up on this project of my own."

Igor nodded. "I understand. You really can't digress. I find that with mine."

If I hadn't heard him I wouldn't have believed it, and listening to him was as exhausting as trying to follow a foreign language. He left shortly after and at the door he actually addressed me.

"There aren't many with his flexibility. He'll go a long way."

"Lucky me," I said. "How right you are."

He left.

"He's got to be kidding!" Eric's shoulders were heaving with laughter. "My flexibility! Darling, tell me it's not true! Say it isn't true!"

I looked at the remnant of my cake.

"He's true all right. I suppose you think you're pretty damn smart sitting there like you're James Joyce or somebody."

"A little Christian charity, if you please, Amy. What's the matter with old Igor, apart from the fact that he's always bumming cigarettes? For all you know he may be playing Beckett to my Joyce, someday. Anyway, writing is a lonely occupation and an author needs some contact with his fellow man."

He took the dishes to the sink and turned to me.

"Besides, it's flattering to be looked upon as a syllogizer, whatever that is."

Murders

Continued from Page 1

On Wednesday morning when Constable Graham still had not showed up for duty, his superior officers went through the usual routine in the case of an officer thought to be absent without leave.

A pair of investigators, after questioning neighbors and learning there had been no sight of the Graham family since Monday, forced a rear door and looked into the downstairs den. The nearest Royal Canadian Mounted Police detachment was immediately notified and an investigating team sent to the house.

CHAPTER SEVEN. May 15th, I think. I see in transcribing I forgot to put the date down. I read some place psychologists have a theory we do this with unconscious deliberation. I forget why. Also, I am too lazy to get up, find calendar and check date.

However, around May 15th I arrived at the Perry Supply Company on time and was greeted by Mr. Perry, Junior.

"I'm afraid Igor won't be here, but he phoned and asked me to look after you. I'll be glad to help you select your fixtures, if you'll come this way."

I was a little annoyed. Igor could have called me. However, Mr. Perry, who was a personable, polite young man, was very helpful, and together we chose a tub, toilet, light fixture, towel rack, and tiles.

In his office, as we totted up my purchases, the phone rang. It was Igor. Would I drop the invoice copies at his apartment?

Mr. Perry placed his hand over the mouthpiece and asked me if I would mind. The apartment was in the West End and only ten minutes' walk away.

I nodded.

As he saw me out the door, Mr. Perry explained that Igor had been at a reading given by Irving Budd, the new avant-garde poet.

"I wish I had been able to attend it," sighed young Mr. Perry. "I don't know if you are interested in poetry, but Irving Budd is fantastic, Mrs. Burton. Absolutely fantastic. His imagery is out of this world. He hasn't much of a following yet, but believe me, he'll be remembered and take his place with the immortals."

"Does his poetry rhyme?" I asked.

Mr. Perry looked first surprised and then shocked.

"The purpose of modern poetry is not jingles, Mrs. Burton. Anyone can end the first line with cat and the second with bat."

As it happened, I had read an article about Irving Budd recently. His picture showed a wispy, whiskery youth, and his poetry was on a third-grade level, in my hoary opinion.

With Igor's address in my hand, I left Mr. Perry for Igor's apartment. It was in one of those huge high-rise boxes of glass with as much individuality as one egg in a carton of other eggs.

The apartment was on the fifth floor and getting out of the elevator I noticed that peculiar combination of smells of cold cement, hot air, and new carpets that I remembered from our own warren-dwelling days.

My knock was answered by a woman. A young woman. A pregnant young woman.

She stared at me with flat, expressionless eyes.

"I—uh—Mr. Perry of the Perry Supply Company asked me to drop these off for Mr.—," here I paused. I didn't even know Igor's last name.

"Igor?"

I nodded.

"He isn't here yet." She jerked her head in the direction of the interior.

I followed her in. She was a big girl and walked with that heavy grace of pregnancy. I noticed her ankles were swollen.

The living room was simply furnished with a bookcase over-flowing on one wall.

"He'll be here in a minute. Sit down."

It had never occurred to me Igor was married. I sat on the edge of the sofa wondering what to say next. The girl sat in a chair, a straight-backed one opposite me, and picked up some sewing.

She was embroidering baby clothes, and the work was exquisite—the fine, feathery stitches in a formal design of the type often seen on folk costumes.

"What beautiful work you do," I said.

She raised her eyes. They were not exactly hostile. I suppose sullen would describe them. She did not answer.

I began to feel desperate, and when I do, instead of being tongue-tied, I talk too much.

"I'm Amy Burton," I said. "Igor is doing some work for us. We're redecorating an old house. I've just picked out the bathroom fixtures and Mr. Perry asked me to drop off these invoices for Igor."

Somehow I managed to sound as though I were trying to persuade her I was not keeping a tryst with her man.

She searched through the skeins of colored silk, held one up for inspection, threaded her needle and went on with her work.

"You have a lovely view of the bay. My, it's amazing how many apartments have sprung up recently. I imagine it's very handy to the stores and beach here, too."

Like Igor's, her eyes had a slightly Tartar look and I wondered if she came from the same racial stock.

The baby dress she was working on was pink.

"I suppose you want a little girl?"

Why in heaven's name didn't I shut up?

She put down her embroidery.

"My name's Elaina." Her voice was husky and surprisingly well-modulated.

We were interrupted by a key turning in the lock, and Igor walked in. Although he was at least twenty-eight, he dressed like a teen-ager, and with his massive, bowlegged bulk, he looked particularly incongruous in a turtleneck sweater and tight pants.

I stood up.

"Mr. Perry asked me to drop these off."

He looked over the invoices. "Sit down."

Elaina, with bent head, continued her work.

"Got a cigarette?" He was looking at me.

I gave him one and took one for myself. He lit his own; then, quite unembarrassed and obviously as an afterthought, he lit mine. Sitting beside me, he thumbed through the papers.

"Where's that list of figures I left on the coffee table last night?"

The girl rose, went to the bookcase and returned with a paper. Igor read over the figures.

"No," he said. "This tub is too short. We'll have to order one six inches longer. We can get it in the same color and style."

He raised his head and looked at the girl who was back at her sewing. He snapped his fingers.

"Get some coffee."

She rose and went in to the kitchen, but not without throwing him a glance of mocking malice.

I began to feel distinctly uncomfortable.

"You ever hear of Irving Budd?"

I nodded.

"Jeez, he's terrific. Just heard him give a reading of his own poetry."

"Yes, Mr. Perry told me."

His look was shrewd and hard, and I suddenly had a feeling I wouldn't like to cross Comrade Igor.

"You're not much with this modern bit, are you?"

I mumbled I supposed I wasn't and he went back to the invoices.

Finally Elaina brought in the coffee. There were two cups. She did not join us, and after serving it, she went to the bedroom.

I was at a loss again.

"Your wife does very beautiful embroidery."

"She's not my wife."

"Oh," I said.

We finished the coffee, and feeling even more awkward, I rose. Igor stretched and rose too.

"She wants me to marry her. Because of the baby."

"Oh," I said again.

He yawned.

"But I won't."

It's no good saying I wasn't shocked because I was, and it must have shown plainly on my face.

"Hell, why should I? I don't even know if it's mine. With a tramp like her you'd never be sure."

The bedroom door was open and she couldn't have helped but hear him.

"Good-bye," I said. "Thank Elaina for the coffee."

I fled.

When I got home Eric asked where I had been.

"Igor's apartment," I said, and waited.

"Oh. I got two chapters finished today. You know, that's a record for me. This study and the quiet are really paying off. At this rate I may be finished in a year."

I gave him a big kiss on the cheek.

"You know," I said, "you're not so bad. As a matter of fact, right now you look pretty good."

"Hey!" he said. "You want to go to bed? Nobody's here but us."

May 22nd. Laura on way to England. It happened so quickly we didn't have time to be surprised.

One night she was sitting unusually pensive before the drawing room fire when Bernard phoned. After talking to him she hung up, turned around and announced she was "going home." Bernard had arranged for her ticket and Mrs. Mac would mind the shop. The next night she was winging somewhere over the pole.

There were the usual last minute flurries. Laura couldn't get to the hairdresser's without something going wrong, and I really never thought she'd make it on such short notice; but with the indefatigable Bernard's help, she did.

Eric and I drove her to the airport, where she insisted on treating us to a cocktail. Planes were not announced in the lounge and Eric looked worried.

"Don't be so anxious to get rid of me," she said. "You know, you should be afraid I'll run into an adventurer and lose all my money."

"Hurry and finish your drink. You'll miss your plane."

"What's bothering you?"

He said nothing was bothering him, and she said he was her son and she knew him better than that and something was bothering him.

"Well, if you must know, I wish you'd spent a little more time thinking the whole idea over and planning this trip more carefully. It's all so—I don't know—so disorganized."

Laura laughed and tossed back the remainder of her drink. "What an old fogy you are. We are living in the jet age. At least, I am. And I've been thinking it over for nearly thirty years."

"You'll keep in touch with us, won't you? We won't know where you are."

It didn't sound like Eric, but like a little boy afraid of losing his mother.

"Of course. I'll bore you silly with batches of post cards. I might even write you a letter."

We guided her to the "Passengers Only" door, and with a minimum of confusion, kisses, and wavings, saw her off. Driving home, Eric was still worried.

"For heaven's sake, she's not a child, Eric."

She had traveled extensively on the continent before her marriage and had often regaled us with tales of the Grand Hotel era. How the bearded, exiled Grand Duke, cousin of the last Czar of All the Russias, had, in Paris, sent two dozen red roses daily to her hotel and tried to present her with a Fabergé Easter egg.

Or how she was ill with what was thought to be typhoid in Rome and the Italian doctor wanted to cut her hair. "I didn't have to wear wigs then. I could sit on my hair, and it really was my crowning glory. Of course, it wasn't typhoid at all. Really, you might as well call a vet as one of those Italian doctors."

The Grande Bretagne in Athens. She had seen the Parthenon by moonlight. Their party had taken champagne and a picnic lunch. They had eaten salmon and caviar while cold, pale moonbeams had flitted through the ghostly columns, and even now, the memory was dreamlike, a cameo of the past. "Of course, they don't let you do that anymore. It's closed after sundown. Places like that ought to be closed to ordinary people. It's hard to believe, but the tourists had been dismantling it, piece by piece, like a mouse nibbling on a cheese."

And the now-defunct Shepherd's in Cairo. "Those Egyptians burned it down. I must say I wasn't sorry when we lost *that* country. The natives are impossible."

Winter at the Palace Hotel in St. Moritz. "Everybody, simply everybody, was either royalty or related to royalty. Well, not exactly everybody. I remember seeing Otero, the famous courtesan. She was really just a prostitute, but all her clientele were royalty. She was common looking, a coarse, gypsy type, and I never could see what men found so fascinating about her. She took payment only in jewels. They say she lost thirty thousand pounds worth in one hour at the Casino in Monte. She went out, obliged four of her crowned patrons, and returned with enough to play until dawn and win the whole lot back again.

"And the Balkan royalty! We always avoided them. They wouldn't have been allowed in the servants' hall at home!"

"God!" Eric jammed on the brakes so suddenly I almost hit the dashboard. "Are you all right? That bastard nearly clipped me!"

I leaned back and let my breath out slowly. "Eric, you went through an amber light."

"Well, that's not illegal. What else could I do?"

"You could try waiting for the next green light!"

We were at the next corner.

"Eric!" This time I screamed. "You're in the wrong lane for a right hand turn! What in heaven's name is the matter with you?"

We didn't speak again until we reached home.

The house seemed deserted. I made tea and we sipped it in what had once more reverted to the living room. Eric tried to relax against the end of our Madame Récamier sofa, which was scientifically designed to either prang you behind the ear or dislocate your neck.

"This is the damnedest piece of furniture, Amy."

He crawled down, put his head on my lap, and lay with his eyes closed. He looked tired and I stroked his hair.

"I wish you'd stop worrying."

"I'm afraid." He sighed. "Mother may be in for one hell of a shock. She doesn't like to face reality and things are bound to have changed a lot. She's kept part of herself locked up in a castle with spun-sugar windows. I don't know what she'll do if they're shattered."

"Yes, it was awfully sudden. But sometimes people don't do things unless they do them on the spur of the moment. At least, that's what Bernard said. And as far as the spun-sugar windows, isn't that what they use in the movies to give the illusion of glass? People don't get hurt when those break. That's why they use them. The light may be a little dazzling for Laura after all these years, but she'll be all right. Do you suppose she'll visit her family?"

His eyes opened suddenly. "I hope to God she doesn't!" He sat up. "Listen, Amy, I'm done in. I think I'll go to bed. Oh, I nearly forgot. Bernard phoned while you were in the tub before we went out. A prospective boarder is coming out on Friday."

He kissed my cheek.

May 28th. Mrs. Keller, hereafter known as Frau Keller, arrived at nine this morning. I hadn't expected our prospective boarder quite so early and had been weeding Laura's vegetable garden. It was damp out, I hadn't set my hair, and I looked frumpy.

I led her into the living room.

"Excuse me," I said. "I'll just wash my hands in the kitchen."

Frau Keller was solid rather than stout. She was neatly dressed with her hair coiled lump-fashion over each ear, and I had a feeling that she would never be caught with her buns down.

"The kitchen I would like to see also, Mrs. Burton." Her accent was guttural.

Fortunately I had already cleaned up the kitchen, which is not always the case.

"Ja. Very good, Mrs. Burton." Her prominent blue eyes missed nothing, and I half expected her to run her finger over a window-sill. She poked her head into the dining room.

"All meals to be eaten here? Or is the kitchen used for the breakfast?"

"Well, I really hadn't thought about it," I said. "Whatever you choose. My husband and I live quite simply, and generally breakfast in the kitchen." As a matter of fact, now that Laura was gone, we also wined and dined there. "But if you prefer to have yours in the dining room, it will be no trouble."

"No, no!" cried Frau Keller. "We too live simply, Mrs. Burton. Lunch and dinner in the dining room will be sufficient."

"We?"

"Ja, so."

Frau Keller informed me she had a fourteen-year-old son, Rudi, who would also be a boarder. Her husband and two older sons were working in a mine in the interior.

We went upstairs and I showed her what I had come to think of as the Bird's-eye room.

She tried the mattress and inquired as to the whereabouts of the bathroom.

"Well, as a matter of fact, it's not quite finished yet. It's only a matter of a few days until it is, though. But I do have my mother-in-law's room and it has a bathroom en suite. She's gone to Europe and you could have it until the other bathroom is complete."

Laura's room was larger and Frau Keller's sergeant-major's eye lit up.

"This will be sufficient, for Rudi and me."

"Rudi and you?" Together? She *had* said he was fourteen, hadn't she? "There's a bedroom on the lower floor; we could put him there, or in the Bird's-eye room, or one of the other spare rooms up here."

"I have a cot for Rudi," she said. "This will be sufficient for Rudi and me."

A cot. Maybe she said four.

"Pardon me, but how old did you say Rudi was?"

"I have said Rudi was fourteen. There will be sufficient room beside the window for Rudi's cot. The cot is one which you call a—what is it? A roll-away?"

"Yes, that's what they're called."

"Good. That is settled. Now, Mrs. Burton, we will discuss the price for Rudi and me."

Why hadn't I asked Bernard? I had spoken of it to Eric, who had sensibly replied that it depended on whether I was going to feed them steak or macaroni.

"What did you have in mind in the price range?" I hedged.

She named a figure that seemed acceptable.

"Yes, I think that's fair. But really, though, Mrs. Keller, there are the other extra bedrooms and I haven't any other boarders at present. I wouldn't mind a bit if your son slept in the Bird's-eye room or downstairs."

"Ach, Mrs. Burton. I am happy the price is sufficient. Yes. You have of course, laundry facilities?"

"Yes," I said. Hell's bells, was I going to get stuck with that too? It hadn't occurred to me until now.

She must have guessed what was going through my mind. "Of course, Mrs. Burton, I shall not expect you to attend to our laundry. I shall look after it myself."

One up for me.

I had read somewhere, at some time, on some hotel door, that guests were expected to leave by eleven. Trying to sound authoritative, I said, "Your friends will, of course, be welcome in the living room, if they leave by eleven."

One-upmanship was difficult with Frau Keller. She fixed me with a cold Teutonic stare.

"We shall not be entertaining, Mrs. Burton."

We moved downstairs.

"It is a big house," she said.

"Yes, there's a den downstairs, too, where your son could play."

Her eyes softened. "Rudi goes to a special school, Mrs. Burton. He works very hard. Rudi does not play."

"Oh," I said.

"You have—," here she hesitated. "You have help in the house?"

"Help?" I asked.

"Ja, for the cleaning."

"Why no," I said. "I do it."

"You are getting more boarders?"

"Yes, I hope to."

"I see." She let her eyes roam over the front hall, then mentioned the price she had named upstairs.

"That, of course, it is understood, is for both of us."

Oh, no!

"Well, I really don't think we understood each other, Mrs. Keller. I thought that was for each of you."

Frau Keller was unperturbed, even though I was in a sweat of embarrassment.

"No. That is for both, Mrs. Burton."

"I don't think I could manage on that, Mrs. Keller."

She smiled as though everything was now settled.

"But of course, Mrs. Burton, we shall make on that an agreement. For the price I have said, Rudi and I will have one room, not two, and I will help you with the housework." I said nothing. I felt very wary.

"We Germans are very clean, Mrs. Burton. You will be pleased with the way I keep your house."

Us dirty old Canadians. I didn't doubt it would be clean. Whether I would be pleased was another matter.

"It is a bargain you will not regret, Mrs. Burton. Are we agreed?"

"Well, I'd have to talk it over with my husband." Craven, crummy old me. A fat lot of good he'd be.

Frau Keller beamed. "It is good, Mrs. Burton, to do that. Rudi's papa and I always discuss very carefully everything together."

I'll bet they do. How do I get in these messes? I said I'd phone her.

Eric, of course, was no help. He suggested that I call Bernard, which I had already decided to do anyway. After all, he'd sent her.

At this point the phone rang. It was Turner, Turner, Greenbaum, Maples, and Turner. Would I consider coming in for four afternoons a week? There would be a substantial rise in salary.

It's nice to know you are missed, and little wheels began turning in my skull. I could not possibly manage the house and job together, but with Frau Keller's assistance I might come out considerably ahead financially. I resolved to see Bernard that afternoon and to phone them my decision later.

I got an appointment with Bernard for two o'clock. His office surprised me. He himself was so courtly I had rather expected a Dickensian atmosphere—not quite quills and candlesticks, but at least a few roll-top oak desks and heavy ledgers. Instead it was more like a swank country club with thick carpets, leather lounges, and sporting prints.

"Well, Amy, you are looking well. What can I do for you?"

As always, he looked like a big rosy baby, fresh from his bath, immaculately starched and dressed by a doting nanny.

I explained about the job and Frau Keller's offer.

"I haven't had lunch yet. Come on, let's go. We can talk while we're eating."

We went to the King George, where Laura and Mrs. Mac and I had lunched before.

"Well now, Amy, this sounds like the answer to both our prayers. You get the job and free housekeeping, and I get rid of Frau Keller."

That didn't sound auspicious from my point of view. Bernard had ordered double martinis and I sipped mine. He had finished his before I said, "I don't understand, Bernard."

"Drink up, Amy. Don't be a piker. Toujours gai." He beckoned the waiter for more. "Well, it's like this, Frau Keller's husband and sons are into me for quite a bit of money. A business deal I backed that went sour. The three of them are working up in the mines, and making a packet, I don't mind saying; and they're paying me back in installments. They're honest, hardworking people, Amy. Most of the Germans I've met have been, bless their little hearts. Say, how come we won the war? Well, anyhow, back at the old ranch, I'm keeping an eye on Mrs. Keller and the little fellow. You'd be doing me a favor if you could take them in. I mean, particularly if it would help you. The cheaper it is for Frau Keller to live, the quicker they pay me off. And it's a responsibility having her and the boy here. It would be a load off my mind, knowing they're with you."

"Poor Bernard." I patted his hand. "You seem to get stuck with all the lame ducks in the barnyard. As if we're not enough. I don't know what we would have done without you, Bernard."

He ordered his third double and squeezed my hand. He was getting sentimental, which was no wonder, the way he could toss back martinis.

"Don't worry about me, Amy. If I didn't like doing it, I wouldn't do it. It makes me feel wanted."

"You're not married, Bernard?"

His Kewpie-doll face crumpled, then he laughed. "Now who'd

want an old fogy like me? Oh, there was someone a long time ago but—well—it was one of those things."

"I'm sorry," I said, and I was.

During lunch he finished his fourth double martini. I wondered if he always drank this much, but apart from his baby skin being more flushed and his eyes more twinkly, he seemed steady enough.

"Well, that's settled," he said as we rose. "If there are any complications, just yell for old Uncle Bernie. That's what I'm for. Say, I got a nice card from Laura in London."

"Yes, so did we."

He helped me on with my coat.

"Poor Laura. She's had a hard row to hoe." Actually, it came out as "she's had a hard hoe to row." "She's a fine person, Amy. A very fine person. I was so pleased when she came into that money."

"Oh, did you know her then?"

Bernard looked surprised. "Why yes. Only slightly, of course. I handled the lease on her teashop. Mr. Wong, the owner, is a client of mine. Poor old Laura has a bee in her bonnet about him, as if there were a vast conspiracy of two billion Chinese after her."

"I know."

"Well, these old-country people with breeding live in a different era. Empire and all that. Laura's an anachronism, you know. People may laugh at the Lauras of this world; but there aren't too many of them left, and it's a privilege to know her."

We were on the street now.

"I suppose you'll have Frau Keller on your eastern front in a couple of days, but I think you'll find her quite satisfactory, Amy. You'll get along fine. Just let her know who has the whip hand."

"Yeah, her," I said. "Oh!" I put my hand to my head. "Good heavens, Igor will have to get cracking on that bathroom."

Bernard turned and waved a pink forefinger warningly. "Watch that fellow, Amy. Nothing sinister or anything like that, just a case of giving and taking an inch and a mile, if you know what I mean. Can I give you a lift anywhere?"

I thanked him and told him no, that I was walking to the offices of the interminable Turners to accept their offer.

Graham Neighbors Angry

Sightseers by the thousand have driven down the quiet street to the Graham house and neighbors, outraged by a stream of cars driving by at the rate of one hundred an hour, have asked police to put up a roadblock.

One, who asked not to be identified, said neighborhood children are being stopped and asked which is the house. "My wife has had a nervous breakdown because of this tragedy. The children have had enough, losing their playmates. Now they have to put up with these ghouls. The cars started arriving Wednesday, just after the news broadcast of the bodies being taken out."

"I counted 250 cars after the churches finished their Sunday services," said a woman resident. "What are we expected to tell our children? I said that people are looking at houses to buy and Sunday is their only day, but the children don't understand why they have come all of a sudden. My youngest said, 'But how can Bobby find his way back with all these people?' And just what do these ghouls tell their own children whom they bring with them in their cars? It's enough to make you sick. As if we didn't feel badly enough, and one of us already under psychiatric care because of this!"

"It's a miracle none of our children has been run over," said another neighbor. "Until we put a ladder across our driveway, they were using it as a turnabout while the kiddies were playing on it. We are all disgusted and hope some adverse publicity will make these people ashamed to show their faces here!"

CHAPTER EIGHT. It happened the next morning. I could hear Igor bashing about in the bathroom upstairs, and at eleven he came down for coffee.

Eric, who had sent several chapters of his book to a firm of New York agents to see if they would consider handling him, had for the last three days been haunting the letter box anxiously. When he heard the postman slam the little metal door of the mailbox at the foot of the garden, he was off like a child to a birthday party.

Igor, as usual, had bummed a cigarette from me and was sitting sipping his coffee when Eric came in looking disappointed.

"Just a card from mother. She's in Hastings. And this package for you."

It was about five inches square and wrapped in brown paper.

"You order something?" He shook it. "Well, it doesn't tick."

I wiped my hands on a towel and opened it.

It contained a tiny blue-felt baby shoe. A bloodstained blue-felt baby shoe.

I fainted.

I was lying on the sofa in the living room, my head on Igor's lap. Eric, his face shockingly pale, was bending over me, putting a glass to my lips.

"Look out. She'll choke." Igor lifted me to a half-sitting position.

The hand holding the glass was trembling.

Someone was screaming.

"You better call a doctor, Eric."

"No!" The person screaming was me. "I won't see a doctor!"

Eric shook his head. "Come on, Amy, drink a bit. It's mother's brandy." He looked to Igor. "She had an accident several years ago. She's funny about doctors. I'm going to phone the police, Amy."

"No." The screaming had stopped. That other Amy's voice was whispering now. "Somebody knows!"

"Look, Amy, I've got to. This could go on and on. Like blackmail. It was a monstrous thing to do to you and I want to get to the bottom of it."

"No! No! Please, no!"

He sat opposite me, his head in his hands. Even his shoulders were trembling. Finally he raised his face.

"Amy, don't you understand? It could happen again. Someone unbelievably cruel played that trick. I've got to phone the police."

"If you do, I'll leave."

"Knows what?" Igor's voice rumbled in his chest against my ear and I started. "What gives here, Eric?"

"Nothing." Eric stood up. "Come on, Amy. Lie down for a bit in bed. I'll bring you up a nice hot cup of tea and rub your head for you."

He helped me up and took my arm, leading me toward the stairs. Igor, a puzzled look on his face, followed.

My knees buckled. Igor caught me as I fell back.

"I'll carry her," said Eric.

He was still trembling and giving him a look of disdain, Igor carried me up with Eric hovering anxiously at his shoulder.

"I wish I knew what was going on here," said Igor as he put me on the bed. "You oughtta call a doctor."

"She'll be all right." Eric pushed Igor lightly toward the door.

"There's something funny about this house," said Igor as Eric began closing the door in his face. "Something funny. I felt it for a long time. You sure you're okay, Amy?"

It was the first time he had called me by my Christian name.

Eric closed the door quietly and knelt by the bed. "Please, Amy, I know it's terrible for you, but let me phone the police and a doctor."

"What's the use?" I said and turned my face to the wall, which, as in the past, I knew would be there. "I always knew some day someone would find out. When I thought I was safe."

Eric stroked my head.

"You are safe. This time you're not alone." Then, as if to accentuate his helplessness, "I wish mother were here."

Poor Eric.

Madness does not spring full-panoplied from the brow of Jove. Either it lurks, waiting for that special set of circumstances; or one is driven, bludgeoned like an abattoir-bound animal, to it. But this was my sanity, and with long-born cunning, I knew how to protect myself. No doctors. No police.

"What did you do with it?"

"With what?"

"You know what I mean."

"It's still there."

"Burn it."

He nodded.

"Will you?"

He said he would. But did he? He gave me a sleeping pill.

"Go to sleep now. I won't leave."

I felt drowsy and sighed. The horror began to recede. It never fades, but you can live in a state of acute terror for only so long, then the brain's defense mechanism triggers off a blessed dullness.

"Igor was kind," I mumbled. He had been, too, and he had actually seemed concerned.

"So was Deverenko. Until the revolution."

"What are you talking about?"

"Deverenko. The giant Cossack who carried the little invalid Czarevitch everywhere. He was kind. Until the revolution. Then he was the worst of the lot."

"Oh, no! Eric, do you think Igor did it?"

He turned his face from me.

"Who knows? It could be. Who knows?"

"Only you," I said. "I never told anyone but you."

He smiled and continued stroking my head.

"I didn't mean it that way. Don't fight that pill. Try to sleep." He put his cheek next to mine. "Poor Amy. My poor little Amy."

May 30th. They arrived. Light was streaming in the window and I had nearly slept the clock around. I heard a bumping on the staircase, and sitting up and looking through the open bedroom door I saw Eric carrying a roll-away cot.

"My wife is not well today."

Behind him, carrying shabby suitcases, were Frau Keller and a slight blond boy. I don't know how you say "Tsk, tsk" in German, but Frau Keller made the approximate sound. She stopped in the doorway, looking capable and surprisingly kind.

"Don't worry, Mrs. Burton. I will look after the house." She put down her suitcases and reaching behind her, pulled the boy to the front.

"This is my Rudi."

"Hello," I said.

The boy raised his eyes for a fraction of a second, then returned his gaze to the floor.

"Can't you say hello to Mrs. Burton?" She ran her hand over his stubbly head. He didn't reply and she smiled at me.

"Rudi is shy, but in a day or two you will be friends. Yes, Rudi?"

They went on to their room and I lay back and fell asleep.

Shortly afterward, she came up with a tray containing soup, a sandwich and tea.

"Ach," she said. "Everything from a can today, Mrs. Burton. A very expensive way to eat. But tomorrow things will be different."

She did not, I gathered, approve of cans.

"I have taken down to Mr. Burton his lunch and this afternoon he will drive me shopping."

She bustled about, straightening the bedclothes and puffing pillows. "One day in a house a man makes things—how do you say it?"

Knowing Eric I was going to suggest a dog's breakfast, but instead I nodded and said, "A mess?"

"That is it. Now, you lie back and rest. I will look after everything. Mr. Burton tells me you are returning to work part-time."

"Yes. I'm to start tomorrow."

I relaxed. Somebody was taking over and I was glad.

June 1st. If this were April 1st I would have thought somebody was playing a particularly pleasant joke on me. When I returned from the office the house looked as if the seven maids with seven mops had been on duty, and a warm, spicy aroma drifted from the kitchen.

The dining room table was set up with a white linen cloth and the Spode dinner set Laura had given us as a wedding present was laid out. There was even a bowl of lilies-of-the-valley gracing the center of the table.

Eric, who usually eats slumped over his plate with a book propped against the sugar bowl, was wearing a tie and looking miserable. He said little during dinner, while the boy was as silent as he had been the day before.

Frau Keller gently coaxed Rudi to eat. "He doesn't eat enough to keep a bird alive. But Rudi will eat Mutti's strudel, won't he?"

I found it disconcerting when she addressed him throughout the meal in the third person, as if he were a baby or a pet.

Rudi nibbled his food and remained resolutely silent.

That evening I sat up in bed reading, with Eric perched on the edge. He said nothing, but kept looking at me out of the corner of his eye, and I had a well-founded feeling that he had made up his mind to dislike Frau Keller.

"Well," I said, "say it."

"Say what?"

"That you don't like her."

"If you're going back to work, we'll need her. I guess you can get used to anything."

"Hmmmm." I folded the note Igor had sent me and used it for a bookmark. I half thought of telling him and then changed my mind. "Good night."

June 2nd, a hot morning, so I wore a low-cut sun dress. The bay glittered but it was cooler by the water and I wished I had brought a sweater.

As I knocked on Igor's apartment door I wondered why the note said not to tell Eric.

"Come in."

Igor smelled nice. After-shave lotion, I suppose.

"You look pretty, Amy."

My God! From Igor!

The apartment, which I had barely noticed the first time, was like a thousand others in the West End, which was probably why I hadn't noticed it. Hardwood floors, plaster walls, big windows looking over the water. Sailboats were skimming about, I heard a tug hoot, and across the bay the stage-scenery mountains were unusually clear.

He stood looking at me, his hands on his neat hips.

"Sit down. I'll put on some coffee."

Instead he sat beside me.

"You wanted to see me about something?" I felt vaguely uneasy. No. Not just vaguely uneasy. Very uneasy. Whether I liked it or not, Igor attracted me.

"It's early yet. Only ten-thirty. I know when you go to work so don't be in such a rush." He leaned over and removed my sunglasses. "You don't need those in here."

I knew I should get up and leave right then. That very instant. Instead, I sat. Waiting. And willing. Oh yes, willing and remembering that those who do not learn from history are bound to repeat it.

I blushed and straightened up, but already I knew I was lost.

"Could I have a cigarette, Igor?"

Wonder of wonders, he had one.

"Your hand's shaking, Amy." His was quite steady.

Was he going to show me his etchings first?

He seemed to read my thoughts, and gesturing to the bare walls said no, he didn't have any. He puffed his cigarette with one hand and stroked my bare back with the other.

"You wanted to see me alone?"

"Yeah. Not much chance of that at your place now, is there?" His hand continued to stroke me gently, and he stubbed his cigarette. "Amy. Nice name. I know a lot about you, Amy, and I like you, too. Come on, relax."

My neck as well as my face was burning now.

He slid one hand under my knees and lifted me on his lap. "Better?"

Yes, damn it, it was. "I should go," I whispered. In a weak voice. He shook his head and buried his face on my neck. I liked it. I liked the smell of him. I liked the feel of him. I liked the rasp of his freshly shaven cheek on my breast.

"Your skin is beautiful, Amy. It's the first thing I noticed about you."

We stopped talking. He may have been a boor in other ways but when it came to seduction he moved so gently, so steadily, and so surely that it was sleight of hand in slow motion.

Was I dreaming? What was I doing here sitting on this man's lap half dressed, as he kissed with the relish of a professional wine taster? I was thoroughly enjoying it, that's what I was doing.

Up until now it was I who was blushing and breathless. Suddenly his heart pounded and when he raised his face his eyes seemed glazed.

Picking me up he carried me to the bedroom and placed me on the bed. He pulled his shirt over his head and stood over me, his gladiator's chest heaving. Sitting on the edge of the bed he began to remove one shoe.

Then everything went wrong and the flowers of delight faded. Behind him, on the dresser, neatly folded, was the little pink embroidered baby dress.

I had not thought of that girl until now. Igor's eyes followed mine. I sat up and pulled my unzipped and unhooked wardrobe about me, but he pushed me back, pinning me to the pillow with his shoulders.

"Never mind about her."

But it was too late and I shook my head.

"You want it."

"Let me up," I said.

With a mumbled obscenity he did and he looked as though he would like to strangle me. I could hardly blame him. I had had plenty of time in the living room for scruples.

I was sorry, but not for Igor. I was sorry I had so many inhibitions. Considering the circumstances, he behaved remarkably well. He put on his shirt and the one shoe he had removed and he even zipped up the back of my dress for me.

We went into the living room where we stood looking awkwardly at each other.

"I should of known," he said finally. "Well, let's face it, you're not my type. Oh, you're okay, I guess, and your figure's better than I thought it would be."

"I guess I'd better go," I said.

"Not yet." He was nothing if not honest at the wrong time. "We might as well have the coffee. I want to talk to you. Forget about that business." Here he inclined his head toward the bedroom. "I thought it would be easier that way. Easier for you. That's what you want, whether you'll admit it or not. You don't think that's why I asked you here, do you?"

"Easier?"

He was angry and controlling his anger. I suppose I deserved it. Being deserving of something doesn't necessarily make it easier to bear.

"I thought it would be easier for you, that's all."

"Easier?" I repeated. My voice was getting a sharp edge. What was he driving at?

"You're a born old maid with hot pants, Amy. A tough combination, isn't it? When I saw you in that dress showing a bit for a change, I thought maybe things would work out easier for you."

I would have loved to have slapped his face, like women do in the movies. I didn't dare.

"Hell, I was doing you a favor and you would have loved it too."

I ground out the cigarette I had lit. He was so eloquent.

"Just why did you ask me here?"

He leaned toward me until our faces nearly touched again, but this time his eyes were not glazed. They were alert and hard.

"That house. You and I got to talk about that house, Amy."

I was already at the door. I could have spat at him. He thought that package had something to do with the house. I knew it didn't. That package was for me alone.

"I don't have to talk about anything with you."

He realized he had taken the wrong tack and was immediately over me, a hand on either side of the door.

"Come on, now, don't be like that. We got off on the wrong foot, Amy, but you and I are going to be good friends. You'll see. I'll be the best friend you ever had, Amy."

He was whispering and his lips brushed my cheek.

"I can wait." Then, "That's not an old house made new, Amy. That's a new house made old. I'll prove it to you. And I'm going to find out why."

I pushed him away and fled.

He turned up for work at the house the day after our meeting, and if he was self-conscious about what had taken place, he managed to hide it.

My own feelings were so confused that when I saw him sitting at the kitchen table drinking beer with Eric I felt like one of those rubber balls attached to a rubber string, bouncing between desire and dread.

I wished I could discuss it with Eric, but of course, he was the one person with whom I couldn't. I had a feeling I knew what he would say, though. He once told me that only a masochist would willingly put up with him. Maybe he was right. I was weak and Igor was merciless with weaklings. I knew Igor for what he was but I still couldn't think of him without a sinking feeling in the pit of my stomach. He wanted something from me and he despised me. I wanted something from him and I feared him. Who was Igor?

Ambulance Driver Treated At Hospital

Robert Miles, ambulance driver who helped remove the bodies of the slain children, was later given treatment for shock at the General Hospital.

"It was like a battlefield. I have never seen anything like it. Even the house was shot to pieces. It was horrible."

A Royal Canadian Mounted Police officer said that in more than twenty years of police work he had never encountered

Please Turn to Page Two, Column 8

CHAPTER NINE. (June 8th) Weather still grand, and Laura's garden coming up nicely. Puzzled by Rudi. A strange boy. At first I was pleased to have a child in the house, but it's increasingly apparent he's not like other children.

Eric soon dubbed him the wunderkind and after a few attempts at being cordial left him to himself, which seemed to suit Rudi. He went to a special school, being picked up by car at eight in the morning and not returning until nearly four. After dinner, which he always sat through silently, he went to his room, while Frau Keller and I cleaned up the kitchen and did the dishes.

She watched over him with an anxious maternal eye, ready to cater to any whim, only Rudi did not seem to have any whims. His mother tried to coax him down to the living room to watch television after dinner, but no matter what was showing, his attitude was one of stony indifference. Frau Keller, that bundle of energy and efficiency, was reduced to a soft, quivering lump as she tried to humor her grim offspring.

"Damn it all, Amy, the boy's like a zombie," said Eric. "You can't get at him or to him or near him. What's the matter with him?"

I didn't know. He was certainly not a likable child and I felt a mixture of pity and irritation with Frau Keller, whose manner was slavish, almost groveling, where Rudi's welfare was concerned. The reverse of the tigress defending her cub. If his safety or comfort were at stake, she was willing to be a doormat.

So much for our first two boarders. The next, also by courtesy of Bernard, was Elspeth Mackinnon, aged eighteen and a theatre usher. Underneath a calcimined exterior she had a youthful bloom of beauty that was breathtaking, and soft gray eyes ringed with mascara hardened to the texture of argillite.

She also parked her gum on the edge of her plate, left yard-long strands of hair in the bathroom sink, and as far as I could estimate, was courted by every male in the metropolitan area.

She immediately endeared herself to Frau Keller by asking what was the matter with that creepy kid.

When I suggested as tactfully as I could that we would all appreciate it if she wiped off the liquid makeup, mascara and hair that she left in the bathroom, she looked at me cheerfully.

"Yeah. You don't wear makeup, do you?" She then dismissed me with a breezy, "Oh, well, I guess at your age it doesn't make any difference."

Frau Keller, following like an angry bloodhound in the wake of Elspeth's soiled and discarded clothing, hated her. I thought the girl was selfish, immature, loudmouthed and flippant.

Eric said she was the new generation and we might as well get used to a world full of her.

When she learned that Eric was a writer she batted her great eyes and sighed, "Gee, a real writer. My boy friend lent me 'Ulysses.' You read it?"

Eric nodded.

She looked up at him admiringly.

"The language is kinda difficult to understand, but I think he was so courageous for his time, don't you? Do you understand it?"

"Just the dirty words," said Eric.

She amused him and he said we were jealous of her. Who knows?

Strangely enough, Igor and she took an immediate dislike to each other. Neither would be drawn out on the subject, but from remarks passed it seems he thought she was a tart and she thought he was a square trying to be hip.

Or, as she put it, "What's an old guy like him trying to push?"

Thursday started out like any other day, except that I didn't work on Thursdays. Frau Keller, who liked to rise with the lark, got up first and sent Rudi off to school. Elspeth was on night shift and slept in, and by nine I was out in the garden.

The earth here is rich, mulched by a score of autumns' leaves, and everything that Laura planted was flourishing. The dew was still heavy, and as I walked down the neat rows of scarlet runner beans and smelt the air, I thought how the house had changed our lives. As I looked up at it, strong and welcoming, I had that wonderful protected feeling I used to have as a child when I snuggled down with a book under the rafters at home. I wasn't the little match-girl looking in at other people's Christmas trees any more.

It was eleven-thirty before I knew it and when Frau Keller called me in for lunch, I was surprised. I patted our red brick wall which shut out the ugliness of life and on my way to the house I picked some branches from an old lilac bush that was in bloom.

We were not so formal now and ate lunch in the kitchen. Igor, who was paneling the den downstairs, came up with Eric, and smacked his lips when he saw the cold pork, potato salad and a cake called *streusel*-something-or-other that Frau Keller put on the table. Then he bowed his head and buried his face in the lilacs I carried. When he raised his head his eyes looked straight into mine and my heart thudded.

Frau Keller didn't quite know what to make of Igor. Was he friend or servant? Like a lot of Europeans, she had trouble stepping over a certain line. She did not treat him with the deference Eric and I enjoyed, but she kept a servile, if wary, eye on him, and like most good cooks, was flattered that he enjoyed her food.

She had an absent-minded habit of slipping into German that sounded like English, until you suddenly realized it meant something else.

"Es gut," she said to Eric.

Eric nodded. "Yes, it is."

She smiled. "No, no. Eat good. Eat more, Mr. Burton."

Conversations with Eric have a tendency to leap about erratically.

"What brought you to this country, Frau Keller?"

"Canada is a very good country to those who work hard, Mr. Burton. My husband and my sons, they make more money in the mines here in six months than two years at home."

"What are you going to do with all this money?"

Pay Bernard back, I hoped.

Frau Keller's face had a dedicated expression.

"We save to buy an inn. A ski resort. Wolfgang, my eldest son, will be the instructor. Papa will be manager and Dieter will be, how do you say it—a little bit of everything."

Igor looked up sharply from his food.

"Where?"

"In Bavaria," said Frau Keller. Then the color rose to her face and she turned from us.

"Don't you like Canada, Frau Keller?" Eric smiled and I was suspicious. Sometimes he is funny. Sometimes he isn't. "Bavaria. Bavaria," he continued. "Why, Frau Keller, that's Hitler country! Is it not, Frau Keller?"

"Why, of course I like Canada, Mr. Burton! But we were never political. Never!"

"Of course you weren't, Frau Keller."

She turned to Igor and her amiability was gone. "But we saved the world from Communism. No one can say we didn't do that!"

"This cake is delicious," I said, trying to change the subject.

Eric leaned back. "You certainly did, Frau Keller, and I for one am very grateful to you. Aren't you grateful too, Igor?"

I know these moods of his and I hate them. "That's enough!"

"And Rudi," said Eric, as if I hadn't spoken. "You didn't mention Rudi's position in the hierarchy of the inn. Where will Rudi be, Frau Keller? We know what used to happen to the Rudis in

Germany, but what happens to the Rudis in Germany now, Frau Keller?"

She was backed up against the sink and her face paled at the mention of Rudi. Igor was smiling like a wolf.

"Why can't you let me alone?" she said to him. "What have I done to you?" She pointed her finger at him as if he and not Eric was responsible for the conversation. "You are the real murderers! I know what happened when you invaded my country!"

She then turned to Eric. "You blame us for the Jews! They did it! They did it! Ask him what they did to the Jews in the Ukraine! Ask him who were the killers in the concentration camps! We didn't have to kill Jews! They were waiting to do it for us!"

"Igor?" Eric sounded shocked. "But my dear Frau Keller, Igor is a native-born Canadian who has never been near the Ukraine."

"Yeah," said Igor, sitting back and picking his teeth with a match, "and I never killed anybody."

"Some of his best friends are Jews. Irving Budd, for instance," said Eric. "How come you haven't got any German friends, Igor?"

"Stop it!" I hissed. "Leave her alone!"

Frau Keller was trembling with anger, fear, and indignation.

They turned to me like a pair of twins.

"What did I say?"

"Or me?"

I started clearing the table, and mockingly protesting their innocence, they rose and left. Between hammerings I could hear Eric's typewriter click. I felt ashamed to face Frau Keller.

"Leave the lunch dishes for me." Then I went down to Eric's study.

"What's the matter with you? Why did you behave like that? Igor's a slob, but you know better!"

He didn't even look up from his typewriter.

"Oh, go away, Amy. I'm busy."

"You made up your mind not to like her the minute she got here. Well, you can just quit it because she is staying! You make me sick!"

I slammed his study door.

Well, he had certainly spoiled the morning. The inside of the bathroom cupboards upstairs were still unfinished, and after doing the dishes I got out the rags, brushes, and paint.

Kneeling on the bathroom floor, I had my head and shoulders in the cupboard under the sink when something touched me softly on the bottom. I started violently and bumped my head on the pipe under the sink. When I sat back on my heels I found myself looking at the sturdy, bowed legs of Igor.

"Sorry I scared you." He pulled me to my feet.

"Sh! Elspeth's asleep." Her room was next to the bathroom.

Igor smiled and nodded, then leaned over me. "I want to show you something," he whispered.

"No. And please don't be rude like that to Frau Keller again."

"Me? Rude? Come on, Amy. We don't want Eric to know, do we?"

"Know what?"

"What we did at my place. Follow me."

He took my arm and led me into the hall, opened the door leading to the attic and gently pulled me after him.

It was hot and dim and fragrant with the smell of cedar and my heart was pounding.

At first I thought he was going to kiss me, but instead, he slid his hands under my arms and lifted me above his head.

"Smell that wood," he whispered, then he lowered me slowly.

"That's new wood, Amy. New wood. It's not over three years old. And come here."

Where the eaves were low in the corner of the attic he dragged me to my knees and pointed.

"I plastered that hole in the bathroom ceiling, but see, there's still a hole in the wood here."

It was so hot. I felt faint. "What do you mean?"

"Why, Amy? Why? We're going to find out."

He slid softly over on his back and pulled me on to him. His legs twined mine like iron serpents, his mouth was on mine, his breath was mine, and I was his.

Oh God, what had I done! I pulled my clothes together and sat huddled against the sweet-smelling wood.

First Igor stood up, then he squatted down beside me.

"Kielty knows something. But he won't talk. We'll find out, Amy. You and me. Where did the old girl get the money for the house?"

Self-loathing almost choked me.

"Go away. Leave me alone."

"Okay." He sounded agreeable. When he reached the stairs leading down from the attic he stopped; and then, "What's it feel like to be laid by a slob, Amy?"

I remember hearing Elspeth's record player thumping through the house, and I remember she was late for dinner.

As I was getting undressed for bed, Eric, who had been standing brooding at the bedroom window looking over the garden, turned to me. He took me by the shoulders and swung me around.

"I've promised you it won't happen again. What else can I say? I agree I'm a bastard and I don't know what gets into me, but I've said I'm sorry. Can't you forget it?"

What on earth was he talking about?

Model Father, Say Neighbors

Graham belonged to the Little League, P.T.A., and was an usher in church. The family went fishing nearly every weekend. Fishing rods, including children's-size ones, were found in the carport storage room. In the carport itself leaned three bicycles and neatly stacked nearby were four bundles of newspapers, tied and ready to be picked up for the local Rotary paper drive. Graham had helped the children to collect them.

CHAPTER TEN. (June 12th) For some reason or other the old nursery rhyme "Boys and girls, come out to play,/The moon doth shine as bright as day," has been going through my mind all morning with the persistence of a singing TV commercial.

Do people realize how sinister that apparently innocent little verse is? Boys and girls don't go out to play in the moonlight unless something is very much the matter.

Eric promised to be nice to Frau Keller. She responded nobly. No grudges. Reason? Rudi.

Rudi, sitting at the table, with a heaped plate of Frau Keller's delicacies before him. I saw it happen.

He suddenly seemed to explode, his head jerking and his arms shooting up suddenly. His dinner sailed across the room.

Perhaps exploded is the wrong word, for it was done dispassionately, a marionette with the strings pulled the wrong way.

With a cry Frau Keller ran to him, then wringing her hands, she turned to us and apologized.

Eric looked at the boy in disgust. Frau Keller, on her hands and knees frantically picking up dumplings, saw his expression. She gave a terrified whimper and crawled to him, her hands outstretched.

"Please! Do not send us away! It will not happen again!"

Eric took a step back. It was horrifying to see this big woman on her knees begging and I realized it was a scene she had played before.

Eric turned his head and took another step back, as though he found her so repugnant that he could not face her.

"It was an accident," I said, taking his arm, then I got down to help Frau Keller. Eric stood with averted face; and Rudi, the most horrifying thing about the whole incident was Rudi. Rudi sat like a little graven idol.

Frau Keller was the first to collect her composure.

"Rudi will take his meals in our room. I am very sorry, Mr. Burton." With her arm about the boy, she led him upstairs.

"He ought to be in an institution."

No! Anything but that! No wonder she had been on her knees.

"What was it Churchill said? Either at your feet or your throat. Amy, she's afraid of something."

I knew what she was afraid of. She was afraid Rudi would have to be put away.

Frau Keller's resilience was remarkable. After taking a tray up to Rudi and doing the dishes, she sat beside the living room fire crocheting, as I recall, a tablecloth. When Elspeth came home from work at nine, Frau Keller called that her dinner was warming in the oven for her, then, rising, she turned to me.

"Good night, Madame."

Yes, it was a strange household. Frau Keller had cleared the dining room table, so Elspeth ate in the kitchen, a movie magazine in front of her.

"What's playing at the theatre now, Elspeth?"

She raised her charming, grotesquely painted child's face and smiled.

"*Becket*. It's good. You seen it?"

I shook my head.

"It's about these two guys. One of them's a king and the other was like a minister. They're both kind of fruity."

"Elspeth," I said, "how did you come to us? Is Mr. Kielty a friend of yours?"

Her mouth was full and she mumbled, "Kind of."

"A boy friend?" He was close to forty but unlikelier things had happened.

Elspeth hooted. "You gotta be kidding!"

She was impossible to talk to and I went upstairs to bed. An hour later I knocked on her door. When I looked in I saw that her clothes were, as usual, festooned from every article of furniture. Books, magazines, and ashtrays were everywhere. On her dresser, flanked by the largest assembly of cosmetics I had seen outside of a department store, was a doll. It had long, skinny cloth legs, a garish flounced satin skirt, and a harshly painted face that looked remarkably like Elspeth.

"Elspeth, would you please turn your record player down?"

She shrugged, gave a cheerful grin and closed the door.

At two o'clock a terrible sound woke me. It began with a shriek, sank and was stifled to a burbling groan; then there was silence.

Eric and I threw back the covers and rushed to the hall. Elspeth was there, her long hair flowing to her waist and her face, innocent of makeup now, was blank with terror. Sobbing, she clutched me.

"What is it? What is it?"

"I don't know," I whispered.

Eric went to Frau Keller's door and knocked. When there was no response, he turned the handle. It was locked.

"Open up!" he shouted. "What's going on? Open up!" He pounded his fist on the panel.

The lock clicked and Frau Keller stood before us, or partially before us, for she only opened the door a few inches. Her hair also was undone and she wore an old-fashioned flannel wrapper over a frilled, old-fashioned flannel nightgown.

Her face was white but composed.

"Rudi has had a bad dream. A nightmare. He is all right now."

She closed the door and the three of us stood looking at each other. Eric put his arms around both of us and led us to Elspeth's door.

"I think he had a fit, Elspeth. Everything's okay now. Try to sleep."

Still trembling, she looked up at him and I saw her for what she was, a frightened kid.

"God!" she whispered. "I never heard such an awful sound."

Eric tucked her in and for a minute I thought he was going to kiss her good night. Instead, from her dresser he took the doll with the floppy long legs and put it in her arms.

"Good night, Elspeth. Sleep tight."

He led me out.

"They will have to go."

I didn't sleep for the rest of the night. I had heard that sound before. In an asylum.

Eric didn't sleep either. But he pretended he did.

They didn't go.

Rudi did not continue to take his meals on a tray. Frau Keller slipped him in to the breakfast table two mornings later. He took his lunch to school, but on Saturday he was sitting with us, his cropped head over his plate, and by Monday he was reinstated at the dinner table.

Frau Keller never said a word about it. It was as if she had fought some silent battle for him and won.

We could not complain of her efficiency. She became, if anything, more formal and obsequious. Unlike mine, her household accounts were always in perfect order. She shopped carefully and frugally. The meals she prepared were tastefully served and mouthwatering, even if they were a trifle heavily Teutonic for our tastes. She kept the house shining. And like the perfect servant, she watched Eric. If he worked for more than four hours, a tray covered with a starched linen cloth was left at his study door with an unobtrusive knock. She polished our old car. She washed the windows. She gardened. She was the first up in the morning and usually the last to retire. She did all my and Elspeth's mending and darning. She ironed Eric's clothing so exquisitely that his shirts and underwear looked as though they ought to have price tags and cellophane still on them.

She was, in short, irreproachable. And it was all done in sacrificial love for that silent fourteen-year-old.

He would have been fifteen.

June 18th. Yesterday, June 17th—my brother's birthday incidentally—I had a date with Igor. I wonder what my brother is doing now. Not that I care. I never want to set eyes on any of them again. Home, sweet home, and the whole lot of them on me like a bunch of jackals. We forgive you, Amy, and we're sorry you've been sick for so long. Sick, hell! They'd choke before they'd say mental institution. They were, in their own way, worse than those kids down the block who found out and shouted Amy's been on the funny farm, Amy's been on the funny farm. Yes, they forgave me until it was apparent I was still Amy. Please, Mother, Father, David, let's face it. I wasn't sick. I had a nervous breakdown. Lots of people do. Well, damn it, you don't have to flaunt it, as if it's something to be proud of. Now, David. Listen, Mother, she walked in that door with a chip on her shoulder. Oh, I know you, you think we're money-conscious and snobbish. Well, by God, we may be, but we stood by you. Oh, sure, you shoved me under the rug like something dirty. Now, Amy. Mother understands how you feel, but you must realize that we've been under a strain too, dear. Amy, I'm your father and there's no need to get your back up with me. You've only been home half an hour and you're acting as if you were never in that place. It's a waste of money if they didn't do anything for you. Yes, and it set him back just eight thousand bucks. Now David, that's enough. I don't begrudge spending money if it's money well spent. We'll say no more about that. You, the whole lot of you! All you worried about were your reputations, you didn't care about me! You didn't care about me! You didn't care about the baby! Amy! I forbid you to speak of that! All right, Mother. Hell, Mother, are you going to let her talk like that? As if nothing happened? You're old, but I'm not! I have to live in this town! Betty wouldn't marry me because of her!

Reputations! It's too bad she didn't give more thought to hers. Just a little cooperation will be appreciated from you from now on. You got in that mess on your own, so don't try shifting the blame on to us! There's a certain amount of truth in what David says, Amy, apart from the moral aspect. I'm an old man, but I've always lived up to my responsibilities. You didn't. Father——. No, David, that's enough. She'll have to live with her memories and that's her punishment, that she'll face day in and day out for the rest of her life. Amy! There's no need to scream at your father and brother! What happened was certainly not David's fault. Now Charles, it's all right. Don't let her get you upset. Amy, you know your father's heart can't stand these scenes!

Anyhow, I had this date with Igor. Our place of assignation was the park, in, of all places, the rose gardens. Then, like Romeo and Juliet, we wandered through the lawns and trees, up to a more suitable trysting place, the zoo.

"Let's go and watch the polar bears," I said. "I hate monkeys."

Igor laughed. "Dirty little buggers, aren't they? Sort of like people."

We stood resting our elbows on the spiky railing of the bear-pit, looking down. I was glad to get away from those filthy little creatures.

I tossed some popcorn to a polar bear who was standing on his hind feet begging. There are five polar bears there and they all joined the beggar.

"You're not supposed to feed them," said Igor. "People throw them the damndest things. They're omnivorous, you know. They eat seals and fish and berries, but you ought to see some of the crap people toss in there. Say, look how yellow their coats are now. Maybe the ice in the arctic turns that color this time of year."

"Is she still at your apartment?"

He didn't turn his head.

"Listen, Amy. I got here from Toronto on March 3rd, and I got a job working for that house-moving company on March 4th. Now listen to this. The house was already moved, first time I saw it. It was on that flat-decked truck, ready to be loaded on a barge and floated across the inlet. You follow me?"

"I guess so."

"What I mean is, whoever moved that house had a reason, and the reason happened before March 3rd. I tried to get in touch with some of the guys who moved the house from wherever it was to the barge, but you know what?"

"What?"

"Kielty had fired a lot of them and hired a completely new crew to load it on the barge. This means he was trying to stop anybody, including me, from tracing that house."

I nodded.

"Now, the way I figure it, that house isn't much over three years old. Our problem is to find where it came from and why it was moved. Somebody's gone to a lot of trouble to see we don't."

"Yes," I said.

"Whose name is the house in?"

"Eric's mother's."

"And where is she now?'

"England."

He turned and stood looking down at me.

"She knows."

"Knows what?"

"Why that house was moved."

"Laura? Why no, Igor. She saw it for the first time that day we were all at the Danby estate, when we met you."

"So she'd like you and Eric to think."

"Look," I said, "You don't know Laura. Eric's as likely to know as she is, and he doesn't. Incidentally, why just me? Why don't you let Eric in on this?"

He spoke with his usual disarming candor. "He's too important. He shouldn't be bothered with material things. Whether you know it or not, you're married to a man who will be famous some day. His function in society is integrated to literature."

He was on his double-talk kick again. God, he can be a bore when he puts his mind to it. On the other hand, maybe he isn't even trying.

"You don't understand him, Amy. If there's one thing I do, I appreciate the arts."

I didn't, of course.

I looked down to the bear pit and thought what a cute little trick it would be to shove him in it. Silly, of course, because even if I could—which I couldn't—Igor would merely strangle all the polar bears with his bare hands, clamber up, and then strangle me.

"What are you thinking about, Amy?"

Don't tell me there's no such thing as ESP. This wasn't the first time he had read my mind.

"I'm thinking how handsome you are."

"I'll bet." He laughed. "Still, I don't do so bad in the sack, do I, Amy? Or should I say in the attic?"

It wasn't going to happen again. I had made up my mind to that.

"Yes, we will," he said. "Whenever I want it."

He put his arm around me, but I pushed him away. He let me go good-naturedly. He never forces women. At least, he never forced me. I suppose he thinks he's so irresistible it's just a matter of time.

"Now I got a plan, Amy. We're going to go through the newspaper files for the last three years, looking for a story about a house. A house approximately three years old. We'll take turns. Okay?"

"Okay," I said and looked at my watch. "I'd better go. I have to be at work in half an hour."

He borrowed a cigarette from me and I last saw him going back to the monkey cages.

I suppose I'd been a good girl to meet him as he asked. I gave the balloon and popcorn he had bought me to a waif who was staring up at the vendor.

I had wondered why Eric hadn't insisted on Frau Keller and Rudi leaving, and now I knew. He had a talk with her after the dining-room affair and she told him everything. He promptly went to the library and came home with all the books he could get on Rudi's condition and he now considered himself an expert.

This, I might add, was not done in the spirit of Dr. Schweitzer. Eric simply could not bear not to know all about everything. Rudi was a conundrum to him and I think he was secretly just a little disappointed with himself for not recognizing the boy's sickness.

In any case, as I have said, he now considered himself an expert. Rudi was autistic, which meant he could not communicate with or form any attachment to other people. He also suffered from a mild form of epilepsy which could be controlled if he took medication regularly.

The autism was another matter and the symptoms were disturbing. Rudi either sat speechless and withdrawn or he became what Eric called "hippety-hoppety," in which case he did senseless things such as waving his hands or jumping up and down endlessly.

He never played in the ordinary sense, but would spend hours purposelessly lining up an infant's set of blocks. The active phase was partially controlled with drugs, thank heavens, because it was enough to drive me, at any rate, silly, just watching him making the same useless arm-sweeping movement for perhaps two hours at a time. Strangely enough, he was one of the most beautiful children I ever set eyes on.

Frau Keller did not want to go back to Germany and she was terrified that her husband and older sons would insist that Rudi be placed in an institution. She told Eric that she felt if he could make contact with one human being there was hope for him and she didn't think this hope existed in institutions, which was why he attended a school for retarded children. Unfortunately the school personnel were neither trained nor able to cope with Rudi's condition.

Eric was sure that he was the boy to unravel this labyrinth of complications, that Rudi would respond to him.

He talked to Rudi constantly now, in a big-brother sort of way that was so unnatural it made my flesh creep. Rudi couldn't bear to be touched, so of course Eric was determined that this was the first barricade to be stormed.

A couple of days later, in the living room, with Frau Keller watching anxiously, he forced Rudi to sit on his knee. I must say it was rather strange to get any reaction from Rudi, but Eric certainly did. Rudi fought like a little animal to free himself; and Eric, with his arms locked about the boy, wouldn't budge an inch. Finally, in despair, the poor kid bit him. I was on Rudi's side in this and I didn't know how Frau Keller could bear it. I thought forcing was wrong, but old Doc Burton thought otherwise. He would have thrown any ordinary biting fourteen-year-old out the window, but with Rudi he said, "That's good, Rudi. Very good indeed."

I know that Frau Keller was willing to try anything in her desperation, but sometimes I don't think Eric's all there.

Although even I had to admit that something strange did happen. Eric borrowed Elspeth's big doll and sat in the living room rocking it in his arms. Rudi sat like a wooden Indian. It's hard to tell if he sees or not. Then Eric put the doll on Rudi's lap and placed the boy's arms around it. Rudi still just sat.

We heard one of Elspeth's swains tootling good-bye to her and then she came bursting in the front door. She looked into the living room and had a very natural teen-age tantrum.

The doll, called "Aggie," she had won at the Exhibition when she was nine and she said it was the only thing she ever got for nothing in her life.

"She's mine! What's he doing with her?"

She bounced in and tried to wrest Aggie from Rudi, but Rudi wouldn't let go. He clung to it fiercely. I must say it was rather thrilling to see him. His rage when confined was understandable, but this was something different.

"Let him have it, just for a little while. Please, Elspeth!"

Eric. Begging.

Elspeth was furious and I don't blame her. He should have asked her first, and after all, it was her doll. Fortunately she thought Eric was, as she so graphically phrased it, "the cat's nuts."

And so, albeit ungraciously, she allowed Rudi to hold it and she flounced upstairs. After about half an hour the doll slipped from Rudi's arms and fell to the floor.

"Take it back to Elspeth, please, Frau Keller." Eric was beaming. "Good boy, Rudi. Good boy. You were right to hang on to it."

Frau Keller also looked at Eric now as if he were the cat's nuts.

Although Eric said that the books stated that most autistic children are of at least average, and often above-average intelligence, there was one thing that bothered me. Sometimes when Rudi got restless he would put his tongue out against the wall and walk around the room. I don't like to sound unsympathetic, but frankly I found it disgusting. How could Rudi ever take his place in ordinary society if allowed to behave like that in front of other people? Eric said discipline would come later, after contact was established with the boy.

Rudi must not stay up in his room by himself, even if he wanted to. He was to be encouraged to wander around the house, and above all, he must touch things in order to establish their reality. By a stroke of luck the house was not exactly overflowing with artistic treasures, but I took the precaution of hiding, in a high cupboard, a pretty little piece of Dresden which was once in the Vicarage in England and which Laura valued greatly for sentimental reasons.

I found out the connection between Bernard and Elspeth. They were both Catholics. She was from the interior and her parents, friends of Bernard's, only let her stay in the city on the condition that Bernard kept an eye on her and that she attended mass.

Heaven help poor old Bernard trying to keep an eye on that one. It was impossible to keep up with her. She did everything in a hurry. I heard her singing one day and thought her rhythm was off until it occurred to me that she did that in a hurry too.

Bernard, she said, went to mass regularly. She only got up in time once, and that for the eleven o'clock service.

And another thing. I hate to sound old-fashioned, but her language! I know things are a great deal freer with young people now, and we're all quite aware that Bernard drinks too much at times, but really, to refer to him as "old brandy-balls." I don't think I even knew some of the words, at eighteen, that she used in casual conversation.

Eric got a big kick out of her. Then. Frau Keller still looked on her with a jaundiced eye and I guess I got used to her.

Eric would not allow either Frau Keller or me to clean his study. Despite the apparent chaos, he claimed he knew where every item was, and he said he did not want her barging around disrupting things or me snooping.

The study looked as bad as Elspeth's room and about once a week, when he was out at the library, I furtively had a shot at it.

What made me start to read the manuscript? It had been sitting around as plain as the nose on your face for nearly a year, and as long as he got the damned thing written I thought I was content to leave it be. But this day as I looked at the completed part lying as neat as a corpse in its cardboard box, I had a compulsion to read it. Maybe it was because he said he didn't want me snooping. Anyway, I did.

I don't know what I expected. No, that's not quite true. I do know what I expected. I expected it to be the manuscript of any earnest young writer, no masterpiece, full of the usual soul-searching and a plethora of what used to be forbidden words.

I think it was the subject matter that surprised me as much as anything. It was an unbearably sad story of a servant girl in prewar England.

The style was spare and bleak, the presentation as masterly and powerful as Thomas Hardy. I sat with a page drooping in my hand and my conscience tried me. I had never had any confidence in him. I had never really thought he would be any good. I had expected introspection and vanity. I found maturity, dignity and compassion. And, I suspected, greatness.

He was standing in the doorway, his arms full of books.

Sister Ann! Sister Ann! Is there anybody coming, Sister Ann?

He looked at me coldly and took the manuscript from me.

"I have expressly forbidden you to do that."

"I won't do it again, I promise you. I don't know what got into me."

"Stay out of here."

I nodded. I never really changed anything in his study. I just dusted around things and removed moldering perishables and dirty coffee cups. If he weren't so unobservant he would have realized I had been doing it for a year. Well, from now on I would not even do that.

How does one reconcile oneself to the Jekyll and Hyde syndrome of the author? When he came up for tea that afternoon Dr. Jekyll was in the ascendancy again.

"I'm sorry I spoke that way, but my privacy must be respected if I am to do my best. You'll be the first person to read it when it's completed. I'll dedicate it to you, if you like."

For the first time I fully realized that the sacrifices I made for him were worthwhile, and I knew that he deserved this chance to prove himself.

June 23rd. Last night Rudi had another attack. I woke up with sweat plastering my hair to the back of my neck and my heart thudding as I listened.

"Eric! Eric! Wake up!"

He sat up and rubbed his eyes. "What is it?"

"Listen!" I whispered, but the sound stopped. "Rudi. He was crying."

Eric got up and went into the hall. He was back in a minute.

"What's the matter with you, anyway? Rudi's sound asleep. I just saw him. Frau Keller must think I'm crazy, waking her in the middle of the night."

"I heard him, I tell you! I heard him screaming!"

"Well, you didn't. You must have been dreaming. Go back to sleep."

He did.

And then, oh God! I heard Black Sutch!

"Eric!" I had never been so terrified. *"Eric!"*

He sat up again. "For Christ's sake, Amy! I'm tired!"

"The dog!" I whispered.

"I don't hear anything."

"I tell you I heard it!"

"Oh ... Jesus!" He sighed wearily. "All right, all right. Calm down."

When he came back he smiled and ruffled my hair. "You'll be looking under the bed for suitors, next. Now for God's sake, Amy, let me get some sleep."

"I heard it!"

"There was nothing there."

He was asleep almost immediately. It must be comforting to be of an artistic and high-strung nature.

I didn't dare wake him again.

A few minutes later I heard it. It was not howling. It was scratching at the front door.

That first night in the house the real implication hadn't hit me, but now it did.

It was trying to get in.

The next morning at breakfast I asked Frau Keller if Rudi had had an attack during the night.

She and Eric were as thick as thieves now, and she turned to look at him before answering.

"No, Madame. Rudi slept well last night."

"You didn't hear a dog howling?"

"No, Madame. I heard nothing."

Why did she stare at me in that strange way? Was she lying to protect Rudi? If she were, she was a good actress. She looked at me as if she thought I were out of my mind.

Guilt Built Up, Finally Exploded

Those who knew him believe John Malcolm Graham was driven to insanity by a terrible sense of guilt. A close acquaintance of Graham says he feels sure Graham committed a massacre because he didn't 'want his wife and children living with the stigma of a father and husband who was a dishonest policeman.

The thirty-eight-year-old constable had not been questioned but he knew he was under suspicion in the robbery of

Please Turn to Page Three, Column 5

CHAPTER ELEVEN. Improbable things do happen. June 30th —exactly a week after the dog incident, I see from my notes— I was alone in the house. Frau Keller had taken Rudi to the dentist, Eric was at the library, Elspeth was working, Igor was presumably at his apartment being nasty to that poor Elaina, and Laura, of course, was in England.

I knew, as soon as I opened the door, who he was. He couldn't have been anyone else. The only thing was, he was supposed to be dead.

He was shorter and heavier than Eric. He must have been in his sixties, but there wasn't a grey hair on his head. His eyes, as brilliant as black diamonds, were his son's.

He was wearing a dark suit of old-fashioned cut and a soft felt hat. His baggy pants were held up by a belt two inches wide, with a brass buckle that looked as though it would make a formidable weapon. He wore a blue and white checked shirt and a loud tie which was pierced by a large diamond stick pin.

He removed his hat with a theatrical gesture and I saw that on his square, powerful hand another diamond glittered.

"Eric Burton live here?"

"Yes. He's out now."

"You his missus?" He had a bold, cheeky expression.

"Yes, I'm Mrs. Burton. You're his father."

He looked past me, his eyes roaming around the entrance hall.

"He'll be back in about an hour. Will you come in?"

"Don't mind if I do." His accent, unlike Laura's, was frankly lower-class.

In the living room he seemed ill at ease, with an animal wariness, and his eyes were still roaming, missing nothing.

"Nice place."

"Would you care for some tea?"

He looked at me slyly from the corner of his eye.

"I could do with a cuppa. Nice place. Cost a lot of brass, eh?"

"You paid for it."

He laughed.

"Did I?"

"Laura said you were dead, that you left her an inheritance."

He shrugged.

"Well, I ain't dead, am I? Yes, I gave her some money."

He appraised me as if I were a horse, then snorted, "You'll do. Laura here?"

"No. She's in England."

"Hmm! Well, I didn't come to see her. Come to see my boy. I suppose she's made a proper toff out of him."

"He's remarkably like you, Mr. Burton."

"He is?" He cackled, took a large handkerchief from his pocket and blew his nose. "Haven't seen him since he was—oh—just a little fellow. So high."

The resemblance was uncanny. "Twenty-two months old, to be exact, Mr. Burton," I said.

"That long, eh? My, my, how time flies. I was fond of him, I was. Used to dandle him on my knee. Take him to the park. Give him his bath. But she spoiled it."

"Well, she did bring him up." I couldn't forgo that one. "I'll make the tea."

He followed me into the kitchen.

"Is he clever?"

"Yes," I said, setting up the tray. "At least, I have a feeling he is. He's a writer. I think he may be a good one."

He nodded. "Not like his old man. Me, missus, I've been a wanderer. Wasn't cut out for married life. Hate routine. Done a bit of everything. Picked hops, sold cars and bikes, groomed horses. Sold baby buggies. Been a stoker on ships and seen the world. You name it, Agar Burton's done it."

I carried the tray into the living room with him following.

"I suppose Laura's given you and him an earful. Turned him against me." He took four teaspoons of sugar.

"I don't think he cares about you one way or the other, Mr. Burton."

This time Agar Burton chuckled.

"I'll bet he don't. I'll bet he don't like routine either. Get up in the morning. Shave. Brush your teeth. Eat. Go to work. Sound like my son?"

It certainly didn't. Eric, who had not seen this man since he was two years old, refused to do anything consecutively. Some days it was noon before he shaved. He would eat a can of salmon for breakfast and cereal for lunch. From sheer cussedness, I had presumed. But here it was, blood thicker than water.

I laughed. "Yes. He's your son."

Agar Burton laughed. If those teeth were his own, they were remarkable.

"It's the gypsy blood. He had the eyes, too. Here, look." He fumbled through his pockets, brought out a wallet and extracted a yellowed snapshot. It showed a young, short Eric holding a black-eyed baby, with a mean, shabby street in the background.

"Her always wanting to stay put and me always wanting to move on. It couldn't work out."

"Gypsy? You mean, really?"

He gave me a scornful look.

"You ever seen eyes like mine or his on farmers? Yes, we're gypsies. Real gypsies. English gypsies. At least, my mother was.

My father?" He grinned, then, "Well, they come in all shapes and colors now, the English gypsies. Red hair, blue eyes and most of 'em barmy—got the blood of every by-blow and half-wit in the country in them. But it used to be different in my grandmother's day."

What an incredible man!

"My grandmother, Hagar Burton, spoke their lingo. She'd put one over on the gorgios every time, quick as she'd look at you."

And I'll bet Agar Burton would too.

I gave him another cup of tea which looked like syrup after he had filled a quarter of the cup with sugar.

When he finished it he stood up.

"You're not going? Eric should be home soon."

"I changed my mind."

"Would you like to leave your phone number so he can call you?"

"I'm shipping out tomorrow, missus."

I stood up. "Would you mind telling me something, Mr. Burton? Why did you come here?"

The bold, familiar eyes were laughing.

"I was just passing through. Thought maybe Laura had collected something I could lift. But there's nothing here that strikes my fancy. Nothing here but you, missus, and you're another Laura."

"Shall I tell him you called?"

"Suit yourself."

Elemental, shifty, and probably dishonest, Agar Burton, tramp extraordinary. But not a blackguard as Laura had described him. A scoundrel, perhaps. Yes, that has a cheeky, likable, debonair ring to it. No wonder the highborn Pontifaxes had been shocked. Mendel's law is certainly subject to some twists. How had those two produced an Eric?

I took a certain relish in being casual about it.

"Your father dropped in today."

The cigarette fell from his fingers and smoldered on the kitchen table. I put it in the ashtray.

He stood up.

"Amy, my father is dead."

"On the contrary, he is very much alive."

He sat down and I told him about Agar Burton's visit. When I was through he seemed as isolated as Rudi.

Then, finally he said, "Amy, if what you say is true, something is very much amiss."

"What do you mean, if what I say is true?"

"Well, you must admit it's a very improbable story."

My face flushed. "Well of all the bloody nerve!"

"Listen, just take the facts as you have told them, one at a time. Agar Burton, supposedly dead, turns up. After twenty-seven years. He comes to see me, his only son. He produces an old snap-shot of me and has a cup of tea. Then, just like that, he gets up and leaves. Having come halfway around the world to see me, he won't wait an extra half hour. He won't leave a forwarding address. He looks like a tramp but he wears two huge diamonds."

"That's right." My lips were stiff.

"This bum, my supposedly dead father, left my mother a fortune four months ago. The house is proof of it. Does it make sense to you?"

"I just reported what happened! Is it my fault if you come from a crazy family? And let me tell you something else, Eric Burton, I don't like being called a liar!"

"That isn't what I meant." He sat back and looked at me strangely. "Amy, did you sit down and doze off this afternoon? You, of all people, know how real dreams can seem."

It's a wonder my coffee cup didn't break on the table, and I went out to the garden before I said something I would later regret, but I was too angry to stay outside. I came in and slammed the door behind me.

"Maybe he didn't leave your mother a fortune. Has that ever occurred to you?"

"Then where did she get the money? Don't be so damned silly!" It was his turn to leave the room angrily and I heard his study door close with a resounding bang.

Frau Keller came in with Rudi and poured him a glass of milk.

"Are you all right, Madame?"

"Yes, of course. Don't I look all right?"

Rudi's mouth was still frozen from his visit to the dentist and milk dribbled down his chin. She mopped it off and patted his head.

"You look feverish, Mrs. Burton."

"No, it's nothing," I said. My face was still burning.

One of the first officers to enter the house said "We kept finding bodies everywhere. All the floors and walls of the house were blood-spattered. I've seen a lot of dead people, dead women and dead children, but never anything as tragic as this.

"It would have been bad enough if they had all been killed at once, as with a burst of machine-gun fire, but here you had children running everywhere they could, to hide from their own father. One was even found crouched in a closet, and another in the shower.

"I suppose the fear of being caught for the robbery was too much for him and something snapped. No sane person could have done what he did.

"No, there are no new leads on the red-haired woman accomplice."

CHAPTER TWELVE. (July 3rd) I received a phone call from Elaina, the girl at Igor's apartment. Igor had a part-time job at an auto-wrecking firm now, but had left an envelope at the apartment for me. Would I pick it up?

I felt rather sheepish knocking on his door and having her open it.

She was bigger than ever and she looked weary, with dark circles under her eyes. She invited me in and gave me a manila folder, sealed. Then she asked if I would like coffee.

I must have looked surprised because she said, "I just put some on."

When I still seemed hesitant, her manner changed.

"Please sit down. I'm alone here most of the day. I never see anyone. It's good to see another human being."

She laughed, a humorless, bone-tired laugh. "That category doesn't fit Igor."

I sat down and looked about. The apartment was as neat as if Frau Keller's fine Teutonic hand had been at work. It was furnished with the deadly tastelessness of the transient. A studio couch, well-worn, and a cheap chrome table set and chairs. But she had attempted to make it cheerful. There were fresh flowers on the table, and colorful, free, travel posters and some brass camel-bells attached to a velvet ribbon on the bare plaster walls. The view was beautiful, and in front of the open window a set of bamboo Chinese wind chimes tinkled.

"You looked tired," I said. "I hope you're taking care of yourself."

She smiled. What a difference it made. She had beautiful teeth and one of those oval, delicately high-cheekboned Slavic faces.

"Oh, I guess the last few months are always difficult. I'm not sleeping properly. It seems if it isn't your bladder waking you up every hour, it's heartburn. This last week I've been living on antacid pills."

Then she rubbed her swollen belly gently. "And this little wretch can't seem to bear for me to get any shut-eye. The moment I lie down, she starts kicking."

I smiled. I too remembered.

"You seem awfully sure it will be a girl."

She frowned, a mock frown of love and pride, and pointed through the open door of the bedroom to the dresser, which was now heaped with a neat pile of pastel baby dresses. "It had better be a girl. Can you see a boy wearing those?"

She asked about the house as she served coffee, and I told her all we had done and planned to do, and how I had furnished it by going to auctions and sales and answering ads. I recognized the hunger and loneliness of the vagrant.

We chatted about sewing and cooking like a couple of old suburbanites. She was charming. Only when the subject of Igor slipped into the conversation did her expression harden.

She didn't need to spell it out in big letters for me. In her condition it would be no picnic living with a man who had as little consideration for women as Igor.

"Are you seeing the doctor regularly?" I asked.

"Oh, yes. I'm looking after this baby. I used to go every two weeks but about a month ago they thought I had toxemia and they put me in the hospital for five days. Now I go every week. I'm fine, but I have to watch fluids and salt."

Five days. A month ago. That must have been when he had me there.

She sighed.

"It'll be such a relief to finally have her. I get up in the morning and think how tired I am and what a mess I look, and I clean the place up. Then I've got the rest of the day to face. How to spread nothing over ten hours. I'm not complaining, mind you. Lots of women have a much harder time. I was talking to a girl in the doctor's office and she's due a month after me. She has two others. One just walking and the other three, and she says I don't know how lucky I am. 'Enjoy this pregnancy,' she says. 'You'll be too busy the next time.'"

Yes. You don't know how lucky you are. I feel sorry for you. I envy you. I even like you.

"Besides," she said, "during the daytime, when he's not here, I can watch television, and there's a really nice roof garden on the top of the building, and if the weather's nice, I go up and take my sewing with me."

"What do you mean?" I said. "Can't you watch television in the evening?"

"No. He won't let me. He says it's a propaganda medium designed to program the system, whatever that means. And it's my TV set, too."

"Then why do you put up with his nonsense?"

"Huh," she said.

"Look," I said, "When you go into the hospital, have Igor phone me. I'll come to see you."

"Would you?" Her face was like a child's. "I'm from the prairies. I don't know a soul here."

Then the eagerness faded and she looked tireder than she had before. "He wouldn't."

"Surely it wouldn't hurt him to. How could he possibly object?"

This time her face was really hard. "You don't know Igor. He's going to make me eat dirt before he's through with me."

I rose, the manila folder in my hand. "Then you give me a call when you feel your pains start, and I'll see you at the hospital. Okay?"

I remembered the hospital. Being alone. No visitors. Not even my baby left to me.

"Okay," she put her arm through mine as we walked to the door.

"Listen," I said. "I'd like to get something for the baby. What do you need?"

She blushed. "Oh, no. I couldn't take anything from you."

"Don't be silly. What do you need?"

"Well," she peered over her great stomach to her feet. "I haven't been very practical. I've got all those lovely clothes for her but—well—I do need a bath. Just one of those plastic tubs. Nothing fancy."

I patted her arm awkwardly. "I'll bring it to the hospital."

She put her hand on mine.

"Look out for him. He can be nice when he wants. But he can also be the meanest bastard that ever lived, and believe me, it's no effort for him."

Constable Graham Shot Family One By One, Say Police

A crazed policeman with a smoking .357 magnum stalked his children through their luxury home as he wiped out his family of nine and then himself.

Constable John Graham, 38, took ten lives after he came under investigation in a million-dollar bank hold-up.

The awful slaughter started about 3:00 A.M. in the Grahams' Tudor-style home in the quiet neighborhood of Gravesend Gardens, but the tragedy went unnoticed until city police became suspicious when Graham did not come to work and went to investigate. After seeing the bodies of two little girls, police made entry to a ground floor room. One of the children would have been 5 the next day and her iced birthday cake was found on the kitchen table.

Police say that when Graham went on the rampage he was only under suspicion. A middle-aged woman wearing a red wig, or a middle-aged man masquerading as a woman and wearing a red wig, is now being sought for questioning in the robbery.

Police pieced together the terrible minutes between the hours of 2:00 A.M. and 4:00 A.M. on Tuesday. This is what the investigators believe happened.

Death came violently to Graham's sleeping wife, Alma, who was found in bed with the bedclothes pulled up in the top-floor master bedroom, the first to die of a bullet in the head from the powerful .357 magnum revolver Graham had bought several weeks previously.

Graham then shot 18-month-old Kenneth, who slept in a cot in his parents' room. The crazed father hunted down his other seven children, who, police surmise, having heard or investigated the sound of the shots, hid in various parts of the house.

The next to die was Graham's second youngest son, Philip, 6, who was found crouched in the front hall closet, where he had hidden when a heavy slug, powerful enough to kill big game, snuffed out his life.

The other six children were found hiding in different parts of the house. Neighbors report hearing no unusual sounds, but the houses are widely spaced in the fashionable Gravesend Gardens subdivision.

All the children were found shot in the head, but 9-year-old

Neill, who was killed in the upstairs bathroom, appeared to have hidden in the shower in an at first successful effort to evade his father. The bathroom walls and fixtures and even the ceiling had been blasted.

Ian, 13, led Andrew, 10, and Gretchen, 7, to an upstairs linen closet. He had hidden them under comforters and was found lying across them.

Police believe that Graham then stalked the only two left, 12-year-old Sharon, and Linda, whose birthday cake with five candles was standing on the kitchen table. Graham found the last two children in the downstairs den. Beneath a racing car table set Sharon had apparently tried to hide Linda under an old cardboard box and was found dead slumped across the younger child's partly hidden body.

Police think that by this time Graham might have realized what he had done and made his way upstairs, past the scattered bodies, to his bedroom.

He went back to his bedroom in the now silent house and stood beside the bed in which his dead wife lay. He pointed the gun at his head and pulled the trigger.

CHAPTER THIRTEEN. I went up to my bedroom before opening the folder. It contained Xeroxed clippings dated three years before.

I thought my heart would stop.

How could Bernard have done this to us? Oh, God in heaven! What was I to do?

Eric must not know. When he finished the book, perhaps, but not now. No one could write, knowing that they dwelt in that house of horror.

Frau Keller called me down to say I was wanted on the phone. It was Igor.

"I guess you've read it by now. No wonder they wanted the history of that house kept a secret. Jeez, I couldn't eat my dinner last night."

The epitome of horror for him.

"I'm going to see Bernard," I said.

"No!" He was almost shouting into the mouthpiece. "You can't do that. We don't want him to know we know. Don't you see, Amy, the rest of the money, or a clue to where it is, is hidden somewhere in that house?"

"You don't have to live in it! It was misrepresented to us, and it was a terrible thing to do! I'm going to Bernard!"

"Misrepresented, balls!" he shouted. "Whoever bought that house knew exactly what they were doing and had a reason for it."

Oh my God! He was right. I had to be careful. For her sake. But still I had to see Bernard.

He tried to dissuade me, but I refused to be dissuaded.

"All right," he said finally. "But don't tell him you know anything else. All you know is who the house used to belong to and what happened in it. Don't tip your hand about the money. Say, that misrepresentation angle is good. Maybe you can swing a cash rebate on the down payment."

Laura! Laura! Laura! I know why you did it. For Eric! For me! But how could you?

Was almost in state of shock for several days. Couldn't believe this awful thing true. Took me until July 19th to gather my wits and do something sensible. Bernard responsible. Sold house under false pretenses. Phoned, made appointment.

He was his old jovial self as he seated me in his tiny office. But as soon as I sat down, took off my gloves and stared at him, he knew.

His pink face went grey. He tried to light a cigar with an air of nonchalance, but his drinker's tremor, combined with nervousness, made it impossible. He ran a finger under his tight, starched collar.

"So you found out."

"How could you do it?"

He turned his head away for a long minute, then he folded his trembling hands before his chest.

"It had to happen to someone. What I mean is, someone was bound to buy it. I'm sorry it was you, and I'm sorry you found out."

"How could you do it?" It was all I could say.

The periwinkle-blue eyes, framed with the thick sooty Irish eyelashes, were suddenly very bright. His color returned to normal, and his pursed lips were as narrow as a razor blade.

"Listen carefully, Amy. I'm not quite the villain you paint me. You got that house for a fraction of what it's worth for a reason. You know the reason now. If you're not satisfied, I'll take it off your hands and the Trust Company will absorb any loss you may sustain."

"Yes!" I hissed, "and you'll sell it to someone else!"

There was nothing jovial or soft about him now.

"I'm a lawyer as well as a real-estate agent. I was appointed by the Crown to salvage as much as I could from that estate. Don't think I haven't searched my conscience, or that it was easy for me. I have acted as honestly and as honorably as the situation permitted. It was a matter of expediency, not choice, with me, Amy. The people who were robbed have rights too, and I represent them as well as the Crown."

I put my head on his desk and wept.

He was by my side in a minute, kneeling. "Amy, Amy! Don't! Do you think I'm heartless? Do you think I've slept soundly at night? I saw that house directly after it happened. You don't know what it was like then. Now, listen, Amy, if you want to move, I'll see you get out."

"Oh, for God's sake, Bernard! It isn't even our house! It belongs to Laura!"

He mopped my tears. "Don't you worry about that, lover. Uncle Bernie will see you get out, if that's what you want. Is Eric very upset?"

"He doesn't know and he's not going to until that book is finished and his mother is back."

What had I said? But Bernard didn't seem to notice. "Yes, I can understand the effect it would have on a creative mind. We'll see he doesn't find out. Come on, now, Amy. Buck up. Let me pour you a drink."

"That's your answer for everything, isn't it?"

I hurt his feelings. His plump, handsome Irish face crumpled and it now looked as though he would cry. But the thought of a drink pulled him together.

"Hardly, Amy. I want you to know, Amy, that I have been praying for you and Eric, ever since you moved in there."

I tossed back the drink and looked at him, but he was quite serious.

"You hypocrite! You bloody Mick!" I had to laugh. Hard as nails under all that charming-the-birds-out-of-the-trees routine, when it came to a dollar, and then he prays for me.

When he saw me laugh, his eyes became their old soft twinkly blue again.

"Does Laura know?" I asked. I had to ask.

"She knows she got the house as a bargain because there was an accident in it. That's all she knows."

"You wouldn't lie to me, Bernard?"

"Amy!" Then, believe it or not, he actually crossed himself. "In the name of the Father, the Son, and the Holy Ghost, I swear to you that I have not told Laura. I have, as you can see, gone out of my way to make sure that that tragedy was kept from you."

Good. He obviously had no suspicions about that woman in the red wig.

I had often wondered why Bernard was our good shepherd. Now I knew. What he thought was his secret of the awful history of that house. His uncompromising Catholic conscience would give him no peace. I suppose I shouldn't have called him a Mick. I sounded as bad as Laura and her Chinese.

Laura, Laura, Laura. Why, how, did you get mixed up with that poor, tortured policeman? Why was your fate, and ultimately mine and Eric's, twisted up with the robbery and its final, hideous end, the murder of those innocent children?

CHAPTER FOURTEEN. (July 22nd) Feel rotten. A really hot day. It hasn't rained for ages and no outside trash fires are allowed so that that pile of scrap lumber is still piled next to the garden wall where it drives poor neat Frau Keller berserk. Couldn't she just have a kleine, kleine fire, she asked Eric. No. It's against the law. That did it, no more arguments. Ja, ja, she said and barreled off to look for something to scrub.

I ordered a garden swing, one of those with padded cushions and an awning, and it looks very handsome. Rudi immediately, as soon as Eric got it set up, jumped on it and began to swing so violently I thought he would break it. I told him to get off and when he didn't I said I would smack him if he didn't. Made Eric mad. Said there's no need to threaten the child. Lifted Rudi off, carrying him piggyback and jumping all over the garden saying, "Look, Rudi, I'm a swing! This is just as much fun, isn't it?"

Rudi suddenly began to shriek. Eric's a damned fool. It was he who scared Rudi, not me.

Eric says the reason I don't like Rudi is because, like everybody else, I recognize something of myself in him and it frightens me. This is absolute nonsense. If there is anything I can't stand, it's armchair psychiatrists. Anyhow, I don't dislike Rudi. God knows I, like any other ordinary woman, would prefer to have a normal child around; but dislike? I pity him because he is shut off from the rest of humanity, but I certainly don't dislike him. It's just that, well, even with a relationship as simple as that between a person and an animal, there has to be some reciprocity of affection, and with Rudi, there is nothing.

Eric took Rudi in to Frau Keller, who eventually got him calmed down. Rudi's getting worse, not better, and I don't care what Eric says.

That was last week. Yesterday I was sitting in the garden swing writing and trying to keep cool when Frau Keller came storming up to me, so angry I wouldn't have been surprised if she started breathing fire.

"You would tell her, you will tell her, no, you must tell her, she cannot comb her hair in the kitchen!" she sputtered.

I didn't have to ask who could or would or must not.

I went into the living room where Elspeth was sprawled on Madame Récamier's couch, her legs hooked over the top and her head nearly touching the floor. She was patting her cheeks briskly.

"What in heaven's name are you doing?"

"My complexion exercise."

Apparently her aged skin was sluggish and this was best remedied by turning herself topsy-turvy.

"It makes you feel kind of kooky for a couple of minutes after, but it's the best facial there is, all that blood rushing the wrong way. You ought to try it some time."

"Elspeth, please do not comb your hair in the kitchen. It drives Frau Keller stark, raving mad. Use the bathroom."

She mumbled something. Whether it was "old biddy" or "old bitch" I wasn't sure.

"She has a point, Elspeth. It isn't very sanitary. Please use the bathroom as I have asked."

"Huh. There's something creepy about that bathroom upstairs." With her huge, black-rimmed eyes inverted and gazing up at me, she looked like a giant opossum. "I saw a face in the mirror."

"That's natural enough if you're looking in it."

It's difficult to shrug when you are lying upside down, but Elspeth managed.

"It wasn't me. I just got a glimpse of it. Like in 'The Pawnbroker' with Rod Steiger. You know, when they flashed shots from the past for a split second."

"Oh, come now, Elspeth. You're imagining things and it's no wonder you're mixed up, with that sloth act of yours. Doesn't it make your head ache?"

"No kidding, Mrs. Burton." She was sitting up again, her head waving woozily. "I bet it was Rudi. Jeez, there's one creepy kid. It would be just like him to sneak up behind me."

"Don't comb your hair in the kitchen any more, please, Elspeth."

I spoke to Eric about it later.

"It's probably self-hypnotism. That kid spends hours gazing at herself."

"She thought it might have been Rudi."

He sighed.

"Both Frau Keller and I would be very pleased if it were. It would be a big step if he'd take some notice of girls."

"It would be a big step if he'd take notice of anything."

"I thought—," he hesitated. "I wondered, Amy, if I should get him a doll?"

"A doll? For a fourteen-year-old boy? Are you out of your mind? He's bad enough the way he is. Don't make him worse."

"I know." He looked at me pleadingly. "But that doll of Elspeth's is the only thing that has ever riveted his attention. I caught him sneaking it out of her room the other day. Of course, I had to make him put it back. You really don't think he could have a doll, Amy?"

"No."

I had had a horror of the whole house since Igor sent me those clippings, but my horror of the front hall closet was the worst. Philip. Aged six. It was Eric who noticed that the door of it would not stay closed. No matter how often he shut it, it was always open. It's where we hang our coats after coming in and under them is two and a half feet of nothing. Now there is two and a half feet of nothing is what I mean. I could not bring myself to look at that space as I went past.

"It's the house settling," said Eric. "Igor says it could take a year and we may have to rehang some of the doors."

"I wish you'd do it now. It bothers me."

"Amy," he laughed. "I don't know how to hang a picture, let alone a door."

"Then get Igor to do it. It gives me the willies. You get halfway down the stairs and it swings open right before your eyes."

Igor rehung the door. Two hours later it was swinging open again. Igor said it was the vibrations of footsteps on the stairs and Eric said to forget about it.

There were other noises. The crackings, like little rifle shots, always going off when the house was very quiet, it seemed, and the creaking and groaning of drying wood being pulled in opposite directions. Frau Keller, who was not given to fancies, found it eerie.

"This house, it is like an angry old man, always talking and grumbling. Why is it so unhappy?"

It was Frau Keller who suggested we drive out to the valley and pick up some fruits and vegetables cheaply for canning. There was the initial outlay of the canning kettle, jars, and rings; but she assured me it would be a big saving in the winter.

I hadn't seen canning done since I was a child and I had forgotten how you went about it, so she took over and I was her assistant.

It was rewarding to see those gleaming jars all lined up on the kitchen table, and the house heady with the scent of cinnamon and cloves and syrups.

Frau Keller surveyed our handiwork with satisfaction, and sniffed deeply. "Ah, Madame. This is how a house should smell. They are beautiful, are they not?"

Elspeth came in, presumably to comb her hair, and I foolishly confided that the jars made me feel like a little squirrel getting its nuts all ready for the winter.

She was convulsed, of course.

"Gee, Mrs. Burton, you slay me!"

Fruit shelves had been put up in the coolest part of the basement, next to the concrete retaining wall behind the den. I put four jars of the cherries in a row and stood back admiring their color.

Two days later I put half a dozen jars of pickles beside them. As I went through the den I heard an explosion and raced back. One of the jars of cherries had completely disintegrated, and there wasn't a piece of glass left bigger than a quarter, while the ones on each side were cracked and dripping.

Eric came out of his study.

"What was that noise? What happened?"

I felt cold.

"I don't know."

Frau Keller also heard it and came down to investigate.

"That one must have been fermenting and improperly sealed," said Eric. The red juice dripped, thud, thud, thud, on the cement floor.

"Impossible!" cried Frau Keller. "My jars are never improperly sealed."

With her passion for perfection, it was not a tactful explanation; so Eric only shrugged and went back to his study, and I went to fetch a cloth and a basin of soap and water.

I knelt, cleaning up the blood of those fruits, but suddenly I was overcome with faintness and called for Eric.

"For God's sake! No wonder! You're kneeling on broken glass!"

"I think I'm going to be sick," I whispered. I rushed to the small washroom off his study. He followed and held my head. Then I sat on his desk while he put a Band-Aid on my knee.

"It's not bad. But didn't it hurt?"

"No."

"You're still as white as a sheet."

There wasn't an atom of the original downstairs left. It was all new. But only a few feet from where I sat, they had huddled, one under a cardboard box, the other trying to protect her.

It wasn't possible, and yet it was.

I went to work that afternoon, and I didn't feel too badly.

But the next morning I threw up again.

I spent as much time as I could in the garden. At least that wasn't haunted. It was lovely there, and with the espaliered trees and the roses we had planted, it looked like an illustration from the Book of Hours. All it needed was a coiffed dame and a knight with a falcon on his wrist and a greyhound at his feet to complete the picture.

But here was no lily maid of Astolat, nor glass boat to bear me to the enchanted realm of Uther Pendragon. Here was only that house, evil and appalling, the "real toad in the imaginary garden." Waiting. For what? More victims?

If only I could have slept. If only I hadn't felt so sick. It wasn't too bad in the afternoons, and I dragged myself to work. Eric and Frau Keller thought I shouldn't and said we would get along, but I had to keep busy. Maybe it would help me to sleep. I tried not to think about Laura and what would happen if she were caught. I kept telling myself I must not be morbid, that I must get a grip on myself.

Why couldn't Eric leave me alone? Why did he have to nag me? I felt so sick.

"You can't go on this way. I've made an appointment for you."

"I won't! I won't!"

"Listen, Amy, he's not a psychiatrist or a police surgeon. He's just an ordinary general practitioner."

"He'll know!"

"What does it matter? You're married now. If he asks, just say yes. You don't have to give him any details."

"Please, please, no!"

He wouldn't listen.

And Frau Keller. She was as bad as he was. She joined in the chorus. She brought me up iced drinks called spritz made with soda water, sparkling white wine, and raspberry cordial. It was all I could keep on my stomach.

"Now, Madame. You must do what Mr. Burton wishes. Ah, that's better, isn't it? It was the only thing for me too, and my mother before me."

Her large, cool, competent hand was on my forehead.

"Mr. Burton is just like papa. All men are blind. Imagine saying it is nerves! There were twelve years between Dieter and Rudi, and papa forgot. Would you believe it, whenever he heard me he would say, 'Klara, it was the roast pork last night.' Or, 'Klara, your stomach has no teeth. Chew your food, Klara! Chew!' Indigestion, he called it. A new kind of indigestion, ja? But you will be fine. Why, I was forty-one years old when I had Rudi."

This was supposed to console me, but she meant well.

★

Finally I gave in. He was another Irishman. A Kelly this time. Not at all like our Bernard, though. Dr. Kelly was tiny, almost birdlike, with a long narrow nose. Why do people with noses like that always seem to wear rimless glasses? Or do the rimless glasses make them look like they have noses like that?

Oh, yes. It was Bernard who recommended Dr. Kelly. What would we do without him?

I had to wait nearly half an hour and I was shaking with nervousness when I was finally ushered into his consulting-room.

He stood up, shook hands and motioned me to a seat.

"Your husband is quite concerned about you, Mrs. Burton."

He had a long form before him and began the questions.

Measles, yes. Diptheria, no. Yes, shots for polio and small pox. No, nothing else. No, no history of epilepsy in my family. No, no allergies. No, no reaction from penicillin. Weight loss of eight pounds in one week? Mmmm-hmmm. Husband healthy? Occupation? A writer, was he? Well, that was interesting. Someday he was going to take a year off and have a stab at that himself. No, not on medicine. He saw enough of that every day. On mountaineering, his hobby. Now, would I please come into his other office and remove my clothes. Miss Walsh will hang them for you, right there by the door. And now, up on the table. That's the girl. Heart. Blood pressure. Say AAH. Again, please. Once more. Fine, Take a deep breath. Now lie back. Stomach a bit tender? Here? Mmm-hmm. Now try and relax, Mrs. Burton. Of course you can. Nurse, just hold her knees steady. There. Everything is all right, Mrs. Burton. There we are. Now I'm just going to do a Pap smear test. Women over thirty-five should have one every year. Now that wasn't so bad, was it? Yes, we're all through.

The nurse helped me on with my clothes and I joined him in the consulting-room again.

"I'm afraid not, not this time, Mrs. Burton."

The room began to spin. I caught a whiff of smelling salts. Then the nurse withdrew.

"But that doesn't mean never, not by a long shot. I can see, of course, that your first delivery was difficult, and I understand your nervousness. Very difficult. But the repair-work has been well done, and all in all, you are in good physical shape. Nothing to worry about. But you've got to learn to relax, Mrs. Burton. That's the secret. It's an old story to us. A couple, childless for years, come in. Nothing happens. Then they adopt a child and presto! Usually in a year's time! We don't know the answer, but we do know that forgetting about it, the relief from the tension of trying, is at least part of it."

He was very kind.

"Now, there are a few little problems. You are run-down. You are also anemic. I'm going to give you a tonic to bring your blood up, and a very mild tranquilizer to take during the day. This insomnia is a little more difficult. I dislike starting patients on a pill routine, but if you are working and you are not getting your rest, we must take measures to see you do.

"Now, this is what I generally advise. Take a walk before bed-time. Then have a hot bath. Not too hot, just pleasantly warm. Then crawl into bed and read for about an hour. Turn off the light. And try and turn your mind off with it. People keep them-selves awake worrying because they can't sleep. Give yourself a good hour. If you are still wide awake, then take a pill. It works with ninety percent of my patients. When the sleep cycle is disturbed, the best thing is to try to forget it. It will right itself. Nobody ever died from a few nights of insomnia."

It all sounded so sensible.

I walked into the front hall. That ghastly door was open as usual and I closed it. Then I went to the living room and lay down on the sofa.

Eric heard me and came running upstairs.

"You were right, Eric. It was nerves."

He patted my hand. "Did he give you anything for them?"

I fumbled in my purse and handed him the prescription.

"I'll get them for you this afternoon. What else did he say?"

"Just to relax. Sleep. I'm so tired, Eric. Eric, can we go away? For a holiday?"

He didn't answer and when I opened my eyes, he leaned over and kissed me. "We will, as soon as we can, Amy. I promise you. We'll go away together. Just the two of us."

"When?"

"When the book's done. When mother comes home."

Not until then.

I fell asleep and it was nearly dinner time when I awoke. Eric handed me the druggist's envelope and pulled me up.

"You slacker! You need a pill to keep you awake, not to put you to sleep."

I still felt weary, terribly weary, but I managed to smile.

I didn't tell Frau Keller until after dinner. She looked disappointed, then she patted my cheek. She would not let me help with the dishes. I must do exactly as the doctor said. I must go for my walk. She herself would draw my bath. I didn't go to sleep. I tossed and turned and wished I were dead. Finally I slept.

That terrible, cheap hotel room. The cracks in the wall. The couple laughing and drinking in the next room. Then the pains. Sitting in the empty bath tub with a towel between my teeth, biting on it. No one must hear me. What had happened? It was too soon! Six weeks to go! Six weeks too soon. I had come to this horrible little town to hide for the last six weeks. What had happened? I mustn't scream. I must not scream! I must not. I will not scream. The blood. Where is it coming from? Everywhere in the tub. Everywhere in the tub was blood! My blood! What was happening?

They heard. I don't remember crying out, but they heard and they phoned the desk and the manager opened the door with his pass key. The police and the ambulance came.

He was dead. Drowned. In a bathtub with no water in it.

The next morning I did not throw up.

Where Is Bobby?

The Grahams' family dog, Bobby, was found cowering under a table in the kitchen, and had been locked in the house for two days. As S.P.C.A. members were putting him in their van he bolted and though pursued by both the police and the S.P.C.A. he disappeared in the heavy brush bordering Wild Swan Mountain. The S.P.C.A. request members of the public having information on Bobby's whereabouts to please phone their local branch.

CHAPTER FIFTEEN. (August 9th) Couldn't bear to write recently. Everything bothers me. Wish it would rain. Why do I dredge up these old memories? What's the good?

So hot. So hot. Yesterday went shopping. Bought curtains for downstairs bathroom and ordered blender for kitchen. Thought blender extravagance, but Eric saw them demonstrated on TV and wanted one to make milk shakes and frappéed drinks. Assured me Frau Keller would find a million uses for it. I happen to know she hates automation and household appliances. She doesn't even like the vacuum cleaner. She told me just last week that putting rugs on the line and beating them with a spiral wire whip was far more efficient.

Natürlich.

"Well, it's wall to wall and all nailed down, so I guess that's out," I replied.

"Humph!" says she.

If I was hot and tired when I began shopping, I was hotter and tireder when I came out of the department store, so I went to Victory Square to sit under a bush and rest.

The wedge-shaped monument with its chiseled "Is It Nothing To You" shimmered in the heat, and I watched a group of arty-looking young people sprawled on the grass arguing about the world. I envied them. That world they talked about was their oyster. Things were concrete in their universe, casting no more shadow than the war monument at noon.

Another hot and tired housewife sat on a bench fanning herself and she smiled at me as she slipped her shoes off. Between her feet were a bunch of parcels, and she sat with her hands relaxed on her lap, enjoying the sun with closed eyes.

It was a little green island in a sea of cement and traffic, life hummed and buzzed around us, but we seemed strangely isolated. A piece of newspaper, caught by a sudden breeze, pasted itself against the foot of the monument and the headlines read that a famine was predicted in India. Where was India? What did it have to do with us? A sea gull, probably sweating in his feather coat, wandered past, looking for a handout.

An elderly man shuffled up to the matron and sat beside her. She opened her eyes, glared, put her shoes on and retrieved her parcels. It's my bench, the eyes said. She was limping as she went back to the world of traffic and life.

The old man had a shopping bag and from it he took a thermos and into the cap he poured himself a cup of tea. He then put it carefully away and took out a sandwich wrapped in wax paper. I was about six feet away but I could smell the peanut butter as he gummed it around in his toothless mouth. When he had finished he folded the wax paper and returned it to the bag. Then came his dessert, a rotten banana. He was momentarily perplexed about the skin and finally it too went into the bag. He lit his pipe, a real stinky, aromatic old man's pipe, and he smoked peacefully, his eyes on the young people.

He was dressed in heavy tweeds, far too big for him, and I would have been willing to bet he bought them at a church bazaar. On his head was a cloth cap; his old army boots, polished like apples, gleamed in the sun. He should have been sweltering in that outfit, but apart from running his finger around his too-large shirt collar and straightening his tie, he seemed comfortable enough.

His pipe finished, he put it away, then took from the shopping bag another paper bag. He began spreading stale broken crusts of bread around his feet, and gave a shrill whistle. Within a minute there were twenty sea gulls barging about like drunken sailors, pecking, grabbing and shouldering each other.

He turned to me.

"Like people, ain't they?"

That's what Igor had said about the monkeys. These weren't as bad, though their brilliant, unblinking, reptile eyes were far from attractive.

"They seem to know you," I said.

He nodded.

"Do you come here every day?"

"Rain or shine," he said. "They'd go hungry if I didn't."

He was incredibly old, well over eighty, probably ninety, with the fleshlessness and bone-frailty of the aged. I wondered what he had looked like in his youth. Once he had loved and whored and cursed and had muscles and meat on him. Once his cheeks had been firm and his eye bright. I took a second look at him. His eye was still bright, and he was watching me with amusement.

"It's warm today." It was an obvious statement but he laughed as if I had made a joke.

"It don't bother me, miss. I fought in South Africa, and Messpot and India."

"Oh," I sat up and fanned myself. "You were a soldier?"

He nodded.

"Thirty-five years."

I thought of that house.

"I suppose you've seen a lot of dead people."

He looked surprised.

"Now that's a strange question from a young girl on a day like this."

Young girl. Well, I suppose I was to him.

"But," he nodded his head toward the arguing teenagers, "I guess you young ones don't know what war really is. Yes. I seen a lot of dead people in my day, miss."

"Does it bother you?"

"That's all for today," he said to the sea gulls and put the paper bag back with his other treasures. "Oh, it don't do to dwell on these things. But sometimes I remember. My brother, Alfred, he fell at Mafeking. Died in my arms. Sixteen years old. I had to write and tell mother. Broke her heart, nearly, I thought, until Arthur was killed at the Somme; then she never smiled again."

The heat made everything dance, and it was as blurrily unreal as an old picture. The colors were all ochre, sepia, tan, and beige, like an Edwardian photograph.

Speaking seemed to have triggered off a string of memories for the old fellow. He rose and joined me under my bush.

"Ronald was killed in 1914. September, 1914. At Nery, by a forest called Halatte."

Poor old man.

"You lost three brothers? I'm sorry," I said.

"Bless you," he smiled and his bristly old face crinkled, "Ronald was my horse. I was in the cavalry, I was. The Eleventh Hussars."

Cavalry. It was like talking to someone from Waterloo, or, for that matter, Thermopylae, as a jet far above us screamed.

"I'm sorry about Ronald," I said.

He nodded. "He was an old point-to-point winner."

I didn't know what he was talking about, but I nodded too.

"The battles," I said. "Were you frightened?"

"Didn't have time, miss. It was after."

Yes, that I understood.

"Could you sleep?" I asked.

"Sleep?" he chuckled. "Yes, I slept. When you're that tired, you sleep."

"Even on a battlefield? With the dead all around you?"

He nodded.

"But—but—weren't you afraid?"

"There's nothing to be afraid of, miss. I slept on one battlefield with ten thousand dead men beneath and around me."

"And you slept well?"

"Like a log."

I sat thinking. For so long that the old man finally touched my arm, timidly and courteously.

"It isn't often the young ask about these things."

"Tell me," I said, "how would you sleep in a house where eight children had been murdered?"

He looked shocked.

"Oh, that would be different. Grisly. Terrible. Why, you couldn't pay me to sleep in a house like that."

"There were no ghosts on the battlefields?"

"No. Some chaps said they saw an angel once, though. At Mons, it was. Me, I didn't see anything. But then, I wasn't at Mons."

"But you still wouldn't sleep in that house?"

"Ah, like I said, that would be different, miss. That would be a haunted house, wouldn't it?"

I handed him five dollars as I rose. He refused it, so I nodded to half a dozen surly sea gulls, who, still hopeful, paraded around.

"My share."

He touched his forefinger to the brim of his hat.

August 28th. Nothing much in notes to warrant typing up since the 9th, but on the night of August 27th heat spell ended. Igor had been spending more and more time with Eric. I suppose Elaina's confinement was drawing near, although I had no idea when she was due, and his own apartment was one place he didn't want to be.

Oh, well, at least she could watch TV.

He had also taken up yoga, jogging, and chess, presumably because they were all cheap.

He and Eric played a lot of chess, at which Igor was surprisingly good. Eric wasn't. He was always irritably changing his mind after his move, as if some dim-witted kibitzer had played for him. They sat for hours in the evening in Eric's study, gazing at that board. Eric had wanted to teach me, but I thought it was a waste of time. After all, when you're through, what have you got? Eric said it was an exercise in reason and that it cleared his mind so that when the game was through he was able to plan what he would write the following day. I preferred to curl up with a good book. Just why Igor liked it was anybody's guess. Since he didn't have an imagination it couldn't have been to clear his mind for that.

The night of the hall closet incident they were downstairs

playing; Frau Keller and I were in the living room, she crocheting and I reading; Rudi was in bed; and Elspeth was on the late shift at the theatre.

It was so warm out that the doors and windows were open, with all the little chirruping, rustling sounds of the night flooding in. Then there was a sudden hush, so that Frau Keller put down her crocheting and looked about her, and I half-turned a page of my book and sat with raised, listening head.

We rarely get bad storms here in the summer, and we are never ready for them. That odd quietness was shattered by the sound of a rain so heavy it was almost hail. Frau Keller jumped to her feet in alarm. At first I thought she was concerned about Rudi, but she had left sheets on the line and ran out to the back to retrieve them.

The curtains billowed from the open windows and I dashed about closing them, while the wind rose and rose and rose. A branch from a tree crashed against the side of the house with such violence that I wished we had storm shutters. If it had hit a window it would have gone clean through the room.

As a child at home I loved prairie storms—there was something magnificent about them, like warning prophets from the Old Testament—but these coast ones frightened me with their capriciousness.

Frau Keller came in with her arms full of tangled linen.

"The wind has ripped some of them. I am glad I have no one at sea tonight."

We heard trees go thumping down as if a giant belabored the earth with a club and Frau Keller and I exchanged looks of alarm. I thanked heaven our little fruit trees were safe against the sturdy garden walls.

The room became unnaturally bright with a strange bluish light and then we were left in darkness.

"Madame, where are you?"

"Here. Are you all right?"

We heard Igor and Eric stumbling up the stairs.

"That was a transformer that just went." It was Igor's voice.

"This is straight out of a Gothic novel! Rochester's wife will start screaming from her tower any minute. Did I tell you I found Black Sutch's footprints in the front hall this morning? Amy!

Where the hell are you? Have you got any candles?"

There were some, but where?

"I think they may be in the kitchen," I called.

"Candles are always hard to find because you never start to look for them till the lights go out." Igor lit a match and I saw his Tartar eyes gleam in the flare.

I groped my way to the kitchen and fumbled through a catch-all drawer, but they weren't there. Then I remembered. The buffet in the dining room. I realized I had my cigarette lighter in my hand, and for once it worked the first time I tried it. I lit both candles and began to cross the front hall to the living room.

That door. That door swung slowly open.

And huddled in the bottom was Philip. Aged six. On his face with his legs unnaturally contorted and his poor little arms folded across the back of his head, trying to protect himself.

I couldn't scream. I made for the stairs. The candles went out as I ran and I dropped them. I heard Eric and Igor and Frau Keller calling me. I ran straight to the attic.

I don't know how long I was there. Igor found me. He loomed above me, huge and silent, the candle flickering in his hand.

"Don't be afraid, Amy, I'm here. Don't be afraid. Shhh. Don't say anything!"

He called down to the others that he had found me. Eric and Frau Keller took my arms and led me to bed. I was shaking and I still couldn't talk, but I was too frightened to let them leave me and I clung to them, crying.

"What is it? What is it?" Eric kept asking. Then he went to call Dr. Kelly and when he came back he said he didn't know when the doctor would get there because of the blackout.

Finally Dr. Kelly arrived. It must have been the middle of the night, but the lights were still out.

"My God, what a night. Sorry I was so long, but the streets are booby-trapped with trees and poles. Strangely enough, not many people have been hurt. I suppose because they had enough sense to stay indoors."

He sat on the edge of the bed and took my hand.

"Well, Amy, what seems to be the trouble?"

I looked at the circle of faces contorted in the candle light and shook my head. Igor, behind Eric, nodded approvingly.

Dr. Kelly took a hypodermic needle and shoved it into my arm. He pulled the covers up to my chin and patted my shoulder.

"Stay with her until morning, then call me."

"You'd better go to bed." It was Eric addressing Frau Keller. "I'll stay with her."

"I'll spell you off," said Igor.

He pulled a chair beside the bed and sat down. In the hall I heard Dr. Kelly telling Eric that I was under some emotional strain and that I needed help. That as a general practitioner this was outside his field.

The candle flickered on a saucer by my bed, I felt drowsy and thirsty, and Igor sat as immovable as a monolith, only blinking occasionally. And his eyes had all the seeming of a demon that was dreaming and I was so tired, so tired, with the lamplight o'er us streaming. It was a dream, only a terrible dream, and in the morning I would wake up.

My hair had not turned white. It was the same mousy brown.

I couldn't tell Eric the whole story, but I knew I must let him know that something was happening in that house. Not that something terrible had happened. That something was happening.

Eric brought me breakfast on a tray. He looked so weary and pale he broke my heart.

"I'm sorry," I said.

"Don't be," he said, smiling. "You feeling better now?"

"Yes."

"Dr. Kelly thinks you ought to see a specialist."

"A psychiatrist is what you mean."

"Well, yes. Now, be sensible. What's the matter with that?"

"I'm not crazy."

"Oh, Amy! No one, not even Dr. Kelly, thinks that. You're overwrought. Your nerves are at the breaking point. Dr. Kelly says half his calls last night were hysterical in origin. It's quite natural. But he does think you need some extra help. Help he can't give."

"No."

"Well, we'll talk about it later. I'll have to take Rudi to school; the school bus isn't running this morning."

"Then why is he going?"

"He wants to. Routine. Routine is the only thing he can count on. Poor kid, we forgot all about him last night and he was scared stiff."

Igor had stayed the night, sleeping the balance of it on Madame Récamier, and he complained of a stiff neck when he came in to my bedroom.

"I saw one of them. The six-year-old. In the hall closet," I whispered.

The color drained from his cheeks and I saw he needed a shave. He looked over his shoulder compulsively and in a way it was reassuring, because Igor doesn't frighten easily.

I sat up, staring at him.

"You saw him too!"

"Just for a second." He swallowed hard. "We heard you running up the stairs. In the hall I lit a match as I followed you and I saw something. Maybe it was just shadows. Maybe a coat fell on the floor. I don't know what I saw. I went back after we found you, but there was nothing there."

"Igor! What are we going to do?"

He put his arms about me and kissed me. He wanted something. He only kisses when he wants something. His beard hurt and I pushed him away.

"Leave it to me, Amy. Trust me. Don't say anything. Please, Amy, don't spoil everything now."

"But Igor! This house is haunted!"

He didn't try to embrace me again. He never does if he is rejected. He just waits.

"Maybe it is, maybe it isn't. Maybe someone wants to make us think it is haunted."

"But why?"

"Why? There's half a million dollars hidden somewhere, and this house is the answer. It could be anything. A safety deposit box number. A key to a locker in the bus station. A map showing where it's buried. I'm going to find it, Amy, and you're going to help me."

No, Igor is not easily alarmed.

CHAPTER SIXTEEN. After fretting for three days I thought I had better do something and do it fast, before these disturbances had me completely unhinged. There's always a way out, I realized, as I suddenly thought of Mrs. Mac. She was one person who could throw some light on the subject, for the first time she walked into the house, she said it had a disturbing aura.

So, on September 2nd I went to the teashop, which she was now running for Laura, and I smiled as I saw the gold-lettered sign outside.

It was so businesslike. So unlike Laura.

> The English Tea Shoppe
> L. Pontifax, Prop.

Mrs. Mac was delighted to see me, even if I did feel a bit guilty about neglecting her since Laura had left.

As we sat over tea, I asked her if she remembered making that remark about the house.

"Indeed I do, Amy." The owl-eyes behind the thick lenses were kind but knowing. "Has something happened to upset you?"

"Yes."

"Can I be of help?"

For obvious reasons I couldn't tell her everything, but if she was going to be of any use, she had to know something.

"Well," I said hesitantly, "things happen in that house, Mrs. Mac. Things I can't explain. Things that aren't imagination."

She pondered, then, "You've seen or heard something?"

I nodded.

"Mmmm-hmmm."

The place had only three other customers, all women.

"Amy, I don't do much reading now. Physically it's quite exhausting and I find the business of running the shop takes too much energy, but I do have three customers today. Can you wait?"

"Of course," I said. "Don't rush."

The much-maligned Mr. Wong really could have done something with this building. Run down and shoddy, its greatest and I suppose only charm was that it had a lovely view of the bay. Ten rickety tables spraddled about with spotted plastic cloths and dusty paper roses in pressed glass vases. A forgotten remnant of last year's Christmas decorations hung dispiritedly from a ceiling corner, about as cheerful as the banner of a defeated army. But still, in its own wonky way the place had atmosphere, like the stage set for a high-school play.

I glanced at the menu, which never changes. Winter, spring, summer, or fall, you won't be taken unawares at The English Tea Shoppe.

Assorted sandwiches. I remember them. Cheese, ham and tuna, elegantly crustless and cut into quarters. Crumpets. Little, dry iced cakes masquerading grandly as petit fours. They needed a new mousetrap here before they would be beating the public from their door.

The only waitress, new from the last time I had been here and a slattern at that, stood by the cash register looking at the bay with an air of one who has better ways of putting in her time.

Then Mrs. Mac was back and the ladies had left. "Mildred, put on a fresh pot for us, dear."

She turned to me.

"I'm afraid I didn't give them a very good reading today. Some days, with some people, I just seem to be off and there's nothing I can do. Now, about you and this house, Amy."

Her glance was sharp, professional, that of a doctor taking up a difficult case.

"Amy, do you have any adolescents in the house?"

"Why yes, two."

"I see. And is one of them, how shall I put it? Not quite right up here?"

I looked at her in amazement.

"Yes. How on earth did you know?"

She laughed. "Nothing very mysterious, my dear. It's one of the commonest manifestations of the spirit world. You have a natural medium in the house. Is it a boy or a girl?"

"Boy."

"Well, you have three choices. You can have an exorcism ceremony performed by a priest, you can have a séance and warn the spirits away, or you can get rid of the boy."

Well, obviously the last was out and that left me with the two other alternatives.

I somehow couldn't see Eric going for a séance, so exorcism remained. But how did one go about getting an exorcism rite?

First you needed a priest. But where was I going to get one of them? Wait a minute. Bernard. Yes, Bernard was a Catholic. And it was his fault I needed a priest, too.

When I phoned him on the 3rd he suggested we meet for lunch, and I thought I detected a what-is-it-now tone in his voice.

I explained I had to be at work at two that day.

"All right, all right. Meet me at the Pig and Whistle at twelve-thirty."

It is one of those dim grills where you can't see your hand in front of your face at noon. I was on time, but Bernard was already sipping a cocktail when I arrived. He sprang to his feet and declared I looked stunning, although how he could tell in that light was beyond me.

"You look pretty good yourself," I said, watching the match flare on his handsome, sleek face as he lit a cigarette. He didn't look pretty good. He looked nervous and, for Bernard, grouchy; yet he had an air of suppressed excitement that puzzled me.

He ordered me a manhattan, then patted his stomach.

"Me? I'm on a diet. I'm over two hundred again." He looked at the infinitesimal remainder of his drink as if undecided whether to gulp or sip it. He gulped.

He chose a cottage cheese and fruit salad and I had grilled lamb chops, which he eyed longingly and with a glum air.

He patted his stomach again as if it were a beloved but troublesome child. "If you want a more detailed list of my ailments, I also suffer from heartburn. Oh, hell. Cheer up, Amy, what's the matter? You look as if you've seen a ghost. Listen, I've got some news, but it's confidential. At least, for a few weeks. Want to hear?"

What did I care about his news. Good God, I had to find out what to do and I had to find out fast.

"Now keep this under your hat. Not that I think you wouldn't. Any girl who won't even confide her worries to her husband is hardly a gossip."

He paused, his head on one side like a big robin.

"You don't seem very interested."

"I am," I mumbled. "What is it?"

"It's about Graham. They found the money. How does that grab you?"

He nodded as he saw me look up in surprise.

"I thought that would get a rise out of you. Listen to this, Amy. The police had established that Graham had bought an old Volkswagen the day he killed his family. What they couldn't figure out was why he bought it, and what happened to it. Now they know."

Somehow it didn't make much difference. The children were dead, weren't they? But then I thought, Igor. Igor, of course. Igor cared very much about that money. Oh, how much Igor cared.

"What happened?"

"Well, a guy was missing and his wife reported it to the police. A car had taken a sideswipe at the railings on the old Nickomickel River bridge, so the police started diving operations. They didn't find anything there, so they moved downstream about thirty yards. They found a car all right. They found the Volkswagen Graham had bought. He had run it down an old boat ramp. And when the police opened the trunk of the Volkswagen they found money, to the tune of one-half million bucks, that's what they found. So that's the end of that little mystery."

I didn't answer.

"Understandably, our local law-enforcement officers are in a rather sticky position. What I mean is, whatever way you look at it, Graham wasn't exactly honest, was he? So there's a shake-up going on at City Hall and a complete investigation of the whole civic police setup. City Hall wants to find out if anybody else has been dipping fingers in the till. They are particularly interested in finding out if Graham had an accomplice. That's why the news is not being released to the public at present."

"An accomplice? Do you think he had?"

He shook his head. "No. The whole psychology of the case hinged on the fact that Graham was a lone wolf, I think. He wasn't a criminal in the professional sense, and before that crime, ghastly as the outcome was, his reputation was spotless. I personally think he slipped a cog. He just wasn't the sort of person to be in a criminal gang. His subsequent actions bear that out."

But Graham had had an accomplice. One as unlikely to excite suspicion as himself. How they ever got together I don't know, but he had an accomplice and her name was Laura Pontifax Burton.

"Say, are you going to eat that roll?"

I shook my head. I didn't care about the money. But Igor did. What would his attitude to me be when he found that the balance of it had been found? Just what did I mean to him? Well, the moment I told him Bernard's news, I would certainly find out. But I didn't want to tell him. Contrary as it sounds, I was afraid of losing him.

I didn't want to think about the money. Besides, I had other problems. Big problems. Connected with Graham, but not about money.

"I'll have another drink, Bernard."

He looked up.

"A double," I said.

He had finished my roll and had speared his last piece of canned peach, which he gazed at with moody disdain; his expression changed to one of surprise.

"You? Amy? Amy, are you a secret drinker? Come on now, level with me. You been at the cooking sherry while Eric's down there putting Tolstoi out of business?"

He was grinning while he beckoned the waiter and ordered it.

"The house is haunted."

I needed that drink.

"Jesus!" His fork clattered on the table. "Now I need a double." He motioned to the waiter. "Make that two. Amy, what the hell are you talking about? Tell me."

I did.

He sipped his drink, then tossed it back and ordered yet another. Pushing the remainder of his salad away, he sat back staring through the gloom at me.

"I don't believe in ghosts."

"I thought all you Irish did. That you were fey or something. Anyhow, Igor saw it too."

"Igor!" He leaned over the table and shook his finger at me. "I warned you about that fellow. He's no damned good. I wish to God I'd never suggested he go to work for you and Eric. Did he get you started on this ghost nonsense?"

"No."

"Well, what do you want me to do? Get rid of the house for you?"

"No. Get rid of the ghosts. I want a priest."

"A *what*?"

I told him about Mrs. Mac's suggestion and he sat looking at me for a long, long minute.

"Hell, there goes my diet." When the waiter approached from behind with the drink, Bernard reached back and grabbed it from the tray.

"Amy, I think it's about time Eric was let in on this."

I shook my head.

"No look here, he has a right——"

I cut him short. "Eric is not going to know. There's no need for him to. Bernard, you got me into this, now get me out."

He sat with his fingers laced across his chest.

"I think you are wrong to keep this from Eric. And further-more, what you ask is impossible. In the first place, I don't know any priest of whom I could ask such an—an unorthodox thing."

I said nothing.

"And in the second place I wouldn't, anyhow. We're in the twentieth century and there's some natural explanation for this even if you are upset and can't see it now. I am sure Eric would agree with me, and I can't suggest strongly enough, Amy, that you let him know what's bothering you."

"No."

"Then I will," he said. "You need help."

"If you tell Eric," I said, and I meant it, "I'll ruin you. I'll shout what you did from the housetops and you'll never sell that house or any other."

He laid the palms of both his hands on the table.

"Am I to understand that you are threatening me?"

Those damned candlelights. I could barely see him. Maybe it was just as well, because the tone of his voice was frightening.

"You threatened me," I said. "You said you'd tell Eric. Well, I haven't nursed him along this far, on a book that I found out is good, only to have you knock the props out."

"Then it looks as if we're at an impasse, doesn't it?" He motioned the waiter for the check. "Good-bye, Amy. I must get back to my office, and I believe you have an appointment too."

It had been a mistake to try to intimidate him, especially when he was dieting and as irritable as a bear disturbed from hibernation. I should have used my head. I burst into tears and clutched his hand.

"Help me, Bernard! I don't know where to turn."

He stood up.

"I'm here any time you want me, for anything sensible. I'm a busy man, Amy."

I flung his hand away; he shrugged and started for the cashier.

"Don't forget to pray for me!" I was glad the place was dark. No one could see my tears, which were genuine and bitter enough now. He didn't even bother to turn his head.

But I hadn't counted on his conscience. While I was at work he phoned me, gentle and contrite.

"Forgive me, Amy. I lost my temper. You're not the only one whose nerves are shot to hell. That was a bombshell you threw at me."

"Oh, Bernard! I'm sorry too. Will you forgive me?"

He did, but he was adamant about the priest and the hauntings, saying I was overwrought.

"As soon as Eric has finished his book and Laura gets back, we'll make some arrangement. Be a good girl and hang on till then."

I couldn't tell him that if Laura had any sense, she wouldn't come back.

Bobby Still Missing

Mrs. Leona McCurdy of the Animals Have Souls Society said in an interview today, "Bobby is undoubtedly suffering from a deep psychic trauma. However, Mr. Leigh Browning of the Fish and Game Department thinks that because of Bobby's deerhound heritage he may be able to bring down small game on Wild Swan Mountain and survive."

When asked by reporters how she reconciled Bobby's slaying smaller animals with the Animals Have Souls Society movement, Mrs. McCurdy said, "Man is the culprit. The Bobbys of this world never started a war. It is when the balance of nature is upset by man that we can expect our Armageddon. Dog eat dog indeed! Unless we mend our ways, animals will be the only survivors!"

The Animals Have Souls Society was formed two years ago by Mrs. McCurdy and a group of citizens and was previously known as the Pray for Red China movement.

CHAPTER SEVENTEEN. It was a game. A silly game, I knew, and one that I would have been shamefaced to let Eric or anyone else in on. But I was happy when I played it and in some irrational fashion I like to think that it made them happy too. There was no harm in it. One can't eternally snatch dreams away from people without them becoming inwardly as dead as those children.

It all began one morning when I wondered idly how you coped with eight children at breakfast and before I knew it they sprang to life before my eyes. Not really, of course, but like Wordsworth and his field of daffodils.

You might think that that many children would tend to blur and be alike, but on the contrary, in my mind's eye their characteristics became more individual until not only their personalities but their faces were as precise as etchings.

There was Kenneth, the baby in his high chair, banging on his tray with his christening spoon. Sharon. Sharon, the twelve-year-old, ought to be able to handle him.

"Give him his juice and toast, while I check the eggs," I say to the imaginary Sharon.

The problems present themselves automatically. The boys come trickling in, one barefooted, and a little girl wants me to braid her hair.

"You'll have to wait a minute. You know nobody likes hard-boiled eggs here. Andrew, haven't you got your socks on yet? Ian, help him, will you?"

I'm not one of these people always calling out put-on endearments to kids. I'm a realistic mother. They know I love them.

Ian says he can't find any socks for Andrew and I tell him to look in the dryer. Ian's the eldest. A big boy.

The five-year-old is nearly ready for kindergarten, but her dress isn't ironed and I ask Neill to put out the ironing board for Linda's dress.

As I set the table, I look over the cereal, juice, toast, eggs, butter and jam.

"You forgot the vitamin pills. You forgot them yesterday too." Philip. My favorite.

"Don't be cheeky," I say, but I brush his hair from his forehead. I know it's wrong to have favorites, and of course I never let the rest know.

They gobble their food and I remonstrate. Andrew, aged ten, teases Linda and I tell him to quit it.

"I hate eggs," says Philip.

It's a silly daydream, really, I know; but as long as I know that it's a daydream, what harm can it do?

"Last week you didn't like bacon," I tell him.

"You gotta write me a note because I was away on Thursday," says Neill.

"Thursday? Why weren't you at school on Thursday?"

They all stop eating and give me that stare children reserve for obtuse adults.

"I died on Thursday."

Thursday. Was it Thursday? No it was Tuesday. One does try to rationalize and I realize I am back in my own empty kitchen, but in a minute my imagination takes hold and the children bring me to themselves with hoots of laughter.

They know how to play, to pretend.

"Don't you remember?" Ian, the man of the family. "He lay down and pretended to be dead because he didn't want to go to school because he had a spelling test. He said his legs hurt and his heart hurt and his head hurt and he was dead, dead, dead. And you thought it might be his rheumatic fever and were going to call the doctor."

I'm old, that's my trouble. I've forgotten what it's like to be a child, to have an imagination. To pretend. To play.

"Yes, of course," I say. I'm all right now. "Andrew, if you pull the bows out of her hair again I'll smack you."

Gretchen tries to crawl on my lap.

"You know I can't do your hair with you up here," I say, as I take the bows from her. "Did you pick up your room?"

She squirms and says yes. Kenneth howls lustily because no one is taking any notice of him. Ian spoons him the rest of his soft-boiled egg and pats him on his flaxen head.

They're all white Anglo-Saxon children with blue eyes, naturally. I didn't choose them that way. Honestly, that's the way they were and it would be sort of silly to change them to make them more real.

Ian sniffs.

"He's gone and done it again."

"Oh, well, just a minute. Finish your breakfast now. You haven't got all day."

I snatch Kenneth from his high chair and dash to the bathroom. Changed and powdered, I pop him in his play pen.

"Okay," I shout. "Lunches and then teeth."

They all have their jobs and with a minimum of shoving and joking, they perform them. Neill gets the sandwiches out of the freezer. Sharon puts out seven paper bags and seven oranges. Gretchen gets the cookies and puts three in each plastic bag. I fill and cap seven plastic cups with milk.

There's the usual last-minute chaos of "Where's my geography book?" "That's my hat! You lost yours and you're not snitching mine!" and "I have to take fifty cents for our field trip on Monday. Miss Carter said we *have* to get it in today."

Where's my purse? No change. I give her a dollar and warn, "Now don't you lose that, and bring me back fifty cents."

Gretchen and Linda kiss me good-bye, but the older ones are too self-conscious for that, and Philip looks as if he wouldn't touch me with a ten-foot pole. But when the others are gone he dashes back and gives me a wet and furtive smack on the cheek.

They're gone and I hear the boys getting their bicycles from the carport and Sharon yelling for her friend, Carol, down the block, to wait for her.

Suddenly all is quiet. I look around the messy breakfast table and see one lunch forgotten.

I shout out the kitchen window, "Neill, you've forgotten your lunch."

"I'll give it to him." It's Andrew, already on the saddle of his bike, and I toss it to him.

Kenneth is in his playpen chewing on an arrowroot biscuit some generous sibling has slipped him. He hates the playpen now and will only stay in it for short periods, so I have to make hay while the sun shines.

I dash upstairs and start going through the bedrooms, collecting clothes for the first wash. They should put them in the hamper but they forget, and I pick up an armful of shirts, vests, socks and pants and I strip Gretchen's bed. I do one a day and that way don't get too far behind. I also rip everything except the draw sheet off Kenneth's crib as a matter of course. They are supposed to make their beds but I always have to redo the little ones'. I dash down and start a load and hear Kenneth, who has plainly had enough, yelling.

"Okay," I call. I pick him up, take him to the bathroom and put him on the toidy seat. I give him a comic book to look at, which he holds upside down.

"No more of your tricks like at breakfast." I am stern. "You know what you are there for."

He chortles and begins ripping the comic book.

He's good for ten minutes at that so it's back to the kitchen, which looks as if a hurricane had hit it.

I load the dishwasher. (Yes, I have one. With eight children, why not?)

I sweep the floor and wash the arborite top of the kitchen table. Meat! I forgot to get meat out of the freezer for dinner. While I'm downstairs I remember I didn't put soap in the washer, but it's not too late.

Now it's quiet. I pour myself a cup of coffee, get the morning paper and light a cigarette. I'm halfway through when the phone rings. It's Mildred Williamson who says that if Grace Fisher doesn't stop trying to run the whole PTA she for one is not attending any more meetings. We decide we hate Grace Fisher.

"The way she talks, you'd think her kids were perfect. Believe me, once they're out of her clutches, they're the worst brats in the neighborhood. Not that I blame them."

I agree and then remember I have secretly promised myself not to gossip.

It's strange, but in these fantasies there were no parents. The children were real to me but John and Alma Graham were not. It was as if that would be going too far. I didn't even dare let the dream children call me Mummy and there wasn't Eric as a substitute father. I knew they were not real and in their unreality they were mine. This way they stayed noisy and bumptious and alive. They were not perfect. I didn't want perfect children, and so Gretchen whined, Neill told lies, Andrew teased, Linda balked. Ian was too serious for his age, but then that was natural. He was the eldest and had always had more responsibility. Sometimes I asked too much of Sharon in helping with the little ones and she sulked, but in an emergency I knew I could count on her, she who with her own frail flesh had tried to absorb the impact of those hideous bullets.

They never frightened me in the day. Only at night when that demon dog howled and tried to get in and they cried and I knew I couldn't comfort them.

It was lonely when the magic and the voices of the day faded and I was back by myself in the kitchen, with reality in the form of Frau Keller or Eric or Elspeth or Igor barging in. Even that pathetic substitute for a child, Rudi, was an interloper.

One sultry afternoon a few days after I discovered the daytime children and I had just finished playing with them, Eric came into the kitchen.

I had been daydreaming for over an hour and I felt guilty. Frau Keller was doing more and more and I was doing less and less. I got out the ironing board.

"Put that away, for God's sake, Amy. It's too hot."

"No. I always seem to be putting things off. I should keep busy. Maybe I'll sleep better at night if I do."

"Put it away, Amy, please. I want to talk to you."

He took an airmail letter out of his pocket and tapped it on the palm of his hand.

"From Mother."

"Is anything wrong?"

"Yes, there is. There's something I want to tell you."

Well, there was something I wanted to tell him, only I couldn't.

"I should have told you long ago." He looked around in a despairing way. "I tried to, but the words would never come out right."

He tapped the letter on the palm of his hand again and stood gazing out the kitchen window at Rudi, who was sitting beside an apple tree in the garden, looking like part of the landscape.

"Come on," Eric said. "Let's go to the beach for a swim. We'll talk then." He tossed the letter down. "Hey, Rudi! Get your bathing suit on. We're going to the beach."

Rudi looked up, his strange, unseeing eyes showing no pleasure at the prospect. But he did rise.

Frau Keller came bustling in, beaming.

"Ah, that is kind, Mr. Burton. Would you like me to make a picnic supper?"

"No, no," said Eric. "Take an evening off. You deserve it. We'll pick up some fish and chips and pop there."

We heard her speaking German to Rudi in the hall and even we understood the word "schwimm" which she spoke so hopefully and earnestly. When she handed Rudi his towel and bathing suit she attempted to embrace him. He pushed her aside, not angrily or sullenly, but as if she were some troublesome burden he wished to rid himself of.

We were halfway down the stairs when she came chasing after us, still beaming.

"Madame, your bathing cap."

Poor Frau Keller. She would have loved to have had some elegant lady on whom to lavish her gratitude for Rudi. As it was, she was stuck with plain old me.

At the beach Rudi looked pathetically thin and small in his trunks, which was no wonder as he eats practically nothing.

Eric tried to tempt him out to the water, but after getting to his waist, Rudi started shivering and his finger tips and lips turned bluish.

Eric didn't insist. He brought the boy back and tried to dry him off. Rudi snatched the towel from him and dried himself.

"He's abnormally sensitive to both noise and cold."

The beach was packed, but it might have been deserted for all the notice Rudi took of the crowds. How Eric reconciled this with the noise theory is a mystery, but he's one of those people who happily spend a lifetime trying to jam square pegs into lopsided holes. Rudi sat down, sifting sand through his fingers in another one of his endless, meaningless gestures.

Eric went off to get fish and chips. When he returned he offered them to Rudi, who shook his head almost imperceptibly, the slightest negative gesture possible.

"Oh, come on, Rudi," said Eric. "You want to be big and strong like me, don't you?"

"Har, har," I said. Eric is built like an emaciated Iroquois.

Eric put a chip in his own mouth, chewed it and with the awful mock cheerfulness and gusto he always uses with Rudi said, "Ah! Good!"

Rudi continued sifting sand.

Eric held a chip before Rudi's nose. Rudi looked up, gazed right into Eric's eyes and deliberately knocked the paper boat of fish and chips into the sand.

I resisted an impulse to smack him, but no such impulse came to that eminent psychiatrist, Dr. Burton.

"You see that?" he said to me. "He didn't want it and he showed me he didn't want it."

"Yeah. That took a lot of brains."

Rudi stared at Eric and the expression in his eyes shocked both of us. He was waiting.

"I wish you wouldn't be so antagonistic to him," said Eric. "No harm done, Rudi. We'll go and get some more chips. Come on, Amy. You stay right there, Rudi."

As we threaded our way to the food concession Eric turned to me. "Did you see the look in his eyes? Don't tell me that his father and brothers haven't beaten him in the past. He was waiting for it."

"Well, they have my sympathy. He knew exactly what he was doing."

"He can't help it." Eric sighed as he ordered a double order of fish and chips. "You don't understand anything, Amy. If it isn't printed in your book it doesn't exist."

"Oh forget it. What did you want to tell me?"

"Later."

I know him. He puts off unpleasant things as long as he can and when he does decide to face them it's with all the delicacy of a canal horse.

When we returned Rudi was, of course, sitting just as we had left him. Eric put the food down before the boy.

"I wish you'd tell me. The suspense is killing me."

He looked at me and then away.

"It's mother. That letter was from her. Amy, she's a fraud."

My heart nearly stopped. But, as I sat looking at his profile, I realized he didn't say it as if he were shocked or surprised. He said it as if it were something sad he had known for a long, long time.

"I don't understand, Eric."

He stared at the incoming tide, tossing pebbles at it.

"You remember I told you about the assignment I had covering that royal wedding in England five years ago?"

I nodded. He had been there three weeks.

"Well, I did some checking when I was back. Sentimental old me. I was going to surprise her when I returned. The first place I went was the Vicarage. I'd heard her speak of it ever since I was a toddler and I felt I knew every inch of it.

"It was just as she had described it. The lady of the house, when I explained I was a visiting journalist from Canada, was very kind and invited me in.

"Part of the house was sixteenth century. Just as she said. The drawing room with the chintzes and the big Chinese vases and the mullioned windows with the ivy growing around them, and the stone-flagged passages and the rooms on half a dozen floor levels, and the little flights of stairs at odd places. It was like seeing something after dreaming of it for years.

"The woman asked me my name and I told her. 'It wouldn't mean much to you,' I said. 'But my mother's name might. It was Pontifax, and she used to live here.'

"She gave me a funny look and said her name was also Pontifax. Well, I was all ready to throw my arms about her neck and say 'Auntie, I've come home!' when she said she didn't recall any of her family going to Canada.

"I told her it was a long time ago. It was about twenty-one years then. I told her my grandfather had been the vicar. Her expression became quite cold when she informed me her father had been and still was the vicar.

"'There must be some misunderstanding,' I said. Then she asked me my mother's first name. When I said Laura, she gave a peculiar laugh.

"'Oh, yes, Laura. I remember her very well. Yes, she did go to Canada, didn't she?'

"She pointed to the fireplace with its coat of arms carved in stone, and on the mantlepiece was a little Dresden figurine.

"'Yes, as I recall, she stole the mate to that when she left.'

"Amy, she started out there as a scullery maid. There weren't any boating parties on the Cam. Grandfather wasn't an Oxford or Cambridge or whatever it was, blue. There were no weekends with the relatives at Portchester Castle. Oh, she was there all right, as a servant, when they visited. There were no strawberry teas unless you want to count her passing bread and butter. There were no county balls or pink coats. She never refused to ride with the hounds because she felt so sorry for that poor little fox. The closest she ever got to a horse was when she visited my father in the stables where he was a groom. Oh, yes. She traveled extensively on the continent, when she had risen to the dizzy heights of a lady's maid to that very woman I was speaking to.

"It was all a dream. She came from the slums of Manchester, and her father worked in a cotton factory. I checked. They were decent enough people. Poor. But that's no crime, is it? Her name was Potter. Laura Potter. She was one of eight children and they lived in a row house with two bedrooms and she went into service at the Vicarage when she was fourteen."

Suddenly he stood up.

"Hey!"

The fish and chips were all gone. Rudi stood up too. He pointed to the water and tugged on Eric's arm.

Eric was so excited he could hardly speak.

"Yes, Rudi, yes! But you must ask me! Go on, try!"

Rudi's mouth worked but no sound came out. He tugged and tugged on Eric's arm, but Eric wouldn't budge.

"Ask me, Rudi! Go on, ask me!"

Then, in a hoarse voice, Rudi croaked,

"Schwimm, bitte, Eric."

We sat up in bed smoking and talking for a long time that night.

"Do you hate her for it?"

"No, of course not. It's not wicked, Amy. It's sad. And I'll tell you another thing. She never stole their —— figurine."

I won't use the adjective he used.

"And I understand why she took it. It was the one concrete element of refinement in her life. There were no Dresden ornaments in the Manchester row-house. It was a gesture. Not a wise one, but then, mother's not a wise woman; but she is honest, Amy. She's never stolen anything in her life."

Oh, God! What would he think or do if he knew?

"The reason I've told you all this is that she's more deluded than ever. She's met a lot of well-bred people back there and they've accepted her, and that phony past is more real to her than ever now. I want her to come home before she's unmasked. I don't know what it would do to her if she were. I think it would break her heart if she thought I knew. She herself has come to believe that I'm some sort of little Crown Prince."

And the one place she couldn't safely come was here. Someday, someone was going to put two and two together, and someday she was going to slip up. She was more secure with her pitiful masquerade in England than anywhere else. What was I to do?

Poor Laura. We all have our dreams and our spun-sugar worlds. Was she so different from us? Eric escaping into the realm of literature, a form of make-believe. Bernard and his liquor. Frau Keller and her undying, blind hope for that hopeless child.

Igor? Igor's outside the pale of all fantasy or normal human relations. Eric once said Igor had a primitive nature, a dinosaur with a tiny pineal brain in his skull and another in his tail, needing both to propel himself through life. And yet, Eric is fond of Igor. When I asked him why, he said somebody has to like dinosaurs. Then he said something rather odd. He said he preferred Igor to Bernard.

"Eric!"

"But Amy," he replied, "I'm not saying I don't like Bernard. I'm just saying I prefer Igor. Igor's a man. You're too hard on poor old Igor, Amy. There's no give to you. Things always have to be black or white. Bernard the good guy and Igor the villain. Oh, I know Igor's stingy and he's a bit rough around the edges and he's a bloody bore about culture, but so what? Who's perfect? Igor's not all bad."

"Huh!" I said. Men always stick together.

That night the voices started in earnest. It was no good waking anybody up and I lay clinging to the sleeping Eric, too terrified to move. I could have sworn one of them was sobbing even in the attic directly over our heads. The newspapers hadn't mentioned the attic, but God knows how many stories there were that we hadn't read. Only one thing was certain. There were no survivors. Even the baby. He'd been in his crib not six feet from where I lay. Oh, it doesn't bear thinking about! There wasn't a corner of that accursed house that wasn't haunted.

The next morning Frau Keller looked pale and said Rudi had had a bad night.

"You're not kidding," said Elspeth.

"Perhaps, Mr. Burton, we counted on too much yesterday, and the excitement was more than we realized."

"Yes," said Eric, rather crestfallen because he and she had been so elated about Rudi's progress at the beach. "Maybe we're rushing things, Frau Keller. We must let him set the pace."

I said nothing. Why destroy their hopes? Even the doctors do not know a cure for autism, and Frau Keller and Eric will go on and on hoping until he's grown up and hopeless and has to be put away. It's cruel to think it and to face it, but it's crueler to leave Frau Keller nothing.

Bobby Sighted On Wild Swan Mountain, Say Two Bird Watchers

The S.P.C.A. again renewed its request for information concerning "Bobby," the family dog of the Grahams.

Mrs. Leona McCurdy, of the Animals Have Souls Society reported today in an interview,

"We have been swamped with offers of good homes for Bobby and have received donations totalling $800, which will be offered as a reward to anyone bringing Bobby safely to the S.P.C.A."

Neighbors say Bobby was a large, gentle dog loved by all the children in the area, who used to ride on his back. He is described as half Scottish Deer Hound and half Newfoundland and is black with one white left foot. Bobby was given to Ian, the eldest Graham child, on Ian's sixth birthday. Bobby is now seven years old.

See Page Four for Pictures

CHAPTER EIGHTEEN. (September 15th) Been remiss about notes for couple of weeks and no wonder. Must take some definite action. Things, peculiar things, going on. Elspeth affected by psychic manifestations?

She came dashing into my room a couple of days after I saw Bernard and grasped my arm in a grip that made me wince. With that mask of tragedy makeup kit of hers she looked like Eleanora Duse.

"That damned kid! You make him stay out of my room! He looked over my shoulder again! I saw him in my room!"

"Take it easy, take it easy," I said. "I'll speak to Frau Keller now."

Elspeth stamped her foot and ran off.

I went down to the kitchen where I found Frau Keller concocting something called chocolate Napfkuchen.

"I'm sorry to have to mention this, Frau Keller," I said, "but please do not let Rudi go into Elspeth's room. He frightened her rather badly looking over her shoulder suddenly."

Frau Keller bridled and patted her braids with floury hands. "And just when, does she say?"

"Why, I don't know," I said.

"Please, you shall ask her."

So I did and I reported back.

"About an hour ago."

Frau Keller gave a wintry, triumphant smile. "Rudi was not home an hour ago. And," here she gave a sniff and a combative jerk of her head, "she did not sleep in her bed last night. Nor twice last week. There's something wrong with that one, Madame. She'll come to no good. You'll see that I am right."

I'm fond of Frau Keller; but damn her, she always is.

I told Eric I thought Elspeth was running a bit wild but he said we had better mind our own business. "After all, she's eighteen and only boarding here, and not our responsibility. Why don't you call Bernard?"

But I had already bothered him so much I hated to do so again. Perhaps it would have been better if I had, because not many days later the phone rang.

A male voice that identified itself as a member of the Royal Canadian Mounted Police asked if this were the residence of Elspeth Mackinnon.

With a sinking heart I said yes. My first fear was that she had been in an accident.

"Are you her legal guardian?"

"What has happened to her?"

The voice again asked if I were her legal guardian.

"No. Her parents live in the interior. She boards here. Will you please tell me what this is all about?"

Elspeth had been picked up on a drug charge. Also, she would not be eighteen for two weeks. She was still a juvenile.

I told the police I would get in touch with our lawyer, Mr. Kielty, and I asked him to tell Elspeth Bernard would soon be there.

"Oh, my God!" said Bernard, when I called him. "Her poor parents. I'll go right down now."

When they arrived home later, Elspeth, with a distraught face, ran straight to her room, while Bernard followed Eric to the living room. With a certain grim pleasure, Frau Keller served coffee. I didn't have any and went up to Elspeth's room.

"What do you want?" Her voice was sob-ridden.

"Elspeth, I want to talk to you. Can I come in?"

She didn't answer so I went in anyway. She was lying on the bed with her arms around Aggie, weeping as though her heart would break.

"Tell me what happened," I said, sitting on the edge of the bed.

She looked thirty years old when she raised her face.

"Where's Uncle Bernie? Is he still mad?"

"He's downstairs. I don't know."

There was another torrent of sobs and then Bernard came in. He was quite sober and very angry, a study in outrage, as a matter of fact.

"What have you got to say for yourself?" He was shouting. "Sit up and tell me everything!"

We were engulfed in more tears but finally she pulled herself together. If it hadn't been sad it would have been funny and it proved once again how strangely our destinies are controlled by small incidents.

She and one of her boy friends had driven up to the foot of the ski-lift, parked, and were having a quiet smoke of marijuana. As she herself put it, unbeknownst to them two little kids had gone for a hike on the mountain and had got lost. Their alarmed parents had phoned the police who sent a squad car out. A policeman had rapped on the car window to ask if they had seen two small boys, and when her boy friend rolled down the window, the police got a whiff, and that was that.

"You can thank your lucky stars you're not eighteen yet." Bernard's face was an unhealthy cerise. "You're to appear in Juvenile Court on Thursday. You'll probably get a suspended sentence, because of your age and this being a first offense."

He took out his wallet and threw a twenty dollar bill on her bedside table.

"That's for bus fare home. If you're not convicted you're going to be on that bus an hour after you leave court."

She let out a wail.

"I'm not going back to that hick town!"

Either from anger or to stop her crying, he slapped her face smartly.

"You'll do exactly as I tell you."

"I won't! I won't! Amy!" She turned to me. "Don't let him send me back there. I'd rather die! You don't know what it's like. There's nothing to do! Nothing!"

I didn't know what to say. Coming from a small town myself I had a certain sympathy for her. Eric had come up and stood in the doorway, looking over Bernard's shoulder.

"Mr. Burton! Mr. Burton!" She ran to him. "Mr. Burton! Don't let him make me go back! Please!"

Eric gave a helpless shrug and turned to Bernard.

"I won't go!" she screamed, and wheeling to Bernard, "and you can't make me. I won't go!" She stamped her foot and flung herself on the bed again.

Bernard reached down, grabbed her by one arm and hauling her to her feet, shook her as if she were poor old Aggie.

"What have you been trying besides pot?"

"Nothing! Nothing! Honestly, Uncle Bernie!"

He shook her even more violently.

"What else?"

She was sobbing uncontrollably now.

"I tried speed a couple of times."

"And?"

"Acid. But only once. I swear to God, Uncle Bernie, only once."

He threw her back on the bed and ran his hands through his curly black hair, then he straightened up.

"Listen carefully, little lady. You're going to be on that bus and you're going home. You have one other choice, which I've discussed with your parents on the phone. You'll do exactly what I tell you, or I'll have you declared incorrigible and made a ward of the courts. We'll see how you like life in the Girls' Correctional Institution. Believe me, the ranch will look pretty good in comparison."

She hiccuped in horror.

"Uncle Bernie! You wouldn't sent me there! Why—why, those girls are awful! I'm not like *them*! Uncle Bernie, you wouldn't!"

"Just try me. If you've got any brains at all, be on that bus." He turned on his heel, then stopped. "And apart from going to court, don't leave this house. I'll be there on Thursday morning."

I had no idea he could be so implacable.

When I went downstairs, Frau Keller was setting the dining room table.

"Will *she* be here?"

"Yes. She still has to eat. What's for dinner?" I walked into the kitchen, with her, waving a wooden mixing spoon, following in my wake.

"Cabbage rolls. I warned you! She ought to be in jail. These young people! They know what the law is and still they break it. Then they cry! Jail's too good for her. She broke the law!"

I lifted a pot-lid on the stove then turned to her.

"Please, Frau Keller. What if it were Dieter or Wolfgang?"

The thought was so untenable that she banged the spoon on the counter. "Please, Madame!"

Everybody seemed to be implacable that day. Eric was lying on Madame Récamier in the living room, smoking and staring at the ceiling.

"It's too bad——" I began.

"Too bad, hell! These kids ask for it. The little goose. As Bernard said, she can thank her lucky stars she's a juvenile."

She refused to come down for dinner and when I took her up a tray her face was still swollen from crying.

"I'm not hungry." She gave Aggie a sullen punch in the ribs. "Who the hell does he think he is, anyhow? All the kids smoke. Just because I got busted he thinks he can play God!"

She obviously hadn't learned a lesson from the incident and her manner was so rebellious that I felt like telling her it wasn't my fault. Instead, I said, "You'd better do exactly as he says. He means business."

"That fat-assed creep!" She began to cry again; then, as she saw me leaving with the tray she sniffed and said, "You might as well leave that. I can't go anywhere and I suppose I'll have to eat *something* eventually. If that old bitch hasn't poisoned it."

She was quite unrepentant, and with these gracious words she buried her face in Aggie and wept some more; so I left the tray and went downstairs.

In the days following, until her trial, all hell broke out on several nights. There were screams, shouts and poundings. Elspeth said it was Rudi. Frau Keller said it was Elspeth. Only I knew better. Even Eric heard the noises.

Her bag dutifully packed on Thursday morning, Elspeth left with Eric for court, and then, with Aggie under her arm, he watched her get on the bus.

I know it sounds strange, but I missed her. Her room, finally tidy, looked bare and lonely and the whole house had an empty feeling. She was more like a tornado than a breath of fresh air, but she was young. She was vital. She was alive.

And the noises didn't stop. They got worse. We were all jumpy. Eric said we were letting our imaginations run away with us. But Frau Keller knew. Rudi was bringing them back. She pretended not to know, but I knew she knew.

Week of September 20th. I think. Dates mixed up sometime around here. Too much to think about.

Well, I tried everything within reason, and nothing worked. Then I phoned the priest. On my own, saying nothing to Bernard. He refused, the priest, I mean, and I think he thought I was crazy.

So that left me with the séance. The memory of that will haunt me to my dying day. If I were ever to lose my mind, I would have, that night.

I wasn't prepared for what happened. All Mrs. Mac told me was that she had arranged for a séance with a medium named Alex, and that his spirit control who took over when he went into trance was an Indian holy man named Ram Lal, who had "passed over" several centuries before. It sounded phony, of course, but Mrs. Mac assured me that astounding phenomena had taken place when Alex was under the control of Ram Lal.

I had been brought up in a family who considered spiritualism as a province of the devil, and I wondered what they would say. I didn't wonder about what Eric would say. I knew. So as far as he was concerned I was merely having dinner and spending the evening with Mrs. Mac.

Eric admitted the dog's presence, but of course I had not told him of the hauntings. The noises at night were, he thought, Rudi; and Frau Keller certainly did nothing to enlighten him on that point.

We arrived at the medium's home, a neat bungalow in the sub-urbs, at eight o'clock, and were met at the door by two pale and pimply young acolytes who led us into the living room.

What a strange room it was for the bachelor this Alex was supposed to be. The mantelpiece was covered with Dresden figurines. Opposite the fireplace was a spinet piano, standing on a bear skin rug. The piano was laden with cut glass, tastefully grouped arrangements of flowers, and Doulton statuettes. In one corner was an electric organ, also covered with china orna-ments and glass odds and ends, and in the other, on a pedestal, was the roughly sculpted head of a turbaned man.

"Ram Lal," whispered Mrs. Mac. "Alex did it himself in clay." She paused. "From memory," she added in a tone of reverence. "He occasionally sees Ram Lal when he is not in trance, and he says he is as real as you or me when he materializes."

Double sliding doors, pushed back, led to a dining room also crowded with gewgaws. Every conceivable inch of space in both the dining room and living room was covered with bric-a-brac and the whole place looked like the abode of an elderly spinster.

The two priestlings, in the meanwhile, had excused them-selves to go to the kitchen and prepare tea.

"Are you sure he hasn't a wife?" I whispered to Mrs. Mac.

"Quite sure," she whispered back.

"I have always loved the finer things of life."

I jumped. I hadn't heard him come in. He stood in the doorway, a heavy-set man in his middle thirties, with a thick Scottish accent and the face of a Caliban. He walked to the dining room and caressed the magnificent china statue of an Arab mounted on a richly caparisoned horse.

"I just got this last week and a pretty penny it cost, too. The papers say I am a fraud, but I do well for a fraud, don't I? Do you think I am a fraud?"

His moonstruck eyes frightened me and I wished I hadn't come. Mrs. Mac squeezed my hand reassuringly.

"Last week," he continued, without waiting for an answer to his question, and his manner was petulant, "last week I had a woman come here who wanted me to get in touch with her dead son. As proof that I had contacted him she wanted me to give her the name of his best friend, also on the other side. 'So, Madame! Two for the price of one,' I said. You can be sure she paid through the nose for that! I tell you, if I had a machine gun in my hands when some of them are going down those front stairs—" He paused, and like a small boy imitating a gangster movie, he raised his hands into shooting position and shouted, "Br-r-r-r-r-r!!!"

I nearly jumped out of my skin. The two assistants, casting adoring glances at him, came in with tea.

He was a compulsive talker who neither wanted nor waited for an answer.

"I've always loved the finer things of life. I don't mind hard work. I was a sailor once. A stoker. It wasn't the work I minded. Those filthy men! Having to eat at the same table with them! Half of them had syphilis. You wouldn't believe it. If I hadn't had my accordion with me, I would have gone mad. But music doth soothe the soul."

He paused for breath and accepted a cup of tea which he placed before him on a low table. "It is difficult to be a medium. We suffer from vibrations that you—," and here he paused, pointed a finger accusingly at me and shouted, "that you are incapable of feeling!"

On and on he went. Some of it made sense, most of it sounded like gibberish. I wanted to go home; instead, I sat beside Mrs. Mac, mesmerized, drowned in a tidal wave of words.

"And they come to me. Women, wanting to know who they will marry! What do they think I am? A teacup reader? Only the spirit is important. But the Jezebels keep coming! I hate this city. I've been here two years and never have I found people more unfriendly!"

Myself, I could scarcely blame them.

"It's a horrible place. If it weren't for my disciples I couldn't bear it!"

One of the disciples knelt before the master, serving cream and sugar and the medium cast him an affectionate glance.

"What would I do without them?" As if giving benediction, he laid his hand upon the youth's head, and his swarthy face was tender.

The young man, to me at least, was singularly unattractive; and he beamed at the medium, becoming, if possible, even less appealing.

The master gulped his tea.

"Shall we go up now, ladies?" I wasn't sure whom he addressed.

As he rose he flicked a speck of dust from an ornament and centered its lace doily more precisely on the table.

A carpeted flight of stairs led from the front hall to the second floor and we all obediently trooped after him.

We were led into what appeared to be a windowless room heavily draped in red velvet. A table, surrounded by eight chairs, stood in front of a recess in one wall. In the recess was a statue of the Virgin banked by two red votive lights.

The front doorbell rang, and one of the attendants went down. He returned leading three more people, two women and a nondescript looking man. We were not introduced, but it was obvious that they had all met before.

With a princely wave of his hand, Alex bade us all be seated, then he fastened those crazy eyes on me.

"You're afraid of the dead, aren't you?"

Well, who isn't? Anybody in their right mind, that is. I nodded.

"There's nothing to be afraid of. They are as real as you or me."

Mrs. Mac, who had attended séances for years, nodded comfortingly. "It's quite true, Amy dear. There's nothing to be afraid of."

"First a hymn and then a short prayer."

We sang "Just a Closer Walk with Thee," and then we lowered our heads as he mumbled what sounded more like an incantation than a prayer.

The assistants bustled about, and one placed a silver trumpet on the table.

"Well?" Alex fixed Mrs. Mac with his bright, maniac's eye.

"This lady," said Mrs. Mac hesitantly to the group, "wishes to contact some children who went to the other side most suddenly. They are being brought back by an unconscious medium, a young, mentally disturbed boy. We wish to assure them that all is well in their present state and that if they feel lost, they will soon be attended by a spiritual guide on the other side."

The group nodded soberly, unsurprised by this request. An overhead light threw odd shadows on Alex. Downstairs, while I wouldn't have described him as ordinary looking, he was not ugly. Now he looked grotesque. His complexion was pitted and large-pored, his nose seemed huge in the shadows, and his mouth lipless.

"He is about to go into trance," whispered one of the assistants, and glancing at me, "when he does, please do not speak. We will turn off the center light."

Alex's head sagged, then sank on his breast, and after about a minute he appeared to sleep. Then, very slowly, his body began to jerk and a spasm traveled up from his legs, through his chest and neck and shoulders to his face. He sat upright, his appearance changed. His features had altered subtly, the taut muscles giving him an ageless, almost Oriental, appearance.

The group nodded to each other, and silently, by some prearranged signal, they all fumbled for each other's hands, and I found myself damply grasping Mrs. Mac's on one side and a strange woman's on the other.

"Ram Lal," said one of the assistants, "we are here to seek your counsel on this lady's children. They left our plane suddenly and she fears they are confused."

I opened my mouth to explain that they were not my children but the group turned on me as a whole, every pair of eyes warning me to silence.

One of the assistants rose and turned out the light. Only the flickering ruby votive lights were left.

"Ram Lal, are you with us?"

The medium's head nodded, then he spoke, strangely enough without a Scottish accent.

"Yes, I am with you."

"And are you in touch with the spirit world also?"

The medium or Ram Lal, or whoever he was now, folded his hands across his chest like a Mandarin, and the voice became stern and tutorial.

"We are all of the spirit world. Ghosts yet walking the earth. Ghosts, traveling from one point of infinity to another. Souls seeking perfection, souls that pass in the night, sailing through planes of eternity to that great Central Being, the source of all light."

"The children, Ram Lal? Can you contact them?" Mrs. Mac's gentle voice.

"The children. Yes. Children. Yes, they are here."

"Are they unhappy, Ram Lal?"

I didn't want to know. I wanted to get out of that room.

Suddenly, the trumpet which had been gleaming dully on the table, sailed jerkily across the room.

"One of them wishes to speak," said Ram Lal. "Speak, little one. Speak through me."

I tensed and felt Mrs. Mac's hand grip mine.

There was something monstrous about this. The silver trumpet twitched crazily over our heads and finally came to rest in midair, near Ram Lal.

"Speak, child, speak. Be at peace."

Then, what seemed to be a child's light voice lilted from near Ram Lal.

"Do not grieve for us."

"Are you happy?"

"Happy?"

There was a pause, then, "I will ask my brother. Brother, are we happy?"

Another voice, slightly deeper in timbre, now lisped through the room.

"We are happy. Do not grieve for us. But it is the boy, that strange boy, who brings us back."

This voice was stilted, falsetto and unnatural. How did I know that this Alex was not just a ventriloquist?

"Give me some proof," I said. "Give me some proof that you are really here and that you are them."

"No, no!" whispered the group.

"Materialization can be dangerous for the medium if he is not sufficiently prepared," said one of the young assistants.

But the medium, or rather, Ram Lal, spoke.

"I will bring you proof."

His body straightened further and he seemed to rise slightly in his chair.

"Show yourself, child. Let us see you. Do not be afraid. We are here to help you."

I heard one of the assistants stirring, but he did not leave the table. Then, in the far corner of the room a light began to hover, and gradually a diaphanous shape formed in the darkness.

"More clearly," coaxed the spirit guide.

Suddenly there was an explosion exactly like a camera flash bulb going off and the corner of the room was brightly and redly illuminated.

Whether it was the light that was red or the reflection of the velvet hangings, I'm not sure, but you know how it is when a flash bulb goes off.

For one split second we all saw it redly, like a bloodstained paper kite, suspended in mid air. The dim, red-blotched form of a small body.

I screamed, then Ram Lal gave a loud, hoarse moan and some-body turned on the lights and we were all blinking at each other, still partly blinded by that small, bright, bloody explosion.

I was so shaken Mrs. Mac had to take me back to her place in a taxi and Alex, or Ram Lal or whoever he was, didn't seem to be in any better shape.

We left him with his priestlings putting cold cloths on his

sweating brow while his eyes rolled wildly and accusingly at me as we retreated.

"You shouldn't have screamed, Amy. It is very dangerous to bring a medium out of a trance quickly," said Mrs. Mac with mild reproach as I stretched, trembling, on her chesterfield.

Those voices! That light! Was it a fraud, and if not, what in the name of God had I seen in the corner?

And if I had seen—oh, you know what I mean—I can't bear to say it, had the séance accomplished its purpose? Were they at rest now?

"It was a very dangerous manifestation, Amy. Those who go over quickly and violently often materialize that way. Poor Alex."

Poor Alex! What about me? There I was, so frozen with sheer terror that I couldn't move, which was probably just as well, as I wanted to bang my head on the wall to free it from that awful vision. Strangely enough, apart from the trembling, I appeared calm. But that's often the way with me. Frightened into immobility.

"I'm afraid the only answer now, Amy, is for that boy— Rudi, is that his name?—for Rudi to go. We couldn't risk, for Alex's sake, another session like that."

But I'd done it for Rudi! Was it all for nothing? I didn't want him to have to go. Why is it that nothing ever works out in my life? I'd tried everything and nothing worked. What else could I do?

And I don't care what anybody, including Mrs. Mac, says—that Alex is crazy. Crazy, crazy, crazy! If he has occult powers, he has paid for them with his sanity. I never want to see him again. He's horrible! The whole thing was horrible!

I was so upset that I spent the night at Mrs. Mac's. She phoned and told Eric I didn't feel too well, which was not an exaggeration. We didn't tell him about the séance.

Oh, I already said that, didn't I. Confused. Repeating oneself is a sign of old age or something. Drink. That's it. Bernard repeats himself endlessly when he's drinking. Dear Bernard. If only I had had enough sense to take his advice. Where was I? Yes, repeating oneself. Bernard repeats himself when he's drinking.

Only I don't drink.

There was something else I had to think about. Rudi. Poor little Rudi. It was sad, but there was no alternative. Eric tried to talk me out of it but I had no choice. Then he realized I was right. I heard him tell Frau Keller that it was best for Rudi's sake, which of course, it was. She took it very well, I must say, although she burst into tears.

It was about now that time seemed to be telescoped.

They were leaving. She took my face between her hands and kissed me, so I guess there were no hard feelings.

Poor little Rudi. He was wearing a pair of those short leather pants that had belonged to one of his brothers and they were too big for him. With his cropped head and skinny legs he looked more like ten than fourteen years old.

I was surprised to see that he wept and clung to Eric when they had to go. It was, as I have said, sad, and I was sorry, but what could I do?

The thought of those battered suitcases that had accompanied them on so many weary trips, and Frau Keller's shabby coat, still makes my throat ache.

But there were no more avenues open.

Eric was angry. I knew. He didn't say anything. He was quiet. Very quiet.

Then we were alone. Just Eric and I, and it was about this time that Eric began to act rather oddly. But more about that later.

**Police Close File
On Graham Case**

After three years Police Chief Arthur Whitely stated today that the Graham case is now offi-

CHAPTER NINETEEN. (October) Ages since I last bothered to write. Yes, it's autumn, and what a mess the garden is. Mums tattered and drooping from their tubs; and the marigolds which stank in summer, smell like unburied corpses now they are withered. Slugs have been at the petunias, which I always thought of as slip-shod flowers anyway, and the fruit is rotting on the apple trees. The dried-up runner beans curl around their poles like rubber bands that have gone slack, and clumps of lobelia are discarded bouquets. My, we are poetic today, aren't we? Only the roses are flourishing, putting forth a second crop. They remind me of ancient courtesans, the way each strives to be the star and yield the most perfect last bloom of summer. The old tarts.

It all makes me realize how little time it takes for a garden to backslide—snakes and ladders again—and how obviously this one misses Frau Keller. I really ought to get out there and do something, but I can't.

I can't be bothered, that is. God, life is a bore. If only I had something to look forward to. Igor was around last week, although it didn't liven things up much for me. He ignored me. I shouldn't have been surprised. Ignorance is Igor's strong point. I don't care. I really don't. To hell with Igor.

I keep telling myself I've got a roof over my head, I'm healthy, we're reasonably well off, etc.; but it doesn't help. Everybody *has* to have something to look forward to.

Oh, well, because I feel guilty about those abandoned flowers, I'll assuage my conscience by bringing diary up to date. The forsaken garden. Somebody wrote a book about that. No, it was a poem. Who wrote it? Heavens, my memory is getting terrible. Swinburne, yes, that's it. Charles Algernon. With a name like that, no wonder he was peculiar. Although no insensitive slob could write "Here now in his triumph where all things falter, / Stretched out on the spoils that his own hand spread, / As a god self-slain on his own strange altar, / Death lies dead."

Morbid. Though, as Igor would say, "it begs the question" as to whether it is better to be peculiar or to be insensitive. Oh, to hell with Igor. I already said that, didn't I. Well, I repeat, to hell with Igor. I don't give a damn about him.

How lonely with just Eric and me in the house. The kitchen—cheerful, bright, and spotless—isn't a room to be lonely in. And why shouldn't it be spotless? There's no one to mess it up.

When I mentioned this to Eric, he only shrugged and acted as if I had only myself to blame.

The sun shone through the windows over the sink, and I pushed back the café curtains to water the geranium Frau Keller had started from a slip. It was turning brown around the edges. I watered it dutifully but I knew it wouldn't survive. Nothing flourished in that house.

I tried to recall the cheerful bedlam as they came rushing in from school. Remember, I would say to myself, how Philip's shirt was torn because Rodney, the boy he said yesterday he would never speak to again, had a fight with him when they were playing at recess today?

I pretended. And I made cookies. Peanut-butter cookies. So what, I thought, as I put them on the table. Who would eat them? I had scarcely any appetite now. Perhaps Eric liked peanut-butter cookies. I couldn't remember.

I kept on trying to pretend. Little Linda, so pretty with her long, golden braids and gentian eyes. Linda giving me a card with colored macaroni glued on it that she made at kindergarten. It's not much, but she's so proud of it and says it is a garden. Philip, cheeky as usual, says it isn't. "I made it just for you," she says. She's been jealous of the baby ever since he was born, so I take her on my lap and rock her and whisper that she's my baby.

Sharon comes in wanting to know if she can go ice skating with her friend Carol at the Community Center after dinner. Can she have fifty cents? That's what it costs. I say all right and where's the fifty cents change from the dollar I gave you this morning? They all laugh. That was Gretchen, they shout.

But it didn't go right. It was like watching a movie a second time. No spontaneity, no sense of wonder or surprise. And no fun.

What are we, the real us, I mean, Eric and me, to have for dinner? Wearily I opened the freezer at the top of the fridge and gazed at a sirloin tip roast. Roast, Yorkshire pudding, baked potatoes.

For two people? No. It was too much trouble. I'd scramble some eggs and open a can of vegetables. Eric never cared what he ate anyway.

What was it? Had the fright of that séance driven them from my brain, like the old snake-pit theory? I could remember remembering them, if you follow me, but I couldn't *recall* them as I had in the past. They were one-dimensional, transparent and unreal.

Then I realized it was me. I didn't want them to come back. I was afraid. Afraid they might *really* return. Return in the ghastly fashion that that one had in the séance. Had it been Philip?

It was too awful for any normal mind to contemplate, and I knew what I wanted now was not ghost children, but living, normal children.

I never heard or saw them again.

I was normal and I wanted living, normal children. Is there anything wrong with that?

Later, everyone tried to make me feel guilty about what happened after this. They did, you know. But thank God I knew that I was normal and I was right.

I sat in the kitchen feeling more lonely and despondent then I ever had before in my life.

Eric came in again.

"I thought you were working this afternoon?"

Yes, I was. And I was tired. But I was tireder yet when I knew that they were gone, their little ghosts truly laid. By me.

"There are some peanut butter cookies on the table."

He looked at me and shook his head.

"Amy, if there's one thing that makes my gorge rise it's peanut butter in any form. I was practically raised on it, as you may recall."

I didn't. I really have been forgetting a lot of things lately. Which can be construed as a blessing, I suppose.

I was tired that I was tired, and that I am real and must go to work at Turner, Turner and whoever the hell they are. Time is mixed up. The tenses are confused.

They were real and they are not real. They are real and they were not real.

But Eric is real enough. And so is Igor.

He turned up again because the car was suffering from its chronic internal trouble and Eric had phoned him.

We had been alone so much together since Frau Keller and Rudi left that we were both glad to see him. Yes, I admit it. Oh, not *him*, but just anyone. I don't care about him but he made me realize how constricted our circle of acquaintances was.

Though we were both glad to see him, true to form it didn't last long.

Igor was out of breath and Eric stared at Igor's broad, heaving chest.

"Do you mean to tell me you jogged all the way here from the West End?"

"Yup," said Igor. "The yoga helps too, of course. Your body and mind have got to be in concert. You ought to try it."

Eric was in his element. He made a rude remark about the lotus position and asked what was so beneficial about being able to touch your forehead with your tongue, which started Igor off on a tirade about Karma, Vishnu and the wheel of life. So Eric demanded to know why, if it was so damned good, had India such an astronomical rate of disease, starvation and illiteracy.

Igor looked surprised, then hurt. I suspect he had thought Eric would give him a pat on the head for trying to develop his Karma.

Relenting a bit, Eric added that jogging did make sense. "After all, it's the big boys like you who keel over with heart attacks at forty-five. But what's in it for me? I'll probably be snatched up to my Maker with lung cancer, although I think you're reasonably secure from that."

An oblique reference to Igor's habit of borrowing cigarettes.

Igor never gets mad at Eric. Instead, he gets mad at the government.

"What's the matter with India? Is Canada any better? You think people get a square deal here? That this is the land of milk and honey? The government doesn't implement the formation of a just society. I got half a mind to go to the States. We ought to be one big melting pot like they are. But are we? We sure as hell are not. Here you're French or English or a Hunkie. That's what they call me. Well, I'm not. My parents were Ukrainians. Ukrainian Cossacks. They shouldn't put labels on people like they do here."

O'er the lonely Volga prairie, rides the Cossack bold but wary.

He was too. He took very good care of himself. Rarely drank, seldom smoked, in perfect physical condition, a big, sleek creature of the jungle.

Yet even he seemed edgy now.

"What's eating you, Igor?"

"Nothing." He turned from Eric to me. "What was your name before you were married?"

"Me?" I said in surprise.

"Yeah, you."

"Robsart," I said. "Amy Robsart."

I knew he wouldn't know who she was. As a matter of fact, if I hadn't recently read a biography of Mary, Queen of Scots, I wouldn't have known myself. But old pachyderm Burton remembered and gave me a distinctly dirty look. He doesn't think it's fair to tease Igor and he's right, of course, but it's my only defense. Like the tethered bait-goat being able to bleat while it waits for the tiger to spring.

"Amy, you're a scream," said Eric.

"That's me. Screaming Amy. Actually I'm not being quite truthful, Igor. I was really Mary, Queen of Scots."

Igor's eyes narrowed, then he shrugged and smiled. "You're nuts. Well, I better look at the car."

If I had not been so naïve I would have guessed what was eating him. After he had fixed the car he came into the kitchen to wash his hands.

Eric had gone down to his den to work and Igor turned, leaning nonchalantly against the sink and staring at me.

"Come here, Amy," he whispered.

I went, like an obedient automaton. He took me in his arms and pressed me to him.

"You're so slender," he whispered. "You're really stacked, Amy, and yet you're so slender. Like Sophia Loren."

I guess *she* wasn't at this particular time. My heart was pounding as no respectable matron's should be and I could feel his thudding through his chest as though it were part of myself.

He whispered in my ear.

Meet me at the Pauline Johnson Memorial in the park, he had said, and there I was, sitting in our old car, waiting. And wondering. Why did I always do his bidding? Did I love him? No, I don't think I even liked him, but nevertheless I was there. He whistles and I follow. Who is Igor and why is he so achingly attractive and why does he excite me as Eric never has?

It was nearly November, the trees were leafless, and apart from the odd sports buff and birdwatcher, the park was almost deserted. With the approach of winter Mother Nature certainly looks like a skinflint, everything bare and stark.

I saw him come padding along the footpath, clad only in an old pair of British Army shorts and sandals.

"Good lord, aren't you freezing?"

No, he said, getting in the driver's side and nudging me over. Where was his car? He had sold it. The difference between Eric's driving and Igor's probably illustrated some important psychological point. Even our old heap responded as if it knew it couldn't kid around with Igor. He drove to a dead end and parked, took me in his arms, and we loved as we never had before; and I had a strange, weightless feeling as if I defied the laws of gravity—my hands seemed huge and far-off, and my head floated. Finally he opened his eyes and said it had been a long time, a long, long time. I nodded and then I said what about her?

"Her? I couldn't touch her with a ten-foot pole the way she is now." I had never credited him with such qualms.

"Haven't you a shirt?" It was a stupid question because I had seen him arrive with nothing but the shorts and sandals and his wristwatch.

He shook his head to my question. I had nothing more to offer him than a Kleenex and said he was likely to catch a cold.

"Not me. I'll go for a sprint. Meet you at the zoo in ten minutes. I want to talk to you. Ten minutes. Okay?" I watched him jogging off down the footpath that cuts through the center of the park. He would probably be at the zoo before I could drive there.

Why didn't I feel guilty? How could I do this to Eric? Eric always said that my conscience was lashed around my neck like a dead albatross. Had it, like the Phoenix, revived and suddenly taken wing?

By the time I reached the zoo and parked, he was already standing lost in meditation in front of those damned monkeys.

When I slipped my arm through his he looked down at me with scorn.

"For Christ's sake, Amy, a good screw is a good screw. And that's all it is."

That beast. Maybe it was tit-for-tat for Amy Robsart. I suppose one shouldn't provoke tigers since this one has just enough cunning to know when he has been teased.

I withdrew my arm from his.

"Why can't you accept things for what they are? You always have to make a song and dance about everything, don't you?"

I turned to walk to the bear pit, but he caught me and swung me around.

"Look at them, God damn you! Just for once in your life face something!"

He lifted me off my feet and held me across the iron bar on the mesh fence that separates the public from the cages. I guess they thought we were going to feed them because a dozen hairy, grasping little arms reached clawing through the bars. I felt as if my ribs would crack from the pressure on that iron bar.

"Stop it! You're breaking me in two!"

All those hideous faces guffawing, they bared their sharp, dirty little yellow teeth, and the stench of them made my stomach turn.

He pulled me back and onto my feet, but he was far from being apologetic.

"What's the matter? Don't you like the picture? It won't go

away! You can close your eyes but when you open them they'll still be there!"

I saw the picture all right. Finally. He wouldn't touch her and he was too cheap to go to a prostitute, so it was me. The substitute for the prostitute.

"They're real, Amy. They're not ghosts. Take a good look at them!"

And for this I had betrayed Eric.

I swear he can read thoughts.

"You and your la-di-da ways! You didn't think twice about being laid, did you? You never even thought of him."

And then he said it. He actually said it, and he meant it. Said it as if *he* were the wronged party.

"My best friend!"

I felt a sudden, hysterical desire to either burst out laughing or screaming. I walked to the bear pits with him following.

"All right. Maybe I shouldn't have said that."

He wanted something.

"Okay. I'm sorry. Amy? I'm sorry."

I waited and of course it came.

"Look, Amy, we're not getting anywhere about that money. Kielty's the answer. I've said it all along. I've sold my car and I'm going east in a week if we don't get a break of some sort."

"Bernard!" I said. "Bernard! You! You're not fit for him to wipe his feet on!"

I lit a cigarette, and when he took it and put it to his lips, I snatched it back and threw it in the bear pit.

The cheapskate!

"You shouldn't of done that! Don't you see the sign? One of them could eat it. And it was lit, too!"

The polar bears were all asleep in one big heap, with their heads and arms and legs resting on each other.

"If you're so sure Bernard is implicated, why don't you ask him yourself?"

"He wouldn't tell me, you know that. He doesn't like me."

"Why ever not?" I snapped. "I suppose you want me to sleep with him to find out."

He laughed.

"Jeez! How dumb can you get? Kielty's the biggest fag in town."

This time I did slap him. Just because Bernard is a gentleman, he'd have to make some filthy remark like that.

"You have the rottenest mind in the whole of Canada!"

And then the strangest thing happened. The polar bears began to stir drowsily and they woke up. Not one at a time, but as if by some prearranged signal.

They stood on their hind feet, twisting those long, snakelike necks and turning their heads with the snooty, Roman-senator noses sniffing the air.

It was so sudden and somehow frightening that both Igor and I took a step back from the spiked iron fence.

We stood watching them writhe and weave and sniff, and the hair on the back of my neck stood on end.

Then we heard a clippety-clop, and looking around we saw a mounted policeman staring at us. Not a Mountie, but one of the city police who patrol the park on horseback.

He looked suspiciously at Igor's bare chest, then to me, as if to ask if this man was molesting me. In this weather, at this season, it did seem odd to see someone dressed as Igor was.

"I've been jogging," said Igor.

The policeman looked at me for confirmation.

"Yes," I said. "I know him."

The policeman nodded.

"What's the matter with them?" Igor inclined his head to the bears. "They were all sound asleep, then they woke up and they're acting funny. It sort of gives you the creeps."

The policeman smiled and patted his horse's neck.

"It's my horse. They smelled him. You see, they're fed horse-meat and every time they get a whiff of him, it excites them. They seem to sense him a long time before they can see him."

When the policeman's horse tossed his head nervously Igor stepped forward and caught the animal's bit. He stroked the horse's head and spoke softly to him and the horse immediately calmed down.

"You seem to know horses," said the policeman.

"Yeah. I used to ride on the prairies."

"What's his name?" I asked.

"Trooper," said the policeman. "Trooper the Third. He's the third called that, you see."

I started to giggle. I couldn't help it. Both men stared at me.

"I—I once knew a horse called Ronald. He was killed at the battle of Nery in the forest of Halatte. Imagine, a horse called Ronald."

I turned my back on them and faced the churning bears. Neither of the men said anything, and I shoved my Kleenex over my mouth to stop that awful giggling.

"So long."

I heard the policeman's horse clattering over the asphalt, going on his rounds, past the monkeys, past the bird sanctuary and the aquarium, and the seal pools; then there was the soft thump, thump as he crossed the grass and left for other parts of the park.

"That was a lucky break for you."

I didn't understand until he put his hand to his cheek. The fingertips of my right hand still tingled.

I started to walk off but he grabbed me again. I had my back against the fence and when I pushed against his chest it was like pushing against a wall.

Somehow I had always known we'd face each other this way.

"You tramp!"

"Leave me alone!"

"You listen, and you listen good! You think you're going to pull a fast one on me? Don't give me any shit about ghosts. You know more about that money than you're letting on. You and that Kielty are real buddies, aren't you? How the hell did you get the cash to furnish that house?"

"Laura gave it to me! Let me go!"

"Laura gave it to me!" he mimicked. "I've wasted enough time around here playing flunky to you. You think I haven't watched you getting rid of the people in that house so you could get your hands on the money? You'd like to cut me out too, wouldn't you?"

Why wouldn't he leave me alone?

But he wouldn't leave me alone and he wouldn't stop talking. I can't bear to think of, let alone repeat, the things he said. I'd always known he was cruel and even Elaina had warned me, but even I didn't know how savage he could be, or how unerringly he could touch where it hurt. Sex, age, appearance, cowardice, inadequacy—he didn't leave anything out, and he mocked me in terms calculated to make a dock-walloper cringe.

"Leave me alone!"

I must have screamed because he put his hand over my mouth and glanced over his shoulder.

"Shut up! Where's that money?"

I had him. For once in my life I had him just where I wanted him. He thought I'd be defenseless, as defenseless as usual, didn't he? Well, I wasn't.

"The money's been found! You think you're so damned smart, don't you? You think you can treat me any way you want, don't you? The police found the money! They found it in an abandoned car that Graham bought! You didn't know that, did you? It isn't in the house! It never was! And I've known it all along! They found it, do you hear me? They found it in an old car in the Nickomickel River, right where Graham drove it, the day he killed his family!"

And then I saw his hands come up toward my throat.

We fought. We wrestled. Oh, God! I managed to shove him aside and I ran. I ran until I thought my heart would burst. Somehow I got to the car. Somehow I got it started, and somehow I drove home.

And when I got home, that demon-dog's footprints were on the front door where it had been scratching.

Eric was in his den working. I called down, pleading a headache, and said I was going to bed. Would he mind getting a TV dinner out of the top of the fridge?

About eleven he came up. I hadn't slept.

"Don't turn on the lights." I couldn't face him.

"Why not?" So of course he did turn them on.

"Black Sutch was here, wasn't he? He always is when there's trouble."

"Oh, for Christ's sake, Amy, I wish I had never started joking about that damned dog. I certainly wouldn't have if I had known you were going to take it seriously. There's nothing supernatural about him. He's just some big dumb dog that can't find his way home. For some reason he picks on us to visit every so often."

I began to cry.

"What's the matter? Be sensible, Amy. Ghost dogs don't leave footprints, and that poor brute certainly does. I tried to coax him in, but he just shivered all over and ran away."

I was sobbing now and I pulled the covers over my head.

"Amy! What is it? It's more than that dog. What is it? Tell me."

"I can't," I sobbed. "You'd hate me. You've been mad ever since Frau Keller and Rudi left, but I was only trying to do my best. Honestly, Eric, I was only trying to do my best! And now this! It's awful! You'd hate me!"

"Don't be silly. You know I wouldn't. No matter what you did. Now tell me. You know you always feel better if you do."

"No matter what I did?"

"No matter what you did," he repeated.

I felt as guilty and as terrible as if I had committed a murder, and like the murderer, I had the same compulsion to confess, as if, somehow, confession would take the load off me.

Still hiding my face, I told him about Igor and me.

For a long time he was silent.

"Eric! He tried to kill me!" I pulled the covers tighter. "Oh, Eric, you do hate me."

"Amy," he sighed and there was a pause, "I don't like sitting here, listening to this. I'm human. But I don't hate you. I love you. And if it's over, as you have promised, I promise you I'll never mention it again. But you've got to forget about it too, Amy. And forget Igor. Forget you ever knew him. Can you do that? He's not evil, Amy, it's just that everything is out of proportion to you now. He didn't try to kill you. He just felt like taking a good belt at you. Women make men want to do that sometimes. So forget about him. Just forget him, will you?"

I nodded.

When the chips are down, Eric is always decent. He tried to turn me around and pull the covers from my face but I wept more than ever.

"Now quit it," he said. "Come on, Amy. Be a good girl." He tugged harder, the covers came down and he stood back. Agar Burton's gypsy eyes glittered dangerously in his son's head.

I sat up and stared with horror at my reflection in the dressing table mirror. My arms and shoulders and neck were black and blue and I did look as if I had been mauled by a tiger.

"Now do you believe me?"

He nodded. "He had better go back east. And stay there. Now forget about him, Amy."

That's all he said. He's an odd one. He brought up tea and sitting beside me read "Sonnets From the Portuguese" out loud until I felt drowsy. Then he got me one of Dr. Kelly's pills.

"Take this and get a good night's sleep. That's what you need most."

I swallowed the little green pellet to oblivion.

"You know," I murmured, "we're not like a husband and wife. We're more like a brother and sister."

He smiled and stroked my cheek.

"That's a hell of a thing to say. Now try and sleep, Amy. As soon as Mother is back, we'll go away for a trip. Just the two of us."

"Why do we have to wait, Eric? Let's go now, before it's too late. Oh, Eric, I'm so sorry, so sorry."

"Shhh," he whispered. "I've got the book to finish. And we can't just walk out and leave the house. She trusted us to look after it. I'll write to her again tomorrow, and as soon as she's back, we'll go. All right?"

But after the pill wore off, about four o'clock, I woke up with a start. There was something I had forgotten, something I had to remember. Something about Igor. I woke Eric.

"Eric, there's something I have forgotten. Something terribly important."

"No, love. Not tonight. It can wait till morning. The only thing that is important now is for you to relax and get some sleep."

"But Eric, I must remember! I think it's about Igor."

"Now, Amy, you promised me you'd forget about him."

I closed my eyes and was quiet, but my mind wasn't. It went round and round. Igor, the faces in the mirror, the screams and moans at night, Black Sutch, Philip in the closet the night of that terrible storm.

It was this damned house! And I mean damned in the literal sense.

We must get away.

New Government Mental Center Opens

The provincial government's new mental hospital, to be known as Fairfields, was officially opened today by the Lieutenant Governor.

Consisting of eight separate buildings set in ten acres of rolling park and formal gardens, the long-awaited four-million-dollar center was described by the Lieutenant Governor as the most modern in North America.

CHAPTER TWENTY. (November 2nd) It is very important that I keep these notes accurately from now on because of Eric's duplicity. This record is my witness.

Elaina phoned and wanted to know if she could take a taxi over immediately and talk to me.

She was here in half an hour and to my amazement she had had the baby. Indeed, she was carrying it in her arms.

I started to lead her to the living room, but she said she'd feel more at home in the kitchen. She appeared to have been crying and was distraught.

"Elaina, are you all right?" I put the coffee pot on and laid out cups and saucers, and then I sat opposite her. The baby, wrapped in a yellow, satin-bound blanket, slept soundly in her trembling arms.

"Oh, Amy!" She burst into tears. "Everything's been so awful. That bastard walking out on me like that."

I looked at the top of the little silvery blond head which showed above the top of the blanket.

"Did you have a difficult time?"

"Yes," she sobbed. "I look as though I'm as strong as an ox, but it was hell! They couldn't give me any anesthetic because the baby's heartbeat wasn't steady. Eight hours of being on the rack, and then those stitches after!"

I let her have a good cry.

"You'll be all right now, Elaina. I know it must have been awful for you, but the worst is over."

I was just going to ask her why she hadn't let me know she was in the hospital when she raised her face, and with her one free hand, grasped mine.

"I don't know what I would have done if it hadn't been for you. You were the only visitor I had."

I sat back and looked at her in amazement. She was obviously still under a terrible emotional strain. She was painfully thin and her eyes had a haunted look, with the dark circles under them even more pronounced.

"It's awful, I know, when you're alone at a time like that."

"Being in the room with the three others! Their husbands came every day, and they all went down the hall to see the babies. You'd think doctors would have more sense than to put someone like me in with them, wouldn't you? But they said the other beds were filled except for private rooms and I couldn't afford one of those. Oh, Amy! I feel as if I'd been torn apart, right down the middle!"

I didn't know whether I ought to try to bring her back to reality or not. She had been through a lot, but she would have to face facts sooner or later.

"Elaina dear," I said as gently as I could, "I didn't go to see you in the hospital. I didn't even know you had the baby."

She looked around desperately, and then got hold of herself. She smiled and squeezed my hand. "Honest to God, I'm so upset I don't know whether I'm coming or going. This decision I have to make. You're so good, Amy. But you don't have to be ashamed of being good to me, or of feeling sorry for me. God knows I need it. I never thought being alone at that time would be as bad as it was. The flowers saved my life. I told them, the other women in the ward, that my husband was working back east and had wired them."

She sipped her coffee. "I still need you, Amy. That's why I'm here. I have no one else to turn to. I'm just about at the end of my rope."

"Of course," I said. "I understand, Elaina. I'll do anything I can to help you. What is it?"

She sniffed, I handed her a Kleenex, and when she gazed down at the baby and smiled, she was a madonna.

"I wish she were awake," I said. "I'd love to hold her. It is a girl, isn't it?"

Elaina laughed, and what a lovely laugh she had. "Of course. I told you it would be, didn't I? Here. She's just had her two o'clock feeding. She'll sleep for at least an hour."

She handed me the blanket-wrapped bundle.

How tiny she was, and how beautiful. Her little pink fingers, resting on the blanket, were as delicate as spider webs.

"Honestly, Amy, I've never felt so close to the edge in my life."

"It's natural to feel as you do," I said. "The doctors have a term for it. It's called post-partum depression. You'll be all right, you'll see, Elaina. Oh, she's lovely, Elaina. What do you call her?"

"Anna, after my mother. It's about her I came, Amy."

I sat rocking the baby gently, looking down at her.

"What color are her eyes?"

"Blue. Like yours."

I looked up. Elaina's eyes were as dark as Igor's.

"It's like this, Amy. There's a fellow from back home, that's Northern Alberta, who's been out here. His name is Steve. He and I—well—we went together ever since we were kids, until I decided to come to the coast. His parents have died and he's got the farm now. They raise wheat up there. It's a big place and a good farm. I know; I was raised on a farm myself until I got too big for my boots and decided to see the bright lights."

She gulped down another sob and then straightened her back. The baby stirred drowsily and I folded the blanket down a bit. She was wearing a little hand-embroidered yellow dress.

"She should always wear yellow," I said. "If she were mine, I'd call her Daphne. She looks like a Daphne. I've always loved that name. It reminds me of spring, and daffodils. Do you remember how long spring seemed in coming on the prairies?"

Elaina was looking tragic again, and I realized that for her sake, I mustn't be too sympathetic. She had the baby, and she was young and would soon be all right physically.

"It's like this, Amy. As I was saying, Steve was out here. He wants to marry me, Amy, and I told him I would. I've had my fill of cities. All I want now is to go back to the farm and be a good wife. There's one thing, though. He doesn't know about Anna."

What was she getting at?

She poured more coffee and put mine nearer to me so I wouldn't have to disturb Daphne.

"He's gone back to Alberta and he wants me to go as soon as possible."

"Yes?"

"Well, I know this sounds awful, put this way, but I wondered if I could leave Anna out here for a while. So as not to be so much of a shock to him, you know, knowing all of a sudden. Once we're married and I've told him, he'll get used to the idea, and then I'll send for her. I know he will, Amy. He's no Igor. He's a really swell guy, and he's always been crazy about me, and I'm not the first girl who's made a mistake."

Surely she didn't mean me? Couldn't mean me? Things like that don't happen to people like me.

"Yes?" I said. My voice sounded faint.

"Well, I was wondering if I could leave her with you for maybe a month. I don't think it would be more than that and I'd pay you, of course. I—well—I couldn't leave her with just anybody. I contacted the Salvation Army and saw two foster homes. They're all right, I guess, but, well, I just couldn't leave my baby in one of them. Would you keep her, Amy?"

I looked down at that beautiful baby.

"Yes," I whispered.

"You'll take her? You will? Oh, Amy!" She jumped up and came over and kissed my cheek. "Oh, Amy! Thank you! God will bless you for your kindness, Amy."

I couldn't see for tears. "Oh, hand me a Kleenex," I said, and after blowing my nose, "You'll be lucky if you get her back!"

We both laughed and Elaina returned to her chair, sat down, and then let her breath out. "Whew! You've saved my life, Amy.

I know Steve will come around. It's just a matter of time and not springing everything on him at once. We'll need a few weeks to be alone and get adjusted, and then he'll be okay, I know he will. Like I said, he's a wonderful guy."

A feeling like cold water began to rise about my heart.

"Elaina, what about Igor?"

"Igor?" For a minute she looked blank, then she burst out laughing again and poured herself another cup of coffee. "Oh, now I get it. That bastard is not my baby's father."

I felt rather shocked.

"But I thought . . ."

"No," she said. "He'd been sponging off me, off and on in the past; and when this happened, I told him she was his because I needed a place to stay. Believe me, Amy, I know it sounds terrible, but it couldn't happen to a nicer guy than Igor, if you know what I mean. Anything he got, he had coming. Incidentally, have you heard anything from him?"

"No. Have you?" I hadn't seen him since that day in the park.

"No. It's just as if he vanished from the face of the earth, and good riddance, too, the no-good crumb."

I hadn't thought about him since that day Eric told me not to, and I certainly wasn't going to start now. And my heart was singing, singing, singing, as I looked down at that lovely little bit of humanity.

"No, Amy. Igor wasn't her father. Her father was a man whose office I worked in last year. He was a real gentleman. I cared about him. The truth is, I loved him. It wasn't anything casual, like it had been with Igor and me the year before. But—oh, well, you know the old story. He was married, had kids, etc. He offered to pay for an abortion, but I wouldn't hear of it. I think they're wrong, don't you? I mean, suppose I had had one. There wouldn't be any little Anna lying in your arms now, would there?"

But when I looked down at little Daphne I got a panicky feeling.

"But Elaina, I don't know anything about babies. Suppose I do something wrong? I mean, about feeding her and all that?"

Elaina jumped up and swung her arms.

"Oh, Amy! That's the least of my worries, now I know she's safe with you. It's not hard, and I'll tell you everything."

Then Elaina smiled as she gazed at me. "How pretty you are, sitting with her in your arms and looking down at her."

For the next two hours we went over the baby's routine until I had everything straight about the formula, the baby foods and vitamin drops, and her bath, and when to take her to the pediatrician to check her weight and get her shots.

It was all so wonderful.

"Can you leave her here now, Elaina?"

She said yes, she'd go to the apartment, get all the baby's things and come back by taxi.

"You'll be surprised at how much there is!"

She was right. There was the bassinet, and her clothes and toys and diapers and soaps and powders and blankets and her plastic bath. This baby had been well looked after.

"I haven't got a crib or a high chair or toidy-seat for her yet. She won't need them for months."

"That's right. We'll worry about them when the time comes."

"Now, about the money, would fifteen a week be all right?"

"No, no!" I was crying again, I was so happy; then Elaina started too. "I should be paying you!"

It was awful when Elaina had to part from her for good. She made three starts for the door and each time she came back sobbing to look at that serene little sleeping face.

Finally she tore herself away and I sat rocking Daphne.

The years passing. Eric, bending over her and admitting that she really was a beautiful baby. Frau Keller bustling around, sterilizing everything in sight and calling her Liebschen. And Rudi, putting aside Elspeth's silly old doll, taking notice of her instead. Rudi, back again and sitting beside me on the chesterfield, while I hold her in my arms.

"Would you like to hold her, Rudi? You can, just as soon as she's finished her bottle." And his eyes shining, as Eric said, "Shove over, Rudi, and let me have a look at that baby."

The day she sat up alone, for the first time, and watching her bat at her toy swans in her bath, in the big bathtub now, and her first tooth, with Frau Keller running and exclaiming.

Oh, I forgot. They're not here now. I do forget things so easily now. A blessing, to be sure. Well, even if they aren't here, Daphne is, and who could forget her?

Her clothes, all handmade by me, spring colors, pale yellows, soft greens, blushing pinks and peaches. And her little shoes. White kid boots. Boots. Why does that word make me feel so strange? I won't think about it.

Going to school, her hair in pig-tails, and clinging to my skirts at the last minute. "Mummy, I don't want to go to school." "But you must, darling. You're six now. Don't be afraid, sweetheart; I know how you feel. Mummy was afraid the first day too, but then I went in and met all those other little boys and girls, and I made friends with them and it was such fun. I loved school, after that."

No. That's not true. It's a lie. But what good would it do to tell a little six-year-old girl of the fear and loneliness, even then? I'll lie to her. I'll lie to anybody, to protect her.

The years passing! Hell's bells! It didn't happen that way at all!

Eric came home. And when he saw her he behaved like a maniac.

"Where did you get that baby?" He was roaring. Actually roaring.

I explained as calmly as I could in the face of his rage that Elaina had given her to me.

It's hard to believe, but he really did act like a madman. He waved his arms and shouted and said I must give her back. Immediately.

He tried to spoil everything. It was impossible to reason with him, and when he kept on shouting, I told him to shut up, and to shut up fast. Imagine carrying on that way in front of a baby. He'd make a nervous wreck out of her, to say nothing of me.

Then he got a sly reasonableness, and in a very soft voice he told me it wasn't my baby.

I explained again, patiently, that I knew that. That Elaina had given her to me, and then he blew up again.

"For Christ sake, are you out of your mind? People don't go around giving babies away! You know it would have to go before an adoption board! We'd be investigated by the child welfare authorities! They check everything! Everything, do you hear?"

I refused to countenance his hysteria any further and I told him if he didn't control these outbursts, Daphne and I were leaving. It was as simple as that, and I meant it.

Then he used the cunning routine again and spoke in a coaxing voice.

"Don't you realize, darling, that it's illegal, and that the reason it is illegal is to protect the baby? Would you want something to happen to that helpless little creature?"

Was that a veiled threat? Or, as I asked him, did he think I was incapable of looking after her?

Oh, no, of course not.

He was impossible, he really was. Like a child. That was it! Why didn't I think of it? Even his mother admitted that she and I had made far too many concessions to him and that he was spoiled.

He was like a spoiled child and he was jealous of Daphne. The Book. Elaina had left The Book on Childcare, and I read it. It was right in the book. It was common for fathers to be jealous of a first baby. I'd have to be more careful, to see that he didn't feel left out of things. It was ridiculous having to treat a twenty-nine-year-old man as if he were a child, but it was necessary, I could see that. It wouldn't be too difficult. I mean, that's what babies are for, for a mother and father to share, and to love. To shower with love, and I vowed that Daphne would never lack love. No matter what I had to do, she would be loved and be first, even if I had to lie and pretend to him that he was.

I bought her a pram, one of those lovely big English ones with the high wheels. It looked like a Spanish galleon in full sail and cost a fortune, but I thought when she was through with it, I could sell it and get a jungle gym set for her to play on in the garden. One thing was certain, she was not getting anybody's old cast-off, secondhand stuff.

I also bought one of those little plastic carriers. I know some people leave their children in buggies unattended outside supermarkets, but I was not taking any chances. I mean, you do hear of women stealing babies. And gypsies. Gypsies steal babies.

She was so beautiful. Oh, I know, all mothers say that, but she really was. Total strangers stopped me and remarked about her. She was very fair-skinned, but her eyelashes were dark, so she didn't have that mole-eyed look of so many blonde babies.

One day as she lay in her carrier in the shopping cart in the market, wearing that little peach silk dress what's her name made her, a woman stopped and remarked on how lovely she was. She gitchy-gitchy-gooed over Daphne, and turning to me said,

"You'll never get your baby mixed up with anybody else's. Her eyes are just like yours."

I was terribly pleased, of course, until this stupid woman leaned above Daphne and actually wheezed all over her. Really, you'd think people would have more sense. I know The Book says babies have to be exposed to a certain amount of germs or they won't develop immunity; but there was this woman, suffering from God knows what, exhaling like a bilge pump all over that child.

I certainly didn't want to sound rude, but for Daphne's sake I couldn't just stand there.

"Please," I said, "don't snuffle all over her that way." I made a point of being very polite.

Well, you would have thought I was deliberately insulting. She drew up her great, whinnying horse face, gave me an icy look and absolutely *swept* past me. As if I cared, the old fool. Fortunately I got her away in time and Daphne didn't suffer any ill effects.

I worried a great deal about Daphne's baptism. I mean her christening. Neither Eric nor I were what you could call religious, but I did want her to be brought up, nominally at least, in what is usually referred to as a Christian home. Eric had been raised as an Anglican and I as a Presbyterian. Well, they were out.

I decided to wait six months and in the meanwhile to give the subject a good deal of thought. After all, whatever my choice fell on would also decide Sunday school and young people's groups and perhaps even her future husband, and for her sake such things couldn't be rushed into.

There were so many, many, decisions about her future to be made. Our life insurance would have to be increased and a policy taken out for her university education. Eric refused to discuss these things so I had no choice at present but to put them off. I did buy a pattern for her christening dress, though, and the finest lawn that could be purchased. I looked forward to the long winter evenings when I could sit beside the fire embroidering it.

Heaven knows the poor child would have no ancestral gown handed down to her. I don't suppose Laura ever got one for Eric and I certainly wouldn't ask them for mine. They had probably burnt it, anyhow. That's what they're like.

But Daphne didn't have to worry. I would look after her.

Eric continued to be unreasonable, and finally his conduct became so peculiar that I was worried. Not for myself, but for the baby. He wouldn't go near her, he wouldn't touch her, but at the same time he wouldn't leave either of us alone. If she cried at night he followed me when I went to her. Even if I only took her out to the garden, he was always there. With an excuse, of course. He just thought he'd have a smoke or a breath of fresh air. One time I saw him sneaking around the backs of cars in the parking lot of the supermarket, spying.

Talking to him seemed to be a waste of breath. He'd agree with me, oh yes, and the next time I turned around there would be that haggard face, watching.

I got so I was afraid to leave her for a second. When I went down to the laundry room to put through her wash (I always did her things separately—you can't get all those ordinary detergents out, and they're much too harsh for a baby's skin) I'd take her with me. But even then he followed me.

His nerves seemed to be in a shocking state, and if I hadn't been so busy with Baby, I would have been worried.

As it was, I didn't have time. Really, you have no idea just how much time babies take, and if he was going to be childish enough to sulk about that, then he'd just have to.

Fortunately she was a good baby and thrived on her food although I was terribly upset once when her temperature rose to 99 degrees. She felt as if she were on fire to me but The Book said not to worry. Right, of course, because the next day she was as right as rain. I don't mind admitting I didn't get much sleep *that* night, though. I don't know what I would have done without The Book, as I came to think of it.

Whenever I had a moment to spare I curled up with Daphne in my arms and read it until I practically knew it by heart. And all this time the voices were quiet. I realized now it wasn't all because of Rudi. My mind had been terribly unsettled at that time and probably helped disquiet them too. Thank heavens I was fine now. It wouldn't be right for a baby to be around a mentally upset woman. And also, they knew, poor little things, that Baby needed her rest. It was quite a rest for me too. If only Eric could have behaved like a decent, ordinary human being, things would have been perfect.

I kept telling him to go and write his *own* book and leave me to mine, but he wouldn't. Said the book wasn't important any more. Just me. What about Baby, I asked? Yes, Baby too, he admitted.

And then it happened. One awful day *she* phoned. It was Eric who answered the phone and spoke to her, and when he hung up he turned to me and said she wanted Daphne.

It was just as much his fault! He never wanted Daphne!

I don't mind admitting I screamed. I could hardly believe my ears. I mean, after all, whichever way you look at it, she had abandoned that child.

Eric kept talking to me in a soothing voice, saying it was her baby and it was time to face facts.

Her baby! Why, she wasn't even sure who the father was!

"Do you really think I'm going to turn that helpless baby over to anyone as irresponsible as she? And this Steve! What do I know about him? How do I know how he'll treat Daphne?"

Eric kept saying stop it, stop it, for God's sake, stop it, Amy.

"What sort of a human being would I be if I failed her now? A farm in Northern Alberta indeed! They probably haven't even got indoor plumbing. Do you think I'm just going to hand her over to those Hunkies? I know what those people are like!"

I'd been silent long enough and now it was time for a few home truths to be heard.

"She and that Steve of hers will probably have a dozen children. Let them neglect their own! They're not getting Daphne! I'm not abandoning her to that irresponsible slut!"

Eric put his hands over his face.

"Yes! That's what I said! Slut! She lived common-law with Igor before this Steve person, and there was another one sandwiched in between them! She's a slut and she's not fit to look after that child, and I'll fight her to the highest court in the land!"

"Amy! Stop it!"

"They're not getting her! Not on your tintype! Why, you must think I'm crazy to even suggest such a thing! For heaven's sake, man, grow up and face your responsibilities!"

Then he wept. I suppose he expected to gain my sympathy. Well, that's an old trick. I had never seen him cry before and it was terrible, but not so terrible as what he did next.

I heard a car door slam outside the house, and before I could collect my wits, he tore, he literally tore the baby from my arms.

He ran outside with her and the car drove away and when he came in she wasn't with him.

I don't really remember too much of what happened after that.

Bobby Shot And Wounded On Wild Swan Mountain.

Identified by license on collar

Hunter Edgar West said today, "I feel real bad about this. He looked so big I thought he was a bear. However, they tell me he's going to be all right. My kiddies want me to bring him home when he's well, but that's up to the S.P.C.A."

Mrs. Leona McCurdy of the Animals Have Souls Society stated today, "We have been most gratified by public response to Bobby and we feel that with love and prayer he will make a full recovery."

CHAPTER TWENTY-ONE. Well, here I am, writing again, this time in a new notebook, a gift from Dr. Rosen.

It was like one of those carved Chinese ivory balls, containing diminishing circles. You had to turn them round and round gradually, to click them into a complete sphere. It doesn't take much imagination, but first you have to realize that there are wheels within wheels.

I really had to get away and it was Dr. Kielty, or rather, I mean, Dr. Kelly, who solved the problem. I had to get away. The situation was intolerable.

A new spa, a lovely place run rather on the lines of one of those health clubs, had recently opened not too far from the city.

It was quite an exclusive deal but Dr. Kelly managed to get me a membership.

Faithful Bernard, as usual, arranged everything and was my first visitor after I had settled in. He had a mixed idea as to what the place was and at first I think he thought it was some sort of religious retreat. Actually, it was far more sensibly run, a great deal of organization etc., and one was expected to be on time for one's exercises and things like that, and on the whole I found it very restful. Actually, if one is religious to begin with, as Bernard is, I suppose religion is all right, but I am suspicious of becoming involved in anything of that nature while under nervous pressure. You never know when it will get the upper hand and you will lose your sense of proportion.

Bernard and I had a nice visit, although he looked very strained and he had tears in his eyes when he left and asked me if I could forgive him. Forgive him for what? Poor Bernard, he is ridden by such a sense of guilt, but I suppose that's one of the penalties of bowing completely to anything as demanding as the Church. Actually, a little bit of that goes a long way.

Actually, I keep wondering why I keep saying actually. Things are certainly actual enough in this life, aren't they?

It was Dr. Rosen, of whom more later, as the Victorian novelists say, who suggested that I continue keeping a diary.

"How can I continue what I have never begun?" I asked.

"Well," he has a rather guilty air, "you know what I mean. Just a few notes to complete those you made while staying at the house. Remember how you used to jot down things, a lot of things, about the house?"

He acts as if my memory were defunct. I realize I'm a bit remiss at times, but really!

"Of course I remember," I said. "But why continue?"

"I think it would help both of us," he replied. "Help both of us to—well—sort of knit together a few skeins that seem to have become unraveled."

What an odd man. I shrugged.

"Why not?" I said. It isn't, after all, as if I had anything to hide.

He beamed at me, sending me to the top of the class, I suppose. Well, it certainly takes little to satisfy some people. Anyhow, hence these hurried notes.

Several days after Bernard's visit, while I was busy starting this diary, as a matter of fact, one of the servants announced Laura.

Yes, it was actually Laura, come to see me! The same poncho cloak, jangling silver jewelry and red wig. I could hardly believe my eyes.

I had been resting when the servant told me Laura was waiting in the Activity Room. (People here seem determined to get their money's worth and keep busy. It's like being on shipboard. Everybody is forever fiddling with pottery or looms or leatherwork. Personally I would just as soon waste my time cutting out paper dolls!) Anyhow, there she was, as large as life and obviously under the misapprehension that she was quite safe.

"Laura!" I whispered, trying to draw her aside before anyone saw her, "are you out of your mind coming here?"

"Oh, Amy!" She took my hand in hers and I was shocked to see how old and tired she looked.

"Laura!" I hissed, "you shouldn't have left England! It isn't safe! Oh, Laura, think of Eric if you won't think of yourself!"

Oh, I don't condemn her for the deaths of those children. How was she to know Graham would crack up? Even the robbery was more in the line of what Mr. Turner used to call "an error of judgement" than a crime, when one considers the participants.

"Oh, my dear," Laura kept staring at me with such a sad expression. I suppose she didn't have much to be happy about. I wouldn't want the results of that robbery on my conscience. "There's a cafeteria here, isn't there? Shall we go and have a cup of tea, Amy?"

"Be careful what you say," I whispered, as I led her there. She held my hand as if she were a child.

"Oh, my poor girl," she said. "What you have been through. Mrs. Mac told us all about that awful séance."

Ah ha. So Mrs. Mac was in on the plot too.

"And then Eric found those Xeroxed newspaper stories and your diary, dear, and Bernard told us the full story of the house. My poor child, how you must have suffered."

I pulled my hand out of hers and ordered tea.

"Amy dear, do you remember one of the clippings stating that a woman neighbor of the Grahams was under a doctor's care and on the verge of a nervous collapse because of what happened?

"Well, Amy, Eric checked with the police and through the postal marks, handwriting, and wrapping, they traced that terrible package you received straight to that woman. She has had psychiatric treatment and recovered now and she admitted sending the package. The police analyzed the blood on the booties and it was beef blood."

Well, of all the balderdash and wasn't she the cool one to come up with a story like that. I suppose that after what she has done and her part in the robbery she has to rationalize somehow, though.

I must not condemn her. If ever she needed kindness and understanding, she needs them now.

"Now listen," I said, as we sat sipping our tea, and I took good care to look around before speaking. (You never know where those microphones may be hidden.) "Listen, Laura. I hate to say this, but I must. You've got to go back to England before it's too late!"

"Amy, dear—," she said.

"No!" I said firmly. "It's for your own sake too, Laura. I know your motives, Laura. It was for Eric. But Laura, I am not a judge and jury and my understanding can't help you. They might be lenient because of your age, and try to remember that time is your friend, not your enemy. That is why there isn't a minute to be wasted. You must go, now!"

Well, she sat there with a stunned look on her face as if she weren't taking in a word I was saying and then suddenly she burst into tears, covered her face with her hands and stumbled from the room.

Guilt. Poor soul. Unhappy creature caught in the web of her deceit. But who am I to judge?

As I promised, back to Dr. Rosen, also a guest here and a close friend of Dr. Kelly's. Dr. Kelly asked him to keep an eye on me, which was kind of him.

Not that I need company; indeed, I rather enjoy solitude after what I have endured. Oh, yes. Dr. Rosen. He's about forty, dark, quiet, with a somewhat saturnine face and a gentle manner. Nosey, mind you, as everybody seems to be around here, but that's a resort for you, people always trying to make as many friends as possible before the holiday is over. Except for a couple of weirdos, whom I don't mind saying I take trouble to avoid. But then, I've never been on a vacation yet without running into a few of them.

This Dr. Rosen and I have had some rather interesting discussions. He has a keen, analytic mind, but like so many brilliant people, he enjoys playing childish games. One, for instance, in which we pretend to float, and then we chat about whatever comes into our minds. Well, if it keeps him happy.

He's very lonely, poor fellow. Have you noticed how often brilliant people are unbalanced? So I've been trying to bring him out of himself and always go along with his games, although I do admit I feel pretty foolish at times.

I have never met anyone who is so curious about the past. Especially mine. His inquisitiveness almost verges on rudeness, and if it weren't for our mutual friendship with Dr. Kelly I'd be a little inclined to put him off. He is, for some reason, particularly interested in, of all people, Igor. Was he like the other one? When I replied the other who, he gave me a coy little look and said, "Now, Amy, you remember the other one. A long time ago."

I thought for a while, then I replied that he was not in the least. He changed the subject. Rather crafty of him, in a way, because then he wanted to know about Eric. Now, really, it would be dishonorable to discuss with someone who, for all his friendliness, is almost a stranger, the intimate relationship of marriage. I mean, after all! Eric and I certainly had our differences, and God knows I tried hard enough to straighten them out. I told Dr. Rosen so, and also that anything further would have to come from Eric's lips, as it won't from mine.

And all I have been able to find out from this Dr. Rosen about himself is that he is married, has two children and is Jewish. I asked him about the latter, as he looks it.

He seemed to be rather sensitive on that point and asked me if

I felt hostile to him. Well, really, as I told him, why go looking for anti-Semitism, that I personally couldn't care less. He seems to think I'm hostile about *something* and actually has made a bit of a bore of himself about it.

This place is really lovely and is, if anything, overstaffed. You can scarcely turn around without one of the servants wanting to wait upon you. There is one in particular who has attached herself to me and is always urging me to eat more. I admit my appetite is not up to scratch, but I do hate being nagged and for all I know, Eric may have had a hand in hiring the staff. After all, it happened before, didn't it? And at the risk of sounding melo-dramatically Borgia-ish, it is just as well to be a little cagey about what one eats. It would be a simple thing to slip something taste-less into one's food. Besides, the food isn't any too good here, anyway. The wallpaper is rather nice, though.

This woman I was mentioning, in order to prove her loyalty to me, has even offered to be my "official food taster." (Her phrase, not mine.) This was supposed to put my mind at ease, but as any reasonable person will allow, it merely demonstrates that the possibility is only too likely. She's a kindly, ox-like girl and to humor her I let her do a bit of tasting. I must say she appears to be enjoying her usual rude health. But of course, she may have been employed by a certain party, in which case she knows the dishes that have been tampered with. The subterfuge and cunning that can be manifest are too apparent to be ignored.

When Dr. Rosen, whom I have dubbed Nosey (privately, of course—I wouldn't dream of hurting his or anyone else's feelings deliberately), well, when he was in the other day, a strange thing happened.

I had been fooling around in the recreation room, pretending to be writing in this diary, but actually, in an unobtrusive manner watching some of the more bizarre guests here, when he asked me if I would like to have tea with him in a private sitting room down the hall.

It was a very pleasant room, chintzy and informal, not at all like some of the private rooms here, which look just like offices, even to filing cabinets and typewriters.

One of the maids served tea, and after both of us had had a cup, he leaned back and starting chatting again about Igor. Really, he is hung up on that subject and can't seem to let it alone. Frankly I'd be ashamed, at his age, to show such a prurient interest in what is, after all, only a shabby interlude between a housewife and a younger man. But not him. You'd think he was trying to gather information for Peyton Place, the way he goes after facts.

Anyway, I told him, as before, that I couldn't remember.

"Eric told you to forget, didn't he?" he asked.

"Yes." I sighed. I had already told him that too. He is really beginning to be a bloody bore and spoiling an otherwise nice vacation for me. I wish I could be blunter about it and tell him to just please mind his own business. Unfortunately, Mother was always very strict about manners and how one should treat people with dignity and courtesy, etc., and one can't forget the habits of a lifetime.

"Let's try and remember more about Igor, Amy. Let's go over that day in the park."

"I've told you all I know."

Damn him anyhow! Why can't some people leave well enough alone! Besides, wasn't it Eric who told me not to think about it? Why doesn't he ask Eric?

But then I got an odd feeling of remembering, and I remembered that after I was in bed that night of the bear-pit incident, I couldn't remember something. Something I had to remember, something I should tell Eric. But I didn't tell Eric because I couldn't remember . . . that's it. And he said again, Eric that is, not to try.

"I'll understand if you don't want to remember, Amy." Dr. Rosen, of course.

Now what have I got to hide, and why shouldn't I remember? "What do you mean?" I snapped. Honestly, he gives me the pip at times.

"Let's try our little game, Amy."

I'm more than a little tired of his little game, but I said, "Well, if it pleases you."

Some people get their kicks in the oddest ways. God, I seem to have spent most of my life humoring peculiar people.

"All right, Amy?"

"All right." I'm afraid I sounded a trifle sullen.

He settled down in his chair as if he were going to have a good snooze, after first pulling the Venetian blinds so that the early winter sun did not shine in my eyes.

"Now let's relax, Amy, the way we always do. Don't be tense. There. That's better, isn't it? Flap your hands, Amy, see how loose you can make them, like a lazy seal's flippers."

I missed my vocation. I ought to be teaching kindergarten. I sat there playing his silly game and obligingly flapping my flippers.

"Hold your arm over your head, Amy. Now let it fall. Just let it plop."

Ah ha. Another convolution of the carved Chinese ball. Why didn't this hit me right between the eyes before? This is what comes of hating to hurt people's feelings. But, what harm can it do? I'm wise to you, Doctor N for Nosey Svengali.

"Look into my eyes and relax. Fine. Now close your eyes. You're doing fine, Amy. I'm going to ask you some questions, but if the questions disturb you, you'll remember me talking to you now and telling you you don't have to answer."

I didn't feel the least bit tired. No I didn't, and I remember everything in his office perfectly. Well, nearly everything.

"Tell me what happened at the bear pit, Amy, that last day. What happened when you and Igor were standing next to the iron palings?"

He was hypnotizing me, of course. Well, I'd go along with it. Willingly. But only because I wanted to. He couldn't force me to. I'm still the master of my soul.

What is it I want to remember, but can't?

"You are standing in front of the iron palings at the bear pit. You have your back to the palings and Igor is facing you."

"Yes."

"You're frightened."

"The palings are sharp. Like spears. So people won't try to climb over."

"That's right, Amy. We remembered this far before. And you told me you were frightened."

"Yes."

"Why, Amy? What are you frightened of?"

"I'm frightened of Igor."

"Igor? Why?"

Didn't he understand? Why?

"Death. Death, doctor. Don't you see? The baby died. My baby. Then all my lovely dream children at the house. They really existed once, but they were murdered. You know that, don't you? Death! Death! People kill each other. It's awful, it doesn't seem possible, but it's true!"

"Yes. I understand. Tell me about Igor."

"I was afraid. I was afraid he would kill me. He had me by the throat. He was angry. He pushed me backwards!"

"Yes, Amy?"

"No, no. NO NO NO!" I tried to shriek. What was the matter? Was that awful rasping noise coming from me? NO, NO, NO.

I get rather confused at this point, but I think I talked some more to the doctor, only I can't be sure.

Then I remember Dr. Rosen leaning over my chair and saying very soothingly, "You are back now, Amy. You are back in my office. You are back and you are safe."

I looked up at him and I don't remember when I've been so appalled by the sudden change in a person's appearance. I scarcely recognized him. He was shaking and sweat poured down his face. Obviously he was in a highly nervous condition.

I didn't feel too good either.

"That's enough for today, my dear. You've been very good, Amy. You're a very good girl."

"Eric said I was to forget. I feel sick," I said. "I think I'm going to throw up."

"No. You're all right now." His color was still ghastly. "I'm going to give you a little medication Amy, because your stomach is upset. There we are. It will relax you and your tummy will feel better. There. You see? You feel better already."

I didn't throw up but I felt rotten and groggy for the rest of the day.

We never had any more chats about Igor and I was curious. After all, it was Dr. Rosen who started them.

Well, thank heavens he had dropped the subject. I certainly

didn't want to think about it. In gratitude for being let off the hook, I've been quite conscientious about keeping up his diary, although I know he's still nosey enough to read it some time.

Eric was for a time visiting me almost daily and of course had an explanation for everything. He didn't look at all well and if I hadn't known what he did, I might have been tempted to feel sorry for him.

As for the explanations, well, you never heard such ridiculous theories in your life.

Take the incident of poor little Philip in the hall closet, the night of the storm. It was Elspeth's doll, according to him. He saw it too and put it back without speaking of it because he didn't want me to know Rudi had had it out. He said I said Rudi was too big to play with dolls, which of course he was.

Did you ever hear such hogwash?

And that jar of blood exploding in the fruit cellar. Oh, that wasn't a psychic phenomenon but merely a fermented bottle of cherries following a natural law. Even the faces Elspeth saw were rational because it was either Rudi or the result of her drug-taking. As I said to Dr. Rosen, "Now, would anyone in their right mind believe that?"

The voices Eric has not been able to explain. I should think not! He is hardly likely to admit he put the microphones and amplifiers in the walls. The one thing that does puzzle me though, is how he figured out how to do it. He is such an idiot about anything mechanical. But every man has his price and no doubt he hired someone. It might even have been Bernard, for instance, though I can scarcely bring myself to believe that that good soul would be party to anything so diabolical.

One of the most tiresomely outrageous theories concerned Agar Burton and Laura.

Yes, he finally admitted that Agar Burton is alive, and that he did visit me. But, and it's such a big but, there is a lot of nonsense about Agar winning a football pool of one hundred and fifty thousand pounds and instructing his lawyer to settle half on Laura. Then, according to his son, it seems Agar lost his half gambling and wanted some of Laura's half back.

Now, I ask you!

About that nightmarish incident of the baby boot, he's hand in glove with Laura on that one. He had some cock-and-bull story of checking with the Mounties and they had traced it to a former neighbor of the Grahams. The woman, he said, had become unbalanced after the murders and thought that whoever bought the house had killed the children. She had watched carefully when the house was being moved and followed it and then sent the parcel.

Yeah, yeah, yeah. He actually expected me to believe it and said he could have the Royal Canadian Mounted Police sergeant come and tell me, if I wanted proof.

I wonder what sort of fool he takes me for. As if I'd trust the Mounties. They were probably in on the plot too. I mean, after all, Graham was a policeman, wasn't he? The vastness of the conspiracy against me is incredible. But I was up to them this time and my reasoning was so irrefutable Eric didn't even try pursuing that line any more. But what can you expect of a man who would literally tear a baby from its mother's arms?

I daren't think of her. I would go mad.

Eric upset me so much with his ridiculous theories that I was finally forced to ask Dr. Rosen to see that he, Eric, did not continue his visits. After all, this is a private resort, and heaven knows that though I don't wish to appear unsociable, I am entitled to my privacy. Dr. Rosen readily agreed that if seeing Eric disturbed me, his visits should be discontinued. He is surprisingly helpful and obliging at times.

Eric had tears in his eyes and tried to kiss me when he said good-bye. Why is it everybody is always crying when they visit me here? Guilt, guilt, guilt, I suppose.

I must not play the part of judge. Their culpability is not my responsibility. My goodness, that sounds like something what's his name, heavens, what is his name, would say.

Anyhow, with Eric, I have it all figured out. His imagination, fine within bounds for a writer, has run rampant and he has completely lost touch with reality. But then, even I must take into account the heredity factor, that dreadful old man for a father and poor Laura as a mother. As I said to Dr. Rosen, Eric is ill with a sickness as real as a broken leg or cancer. And if he were suffering from cancer I would hardly desert or castigate him. It is only that my nerves have been in a shocking state ever since we moved into that terrible house, and what with trying to work at the office and at home and burdened with Laura's secret, it's no wonder that I am in need of a rest.

Good old Nosey is in complete agreement with me in this matter. He is quite sensible when he's not asking silly questions. But then, who is normal? It only occurred to me the other day, that of all the people connected with that house, I was the only one who was.

I mean, take Rudi, or Elspeth, or Eric or Laura or Agar Burton, or what's his name—all of them. Let us face it, even dear Bernard is just a wee bit odd and everyone knows that certain places are filled with people who have "got" religion.

Dr. Rosen insists, incidentally, that Eric's story about Agar and the money is true and provable. That it is entirely consistent and not at all out of character for a man like Agar, with his past history. Well, if that's your attitude, we know whose side you're on, don't we, Doc? And I'm going to put it right here in black and white for you to read.

Oh, you're not so bad, Nosey. As a matter of fact I'm rather fond of you. Where was I? It's so hard to concentrate these days. Even simple reading seems to be difficult. One of the guests said it's because they secretly dope us with these new tranquilizers. It wouldn't surprise me in the least. You're not safe any place.

Religion. Yes, I was thinking about Bernard and religion. Religion is the refuge of those suffering from guilt.

Dr. Rosen, for instance. As I have said, he is Jewish. I asked him if he attended services or whatever the Jews call them and he said that yes, he and his wife go to the temple. The temple. It sounds romantic and rather barbaric to Christian ears, doesn't it? Jesus scourging the money-lenders and all that. Good heavens, that seems like anti-semitism and shades of poor old Laura, doesn't it?

But poor old Dr. Rosen is awfully sensitive about being Jewish and as I well know, it doesn't pay to be sensitive. I really must try to be kinder to him. Empathy. Put myself in his place.

Did I say shades of Laura? Shades. Shades, words, shadings of words. Shades, covers to keep out light. Covers, hidings, screens, shelters. Then the other shades, the ghosts, the phantoms, the shadows, the specters. Oh really, there I go meandering again. I must concentrate.

Where was I. Oh, yes. Dr. Rosen. I asked him why he went to the temple.

"But why not, Amy? After all, I'm a Jew."

Why not, indeed. As if I didn't understand. He's looking for a refuge and also, I know very well that the reason he asks so many questions is that he is looking for an answer to his dilemma. I wish I could help him, poor devil. He is as loaded down with this sense of guilt as poor Bernard, which is saying a great deal.

Oh, honestly, there I go judging people again and it's none of my business. Thank God. I'm alone, finally. Without a care in the world. What a relief to be cut off from the rest of humanity and free from the burden of all their cares and troubles. People do unconsciously try and load you down with their problems, you know.

But it is a hurdle I have overcome and the way is actually so simple. It is really the ultimate goal of any intelligent person. The only way to achieve peace is to divorce oneself from people in order to preserve one's sanity.

Dr. Rosen disagrees with me, but look where messing around in other people's problems has got him. A nervous wreck about being Jewish and turning green and shaking like a leaf after sticking his nose in about what's his name.

"You can't bear to think about him, can you?" I said. "What is it that upsets you so much?"

"In time, Amy. In time. We'll get to it in time."

"With your temperament you'd be a great deal better off not to be so emotional," I replied. "And to follow my example. As I told you, I myself have solved the problem."

He smiled. He smiled very gently, and good lord, improbable though it sounds, I could swear that there were tears in *his* eyes.

You see what I mean? What a bunch of cry-babies people are. As if it did any good.

I never cry any more.

"We must be patient, Amy. Very patient. Little steps before we walk, then bigger steps before we run and jump again."

You know, it's the strangest thing. This is a very large spa, but yesterday when I was walking through the gardens with one of the guests who insisted on joining me (they obviously haven't figured out the ultimate goal around here) anyway, when I was strolling through the gardens, I could have sworn that I saw Rudi walking with Frau Keller. They were in the distance, so of course, I could be mistaken.

How nice that he and Mutti are having a real holiday at last, and not in that terrible Germany where they would lock him up. (Or even worse!)

It seems to me I recall reading in the newspaper, just before I came here, that two of those lovely polar bears died. Really, the public are thoughtless and stupid. Those poor beasts had been eating belt buckles and keys and watches and heaven knows what. I keep dreaming of them, and looking down into the bear pit I see *his* face. Such odd dreams I've had lately. Sometimes it's difficult to separate them from reality. I must ask Dr. Rosen if they have any special significance.

Now and then it seems to me I am about to remember whatever it was I have forgotten, something that keeps jarring at the bottom of my skull like a headache that never quite develops.

Something to do with the bear pit. But what? It won't come clear, but it has to do with feeling surprised—amazed, really—at my own strength. Maybe it's mixed up with the dream. One can be very strong in a dream. Especially a nightmare. One needs superhuman strength then.

I really must cooperate with Dr. Rosen; he may be right about this learning to walk business. Yes, I think he has something there, just what I'm not sure, but I think I should pay more attention to what he says.

Perhaps I've been wrong about some things. Who knows, even about Eric.

It's all quite difficult at present. Yes, as Dr. Rosen says, I must be patient.